UPSTAIRS

M. JANDREAU

UPSTAIRS

OTHER BOOKS FROM M. JANDREAU

My Best Friend, Marty

Dudley Road

My Last Days

A Sour Chord

For Maria and Heather.

Sometimes we're the only ones who see the ghosts who haunt us.
Your ghosts can't haunt you anymore.

You are missed and will always be loved.

CHAPTER 1
THE EULOGY

"IT'S hard to believe he's gone," I said, looking down at my grandfather's casket. Its ornate gold inlays wrapped around the sides, culminating in a floral pattern over the top where his face was lying, just under the closed lid. His coffin, much like the man himself, was over the top and shouted, *I'm rich*. Which he was. Very.

"I know what you're thinking," I continued, trying to distract myself from the sadness by using humor. "Why is there a picture of me next to the casket? Well, there's not. I was lucky enough that the genetics in our family are pretty strong. I look just like my father and my uncles. And they look just like their dad, my Gramps. We all got his good looks. We look like Xeroxed copies of him, I know. The same dark brown hair and blue eyes. He and I were even the same build for our entire adult lives. As soon as I turned eighteen, he joked I grew six inches and gained fifty pounds to match his height and weight."

He and I had been close my whole life. My parents were mostly absent, traveling on Gramps's dime for most of my childhood and adulthood. For most of my life, I spent the majority of my holidays, birthdays, school vacations, and breaks with Gramps. I had my own room in his house until I was old enough to have my own place, though I'm sure my blanket and pillow were still tucked away in a closet somewhere, just in case I turned up to spend an evening. While I still spent plenty of time with him, I hadn't had a sleepover at his house since around the time I met my wife. I suppose on some level, I replaced spending time with Gramps with spending time with Courtney. That's normal, right? New relationships tend to replace current relationships, even if you don't mean them to.

I brushed a tear away from my eye and did my best to continue on with the eulogy.

"He was Gramps to me, and most of you know that already. But for those of you who don't, William Henry Washington was my grandfather. The greatest, most wonderful man I've ever known." I intentionally didn't make eye contact with my father because I knew he'd make a face or scoff. Despite Gramps raising my father—with lots of help from my grandmother, who had passed when I was too little to get to know her—they were nothing alike. Where my grandfather was kind, and warm, and compassionate, my father was cold, and hard, and often cruel. I had always wondered whether he got that behavior from my grandmother or from somewhere else. But the two men were nothing alike. I think that's what drew me to Gramps so much. And also because I didn't have much choice. My parents would leave me at Gramps's house at the drop of a hat. Some urgent trip they had to take. They always made it seem like it was a business trip, but neither of my parents worked when I was growing up. They never openly admitted it, but they mooched off of Gramps's money. I don't know what the arrangement was, but Gramps either set up a trust for my father or gave him an allowance. Whatever the arrangement was, my parents were gone more often than they were home. Did it bother me when I was a little boy? Sure. Why wouldn't it? But as I grew older—into my teens and early twenties—it bothered me less and less. After all, who wouldn't want to spend time with someone as kind as Gramps? Who wouldn't want to run around, playing in a house so big that you couldn't even see every room and explore every nook and cranny in a single day?

"When Gramps got sick, I think I, like most of you, probably didn't want to believe it. People get old, they get sick, but Gramps seemed like he'd live forever. He was strong and able-bodied right until the end." I saw heads nodding in the crowd as I did my best to look up from the pulpit throughout my speech. *Don't want to be like Ross Geller reading his notes for class*, I thought. I made myself chuckle unintentionally.

"He was made of stone and concrete, wasn't he? I couldn't accept it when he got sick, and I am still processing it now that we're here. I still feel a tingle in my stomach when I think of my phone ringing and seeing Geoffrey's name pop up. The only other time Geoffrey had called me was when Gramps fell and hurt his knee a few years back. So, obviously, I knew it wasn't going to be good news." Geoffrey was Gramps's best friend and personal assistant. I think I was around five or six when I first remember meeting him. Sometime in the early '90s, and given how Geoffrey was always tending to Gramps's needs, I recall joking about how he was like Geoffrey from *The Fresh Prince of Bel-Air*. He did *not* like being called a butler, but a lot of what he did was similar, and I always loved a good pop-culture reference.

"I know you all loved Gramps in a way unique to you and

him. I'm sure that , like me, you felt like you were the only person in the entire world when you were with him. He had a way about him. He made you feel special, no matter what." I heard my father clear his throat. Likely to avoid a laugh or bursting out yelling. I ignored it as best I could, but I think I shot a look at him.

"As we lay him to rest today, please do your best not to be sad. Gramps wouldn't have wanted that. He wouldn't have wanted a room full of his closest loved ones crying their eyes out, talking about how much they miss him. And I know. I know how that sounds. Everyone says that at a funeral, right? But I mean it. Let's celebrate Gramps's life today. Let's celebrate his creations. Let's play the video games he created and reflect on the things he did in his incredible life. Let's not focus on the end of his life, but on the journey he took to get there."

It's hard to say goodbye to someone you loved so deeply. Someone who took care of you for years and years, never once asking for any sort of thank you or payback. Never once complaining. Never once saying no when my parents asked if I could come stay with him for a weekend, a week, or a month. It's hard to say goodbye at all, but especially so with someone like Gramps. Someone who was my entire world. Someone who took care of me better than anyone else I've ever known—even my wife. But please don't tell her that.

"As we celebrate him today, please remember the great things about him. Remember his laugh. Remember the same cologne he'd worn since before I was born. Remember the games he created. Remember the times you spent with him. But most of all, remember him, the man. Remember Gramps for the amazing person he was and for all the wonderful memories he gave you."

I folded my speech up and tucked it into the pocket of my suit. The same suit he'd bought me for my wedding. The only suit I owned. It slid into the pocket right behind the folded piece of paper that had my wedding vows on it, chock full of pop culture references, just like I'd always done. Those were the only two speeches I'd ever had to give in my life, so it was fitting that they stayed together in the pocket of my only formal attire.

CHAPTER 2
THE LAWYER'S NEWS

"I CAN'T BELIEVE IT," I said aloud, mostly to myself. It's all I'd thought about for weeks leading up to when my wife, Courtney, and I met with the lawyer of Gramps's estate.

"It's true," he repeated for what felt like the hundredth time. No matter how many times I kept repeating that I couldn't believe it, he kept telling me it was true. Over and over again, on an endless loop.

"Okay," Courtney said. "I think he's telling the truth." She squeezed my arm firmly, but not to hurt me. Just to get me to snap out of the state I was in.

We sat across from the largest wooden desk I'd ever seen in my life. Attorney Statler sat across from us, his eyes darting back and forth between his laptop screen and us. No matter how many times he said it out loud, I was still in shock and somewhat in awe. My Grandfather and I had always been close. Ever since I was a little kid, I'd spent weeks at a time with him and his second wife over summer vacation, while my parents went off on trips around the world. Gramps—which is what he'd always insisted I call him—had remarried before I was old enough even to know that the woman I'd called Grandma wasn't my father's mother. It wasn't until I was in my early teens that my father corrected me, kind of rudely, as it were.

Even into adulthood, Gramps had been there for me. I'd always known he had money from the way he lived. And though I'm not a hundred percent positive, I'm fairly sure that he funded all of those lavish vacations my parents took when I was young. I never knew why, but in my gut I sensed he was the one who took care of those things. And knowing how easy-going he was, he probably did so with no questions asked.

He had everything I ever wanted at his house. Toys as far as the eye could see. Televisions the size of movie theaters, which, when I was a kid, was a feat in and of itself. His back lawn rivaled Central Park. I could run for what felt like days without running out of lawn. I had this amazing box kite he bought me when I was six that I flew constantly out in that yard, while he sat in his Adirondack chair, at the top of the cement steps, watching down on me. Once I got old enough to know what a butler was, I realized that the man who occasionally brought Gramps beverages was one. Never alcohol, to my knowledge. Usually an iced tea, or Gramps's favorite, an Arnold Palmer. Always in a little glass. Always with one of those big, square ice cubes you see on television, or in the movies. An ice cube that was so big it didn't feel real.

Call me naïve. Call me childish. I don't know what you need to call me. But I had never even thought about how my college tuition was paid for. I'd assumed that was my parents. That whatever thing Gramps had done for work to earn his money, that my dad had gone into the same business, because it seemed like we also had money.

Besides the trips my parents went on—now that I'm actively thinking back on my childhood, I think they went on six or seven trips a year, sometimes for weeks at a time—we had a big house in a nice neighborhood. I had everything I'd ever wanted as a kid, too. In the mid-eighties, when Nintendo came to the US, I had one right away. And I had all the games, all the accessories—the extra controllers, too. You know the one I'm talking about. With the turbo buttons and the giant joystick. The controller that was so big you had to rest it on your lap. I had that. But, as silly as it may seem, I think the thing that made me really know we had money, the thing none of my friends seemed to have had, was a television in my bedroom before that was a thing. Back when cable had only a handful of channels. Jesus, I feel old just writing that down.

Now, I know what you're thinking. Kids shouldn't have televisions in their bedrooms until they're old enough to be responsible. Was that close to what you were thinking? And, like I said, I know that's a silly thing. But when I was really young, I didn't know a single other kid who had one in their bedroom—just me. And I had the accompanying VCR to watch any movie I wanted from a collection the size of a Blockbuster that lived downstairs in our family room. I suppose that's another sign that we have money. We had a family room, a living room, and a den in our house. Two of those three rooms, however, were hardly used. They were more for show. When my parents would have a dinner party with their friends, they'd often walk through one of those rooms to show their friends some new piece of artwork they'd gotten, or a new couch, or something. Anything to brag about, come to think of it. My dad would do that thing he did, where he'd interrupt my mother—mid-sentence—and finish the story, as if he'd been telling it the whole time.

Often during those parties, I'd be at Gramps's house. A house that, as of recently, was mine.

Gramps hadn't been sick, which I think is why I was still mostly in shock about what Attorney Statler had told Courtney and I. He was fine when I saw him for our regular Sunday dinner. A tradition that had been in place since I could remember, likely even before I was born. As a child, my parents would take me to Gramps's house for dinner every Sunday afternoon. They'd spend the day catching up on the events of the week, culminating in a dinner that could rival the Royal Family's evening meals. Course after course of appetizers, entrees, and desserts. Food as far as the eye could see. Far more than any four adults and one child could ever need or want. But, like clockwork, we did it every Sunday.

We'd ended that Sunday evening like every other. Gramps said goodbye to my parents, who I generally only saw at these dinners at Gramps's and nowhere else, and, like always, he'd ask Court and me to hang back a minute. That he had something he wanted to talk to us about in private. It became a running joke, because it was always something he needed to talk to us about in private.

He said the same goodbye he'd always said. "You're too good for Max, Courtney." It was their little running joke that I wasn't good enough for her. Which, somewhere deep down inside, I think I knew. At least on some level.

"Oh, shush, you," she'd said, kissing him on the cheek.

"I love you, Gramps," I'd say as we made our way out the door.

"I love you, too, bud." Bud was the only nickname he'd ever given me, and one he called me almost every time I saw him. Ever since I could remember, anyway.

And then we were off. We headed back to our apartment in the city, which Gramps had generously given us a good portion of money for the down payment for. It seemed like everything was fine.

And then the next morning, he was gone. He'd passed in his sleep, completely unexpectedly. I couldn't believe it when I got a call from Geoffrey the next morning. It seemed so strange that something could have happened so quickly in just twelve or so hours.

But Gramps was gone. And he'd chosen me to leave his house to. Well, let me back up a second and call out two points. The first being that it was more of an estate than a house. I can't even think of the right words to describe it to you. But it was enormous. In my entire childhood of running around exploring, I don't think I'd ever even seen all the rooms. And the second point was that I was his only grandchild. His second wife had grandchildren of her own, but they never spent much time with Gramps. I doubt I could even pick them out of a lineup. So, I suppose on some level, it was a default decision that Gramps left the house to me.

He could have left it to my parents or one of my uncles, I suppose. But for some reason, he skipped them and left it to me.

CHAPTER 3

A FOND MEMORY

I MUST HAVE BEEN six or seven, somewhere around that age, the first time I found out where Gramps's money had come from.

We were there for our usual Sunday visit, where my parents would head off to the kitchen to visit with Gramps, while I'd play in the living room by myself. I'd either watch television or, if I were lucky, I'd get to play the Atari that one of my uncles had left out after he'd last played with it. My dad had three brothers: two older than him, one younger. Like our family, they'd visit Gramps on the weekend, too. Sometimes our visits overlapped; sometimes they didn't. It wasn't something that was ever planned; it was just a happy coincidence if we got there and one of my uncles' cars was at the end of the long driveway, parked somewhere in the circular part, where Gramps's prized possession, a 1940s Rolls-Royce, was always parked. It'd been there for as long as I could remember, even well after we stopped going to visit him every Sunday. More on that later.

This particular visit was special because the Atari was left out. My Uncle Matthew—always Matthew, never Matt or Matty —must have visited Gramp earlier that day. If he'd visited on Saturday, Gramps—or one of the housekeepers—would have put the Atari away already. Gramps wasn't a neat freak so much as someone who liked his house to be in order. My father said that it had gotten a lot worse after Gram had passed when I was younger.

So there I am, chugging away at *Pitfall* and trying, for the millionth time, to get past this one tricky level that I could never get past without someone's help. My little fingers tugged on the joystick to the right, pressing that button at the perfect time to get *Pitfall* Harry—don't worry, I just had to look up his name and didn't remember it, either—to the other side of the level. But try as I might, I could never get past the spot where the snake popped up right after jumping over one of the biggest pits in the game. The snake always got me. And now that I'm an adult, I'm thankful I didn't know any curse words then other than "heck" or "darn", because I'm sure I'd have sworn up a storm at the damn frustrating game.

Just as I was about to give up, I heard Gramps over my shoulder. "You have to hit the jump button twice quickly."

It'd startled me, and I turned around to see him standing in the doorway between the living room and the kitchen. He leaned against the frame as if he'd been watching me for a while. "Oh, hi, Gramps," I got out after the initial shock wore off.

Why was I shocked? Glad you asked. You'd think a little boy's grandfather standing there watching him play a video game wouldn't be startling, wouldn't you? You're right. Most times, it'd be nothing. But Gramps never—and I mean never— left the kitchen when my parents were visiting with him. They'd stay in there for hours, talking and catching up on the events of the week. You have to remember that this was a time before cell phones, before texting, or even emailing. Sure, Dad could have called Gramps during the week. But I think there was something special about their Sunday catch-ups. Only occasionally did Dad and Uncles Matthew, Joey, and David all show up at the same time. I remember that visit vividly because it was *loud*. Not in a bad way or a yelling way. Just in a "five grown men in a kitchen talking at full volume" sort of way.

Only Uncle Matthew was married, but he and Aunt Jennifer had never had any children. I didn't find out until much later in life that they had fertility issues. I'm not telling you that to depress you or bum you out, but more so that you understand, I often spent these Sunday afternoons alone. I didn't mind, though. Honestly, I enjoyed being by myself.

Then Gramps did something he had absolutely never done before. He came over and sat down next to me, immediately pulling the Atari controller out of my hands. "Here, let me show you," he said. I can still smell his cologne, thinking about that moment. Aside from his funeral, when I put my hand on his chest in the casket to say goodbye, it was the closest, physically, I'd ever gotten to him for any period of time, more than a quick hug.

"You know how to play?" I asked quizzically. As if no person over ten had ever played a video game before.

"Know how to play?" he almost scoffed. "Maxwell, I helped make this game."

I blinked in rapid succession. "What?"

"Did you not hear me, or did my statement confuse you?" This was one of Gramps's favorite things to say when someone said "what" in response to something he said. I always liked that he wanted to clarify whether you were just being daft or hard of hearing.

"You confused me," I blurted.

"Has your dad not told you the story?" He put the controller down on the coffee table, standing up to reach the console to power it off.

I shook my head.

"Well, then," he began, "I suppose now is a good time."

My father poked his head in through the door, drying his hands on the same dish towel I'm sure he'd been wiping his hands on for years. "Everything all right in here?"

"Yes, yes," Gramps said, almost shooing him away with his eyes. Dad took the hint and turned back to the kitchen, calling out something to my mother that I couldn't quite hear over the excitement flushing through my body.

"You were saying?" I prodded him.

"Ah, yes. I was about to tell you a story, wasn't I?" He took his seat next to me on the couch, turning to face me. "Many years ago, a good friend of mine, David, and I built this video game. It was the end of the last decade, and video games were just beginning to be a thing in households around the world. David—yes, your uncle is named after him—was a storyteller. A genius for taking an idea and making it into a thing. And I was just a lowly programmer. I'd already worked almost my whole life as a programmer for a number of companies that are far less interesting than this."

I found myself staring at him, mouth agape, unintentionally.

"So, one day, David came to me and asked if I'd ever heard of the Atari system. I, of course, hadn't, because I was already an old man at that point. An old man who already had everything he'd ever wanted in life. But shortly after your grandmother passed, rest her soul, I needed something to fill the void I felt. I needed something to do."

He reached across the couch and took my hand. "It was a very hard time in my life," he continued. "Your dad and his brothers were already grown and out on their own. I think, if memory serves correctly, that your father had already met your mother and was on their way to having you. Anyway, I was lonely. I had already finished working. I think they call it 'retirement' now, but I just saw it as having no purpose. I woke up, got dressed, and sat out on the porch, drinking lemonade. By myself. For hours!"

The way he told that part made me chuckle. The idea of sitting on a porch, drinking lemonade, by myself, sounded wonderful to me. But he conveyed such pain in his telling of the story.

"When David presented his idea to me, it seemed preposterous. It seemed like an impossible task. Especially to an old man like me!"

Now, I don't know how you felt when you were seven years old, but I remember feeling like Gramps was at least a thousand at that point in our lives. He seemed like the oldest person who could have ever lived. But in thinking back, and doing some quick math, Gramps was still in his sixties. Maybe in his late sixties, but still not nearly as old as it seemed when I was a little kid. So the idea that he thought of himself as old resonated with me and stuck with me all these years later.

"We met with some other programmers who knew how to make a game for this new Atari system. We met with designers, businesspeople, and lots of other folks in the 'industry'. Folks who knew a lot about a lot. Folks who said they'd help us because they saw the future of video games."

"Did they help you?" I asked, trying my best not to interrupt him, but waiting for a natural breaking point where he needed to take in some air.

"Did they ever!" His face lit up. "It was such a steep learning curve for me, but I figured it out. I learned how to program video games. The first of which, *Pitfall*, is the one you're playing today and have been playing since you could hold that controller."

"No way!" I honestly had no reason not to believe him, but this was also feeling like a pretty far-fetched story, even to my little ears.

"It's true!" He said, poking me in the ribs. "We made this game from the summer of nineteen seventy-nine through the winter of 1980. I remember you were born just about when we started it."

"But how'd you learn?" I asked, genuinely curious.

"A lot of what we call trial and error. Do you know what that means?"

"No," I said, somewhat embarrassed.

"It means you do or make something, try to see if it works, and then try again. Over and over again until you get it right."

"I guess because I'm playing the game now, you got it right?"

"We did," he smiled to himself. "It took a long time, but once I understood how it worked, it wasn't too different from the programming I'd done my whole life. Programming has changed a lot since I started as a boy. Don't get me wrong. It's hard to adjust to change. But I kept at it."

"Wait," I said. "So, did you make more games?"

"Well, not at first," he said. "But once the company that David sold *Pitfall* to realized we had a hit on our hands, we made more games for them and for other companies."

"Have I played the other games you made?" I asked, hoping the answer was yes.

"Have you ever!" He leaped from the couch and pulled the wicker basket out from the shelf next to the television. "Any of these ring a bell?" He held up *Ms. Pac-man*, *Raiders of the Lost Ark*, *Joust*, *Jungle Hunt*, *Mario Bros*, *Kung-Fu Master*, and a handful of others that spilled out of his hands onto the carpet.

"You made all of these?" I asked more in shock than when he first entered the room.

"David and I did," he said. "We made these together."

"Is that how you got this big house?" I asked half seriously.

"Well, yes and no," he said. "Yes, in that video games helped me get the money to buy this house. But also no, because it wasn't directly the video games themselves."

"What do you mean?" I asked, hoping to avoid needing to clarify that I was confused and not deaf.

"When we were building *Pitfall*, I came up with a way to reuse some of the programming. The code that makes the game work. Rather than rewriting it over and over again. I came up with a way to reuse it. It's a complicated and boring technical thing that you don't need to know about. But David was very smart. He found a way to protect the thing I came up with."

"You mean like a copyright?" I asked, knowing full well I was out of my depth with this part of the conversation.

"Sort of!" He seemed pleased that I knew the word, but didn't press me on whether I knew what it meant. "A patent."

"A patent?"

"That's right. It's a way to protect something you invent. And I suppose I invented this way of reusing the programming. Which would save other programmers a lot of time."

"You always say time is money," I added.

"That's exactly right. And that's why David protected our work. He protected it so people had to pay us in order to learn from us."

"But why would they do that, Gramps?"

"You just answered that question," he said. "Do you remember?"

"Huh?" I was so confused.

"Time is money. You said it yourself."

"Oh!" It suddenly clicked in my brain. "Time is money. They could use your… thing… device… doodad?" I paused to see if he'd correct me on what to call it. "Your thing. They could use your thing to make games faster. Which would make them more money?"

"You're such a bright boy, Maxwell." He patted me on the head. "That's exactly right. They could use my invention to make games faster. So they'd pay David and me a small amount of money so they could make a big amount of money."

"And *that's* how you bought this big house?"

"And my favorite car out front." He smiled with one of the biggest smiles I have ever remembered seeing him with. "And here's an important lesson for your life, Maxwell."

He paused, looking up at the ceiling for a moment.

"Yes, Gramps?"

"Money isn't everything. Money can buy you lots of things. It can ease a lot of your problems. It can get you any material thing in the world that you might want. But money cannot and will not make you happy."

The way he said "cannot and will not" has stuck with me my entire life. Had I been older during that conversation, I'd have seen the pain in his eyes when he said it. I'd have known what he meant. I'd have known that he was talking about missing my grandmother. And all these years later, I know what he meant. Courtney and I never had much. We never had a big house or nice cars. We didn't have high-paying jobs. We didn't go on fancy vacations like my parents did. But we had happiness. We had endless moments of love. We had aches in our bellies from endless laughter about jokes no one would have understood but us. We had candlelit meals because we couldn't pay the electric bill sometimes, but we made the best of it.

But all these years later, I can sense the pain Gramps had when he told me that. I think on some level, he'd have given all of it up if he could be with his wife again.

* * *

"DAD?" I called out from the backseat, still reeling from the story Gramps had told me.

"Yeah, pal?" He always called me pal. Well into my late teens, even though I never really felt like his pal. I think I eventually asked him to stop with the nicknames. From that point on, he called me either Max or Maxwell. It never seemed to have bothered him, but our relationship was complicated as I grew up.

"You never told me Gramps made video games."

"He did a lot more than that," my mother called back, turning the radio down. "How'd you find out about that?"

"Gramps told me about it today," I said, still excited.

"Did he?" Dad seemed a little annoyed. "That doesn't mean you get an Atari."

I'd been asking for one for at least a year by that point. Almost weekly. Especially weeks when we visited Gramps, and the Atari was left out by one of my uncles.

He looked to his right at my mom in the passenger seat, who nodded in agreement. "You'll get too consumed with it."

That was Mom's way of saying no to anything I really wanted. That I'd get "too consumed" with it. I suppose nowadays you'd tell your kids that they'd become addicted, which is really the truth of it. We often talk about addiction with drugs or alcohol, but addiction to other things is real, too. Especially in the early to mid-eighties. I think I still have blisters on my thumbs from the Nintendo controller from trying to land that damn jet in the Top Gun game in 1987.

"Gramps has done a lot of things in his lifetime," Dad said. "Making video games is only a small portion of who he is."

"A lucrative portion, but still a small one," Mom added.

I remember looking out the car window as we drove down the long driveway toward the gate. I remember fantasizing about some hidden camera that fed a monitor in Gramps's house and him waiting for us to get close enough to the gate to press a button to open it. I remember wondering whether the gate was automatic or whether someone, somewhere, was really pressing a button to cue it to open so we could leave. I remember counting the trees shaped like three lollipops stacked on top of one another as we drove down the seemingly endless driveway. My forehead pressed up against the glass of the rear passenger seat in our Nissan that, in hindsight, I'm sure Gramps had bought. I remember being so young and so full of imagination. I remember that day as if it were yesterday.

CHAPTER 4

TO SELL OR TO MOVE?

WHEN COURTNEY and I got home from the lawyer's office, we immediately flopped onto our secondhand couch in our too-small-for-just-the-two-of-us apartment. I took her hand and held it close to my heart.

"I can't believe he's gone," I said just quietly enough for it to be audible, but intentionally not loud enough for her to have heard me.

"I can't believe he's gone," she said, reminding me we were always on the same wavelength. "I can't believe he left you his house."

"Me neither," I added. "I'm still in shock from what the lawyer said."

"The estate and everything in it and on the grounds," she said, mimicking the lawyer's less-than-emotional tone.

"Everything on the grounds," I said. "Everything."

"Did he leave anything to your parents or your uncles and their families?" she asked.

"To be honest, I think I blacked out after hearing that he left the property to me. I don't even remember hearing any of the rest of the will," I said.

In my defense, Gramps had a lot of stuff. The story he'd told me about making money from the video games wasn't quite the full picture. It turns out he'd had a full career as a government programmer for most of his adult life. He had already made a lot of money inventing programming techniques for the government and military for over forty-plus years, so that by the time he made video games, he already had enough money to live comfortably on for the rest of his life. And he lived another thirty-three years from the afternoon we had the conversation about Atari.

He was almost one hundred years old when he passed. And while it's sad to lose someone you were so close to and who you held so dearly, it's hard to be too upset because he lived quite a long and fulfilled life. As I mentioned earlier, he went on to re-marry. And while Ginger was lovely—and the closest thing I ever knew to a grandmother—I don't think it was ever quite the same for Gramps as it was with Gram. I know my parents had quite a difficult time with Ginger coming into the picture. It wasn't what you think, though. Although my parents insisted she was only after him for his money, I never saw it that way. It never felt like she swooped in to take advantage of him or his generosity. And while she was younger than him, it was only ten years, I think. It's not like Anna Nicole whatshername and that old guy she married for his money. No, Ginger seemed like a nice lady, and she seemed to really love Gramps. I know he was heartbroken when she passed away. It must have been a similar feeling to when Gram passed, though probably not as tough on him. From the stories Dad told me, Gramps and Gram had been together for almost fifty years when she died.

"I don't even know what to think," Courtney said after a quiet moment of reflection.

"A house like that..." I let my voice trail off. *Big and creepy, like House on Haunted Hill*, I thought.

"It could be life-changing," she finished my sentence.

"It could be life-changing," I reiterated. "We could live for the rest of our lives."

"Wait," she said. "What do you mean?"

"If we sold it," I said.

"Sold it? I meant if we moved there."

We had a moment of staring at each other. I imagine we both thought the same thing in that we'd never really not agreed on something before.

"Move there?" I finally asked. "Are you crazy?"

"Crazy, why?" She pulled her hand back from mine. "Why would that be crazy?"

"We can't live there," I said. "That house is a monster."

"It's big, sure."

"It's not just big," I said. "It's too big. I don't know how Gramps lived there by himself for so many years."

I could tell she was getting a little upset with me. Over the course of our relationship, she'd gotten quite close to my grandfather. When my parents stopped going to see him on Sundays, we filled that void in his schedule without a second thought. In fact, we started going there to meet my parents. We never really saw much of them separately, especially with all the traveling they'd done once they both retired. But we knew when they were in town, they'd be at Gramps's come Sunday afternoon. So we met them there quite often.

But over time, they showed up less and less. Sometimes a postcard would show up in their place, having arrived just a couple of days before. The postcard would apologize for their not being able to make it. That they were having too good a time in Saint-Tropez, or Paris, or Beijing, or wherever they were off to that week.

It never bothered me much, if I'm honest. Like I said, our relationship was tough when I got into my twenties. I often think it was my fault, but I know you sometimes get that way as you get older. You grow up, but also grow out. Sometimes you realize that the adult version of you doesn't necessarily like the older-adult version of your parents. And that's fine. Don't get me wrong, I'm not disparaging my parents. Not by any means. They gave me a great childhood. My mom taught me so much about life, and love, and happiness. But at some point, they decided they wanted to live their lives and let me live mine. Even before I got into my teenage years, they'd go off jet-setting, and I'd stay with Gramps and Ginger. I remember one time I stayed with Uncle Joey, an actor who was in town while Gramps was traveling. That was quite the visit. But I digress.

"How much is it worth?" Courtney asked.

I had no idea. It'd never even crossed my mind to think about the value of Gramps's house. So, I did what any normal person with a smartphone did. I took out my phone, opened the Zillow app, and searched for his address.

It was completely unintentional, but I somehow blocked my phone from Court's view as I glimpsed past the price and went down to the description.

"Holy moly!" I almost yelled.

"What?" She almost yelled back.

"There are four houses on the property."

"What?"

"Did you not hear me, or did you not understand what I

said?" It was the first time I'd ever said that out loud. Though it was ingrained in my inner thoughts, since Gramps had said it so frequently.

"Did you say four houses?"

"Four houses. A twelve-car garage. An Olympic-sized swimming pool. Thirty-four acres of land."

"I'm sorry. Back up. To be sure I heard you. You said four houses?"

"Courtney. Four houses. Four. F. O. U. R."

"Who the hell needs four houses?"

"This can't be right," I said, tossing my phone onto the couch and heading back to the front door of our apartment, where I'd left the paperwork from the lawyer.

Courtney took it from me before I could even sit down and started flipping through the pages, presumably looking for the heading that talked about his last wishes. "Here it is," she said, handing the stack of papers back to me.

"William Henry Washington, of sound mind, blah blah blah," I skipped past all the legalese and found the first mention of my name. "The property located on the grounds of 1 Stone Way, yadda yadda yadda." I continued skipping down the page, looking for more specifics of what this all meant.

"Well?" Courtney asked.

"There it is. Four houses on the property."

"You never knew about this?"

"No," I said, befuddled. "Why would I? The house we've gone to ten thousand times was all I thought was there. It's so massive when you pull into the driveway that I never even thought about seeing anything else."

"You never played in the yard as a kid?" she asked.

"Well, sure, but it was always out front. The front lawn was so big, I can't even ever remember going into the backyard."

"So there have to be other houses back there," she said, ever the quick thinker.

"Oh, here it is," I said, finding more information further down the page. "The housekeeping staff lives in one house, his personal assistant in another, and the third house is a guest house."

"Jesus Christ, Max."

"Jesus Christ," I echoed, not knowing what else to say.

"The staff stay with the house and are to be paid until their deaths from the trust," I read.

"There's a trust?"

"Apparently," I said, still dumbfounded about how I knew none of this.

"Gramps was way richer than we thought he was."

I flashed back to a conversation I'd had with Courtney after we left Gramps's together for the first time. She'd said, "Your grandfather is loaded, isn't he?" It was the first time I'd brought anyone to his house. I'd had other girlfriends, even some serious ones, but none serious enough to introduce to Gramps. I'd never really thought about it before. I knew he had money, sure. But I never had an outsider's opinion about *how much* money he might have had.

It was something we off-handedly joked about over the years. We'd kid that Gramps could give us the coins in his couch and all of our financial problems would be solved. It was just a joke between us for two reasons. The first being that we never thought he'd do something like that. And the second being that I never wanted to get a handout. I never wanted to expect someone to solve any of the problems that I had created for myself or my family.

I saw what the money did to my parents. I saw how it always left them wanting more and more and more. I remembered how it made me feel to be around them, and I hated that feeling.

Yes, Gramps could have solved so many of our problems with a swipe of his pen on one of his checks, but I never asked, and he never offered. Though in a weird, twisted way, he was now solving all our problems. Whether we moved into the house or sold it, we wouldn't have to worry about money ever again.

"Do you seriously want to consider moving there?" I asked.

"Can you imagine it?" Her voice trailed off as if she were daydreaming. "The parties we could have! The balls. The dinners."

"Babe," I said, trying to snap her back to reality.

"Yes, yes. Sorry." She turned back to make eye contact with me again. "I don't think it should *not* be something we consider."

Before replying immediately, I gave it some thought. Yes, selling the property would set us up for a lifetime of lifetimes. We'd have more money than we could ever possibly imagine. Especially if Zillow's estimated value of thirty-five million was even in the right ballpark. But could I live there? Could I live somewhere that I'd only ever spent a handful of hours at a time at?

I guess so, right? We spent about 10 minutes in this apartment before filling out the application paperwork. But was that out of love for the apartment, or out of a need for a place to live once we moved in together?

"Let me think about it," I said, leaving the conversation open-ended. "I'll need to sleep on it."

* * *

A FEW HOURS LATER, after we'd long since gone to bed, I tossed and turned, unable to fall asleep, but also unable to open my eyes. Every time I tried to doze off, I felt my mind wandering, racing. I pictured myself sitting in the living room at Gramps's house. The house had been emptied of all of his belongings, and I sat on a bare floor, just the rug and me, surrounded by bare walls and uncovered windows.

But it was more than an almost-asleep-dream. It felt like I was really there. It felt like the house was summoning me, as if there was something it was trying to tell me. A calling, perhaps. A vision of some sort. Without realizing it, I ran my hand over the top of my blanket. Its surface felt like the rug at Gramps's house. It felt like that once-fluffy but now worn-down, not-quite-shag carpet between my fingers. That carpet I'd spent countless hours on throughout my life. It felt like it was part of me.

With my eyes still closed, I moved my head around, looking at the barren walls of the imaginary house. I saw shapes where the paint was still vibrant from where old family photos that had hung for years and decades had been removed, the faded paint around their frames leaving a perfect rectangle-shaped reminder of the photo or painting that once hung in its place.

From the kitchen, I heard the all-too-familiar voices of my parents and Gramps, and one of my uncles, though I couldn't tell which one it was. Their voices were muffled, but still clear enough that I could hear the topic of conversation.

"Dad, you're imagining things," my father said, clearly trying to hush his voice.

"The house is empty, William," my mother added. In this vision, this memory, this, whatever it was, I was a child. I could sense it in my being. I could feel myself just a little boy. A little boy, eager to know what was happening just through the doorway in the kitchen.

I stood from the bed and took steps toward that doorframe, doing my best not to alert anyone that I was coming closer.

"Max?" I heard Courtney say, but I could not answer her. I took three more steps until I bumped into the dresser of our bedroom, stopping me from moving any further forward. "Max?" she called out again. But still, I was unable to answer her. I couldn't open my eyes and couldn't do anything but focus my hearing on what was happening in Gramps's kitchen.

Doing my best not to trip over the dresser in the real world, I leaned closer to the doorframe in my imagination, tilting my head just to the left to point my ear through the opening.

"There's nothing there, Dad," my father said. "Big empty houses make noise. That's just what happens."

"I know what I saw," Gramps said firmly, slamming his balled-up fist on something that I think was the countertop.

"No, William," I hear my mother say. No matter how long my parents were together, she'd never called him Dad or even Gramps when I came along. And certainly never a nickname. A man of his stature deserves to be called by his full name, she'd once told me. In my head, I sometimes called him Gramps William, but never aloud to him or to anyone else.

"Max?" Courtney called out a third time, this time getting up and walking over next to me. I was still stuck in the daze of my imagination until she put her hand on my shoulder and shook me. It was the third or fourth shake that finally brought me back to reality.

"Huh?" I asked, slightly confused as to why I was standing leaning up against the dresser with my hands on top of it like I was about to scale it.

"What happened?" she asked, now rubbing the shoulder she'd just shaken to bring me back.

"I was…" I didn't know how to describe it. "I was at Gramps'. I must have been dreaming."

"You've never sleepwalked before," she said. "Is that what just happened?"

"I don't know. I'm not even sure I was asleep," I said. "But I couldn't open my eyes when I tried. I think I heard you calling my name, but something in that dream was calling me more than you were."

"What do you mean?"

"I heard Gramps talking to my parents. They were in the kitchen, and I was in the living room, eavesdropping."

"Sometimes I have dreams that are actually memories. Is that maybe what happened to you?"

"I don't…" I fumbled for words, still trying to readjust myself back to reality. "I don't think so."

The light of the television hurt my eyes for some reason. We'd often fall asleep with it on, usually to an old favorite show of ours that we referred to as the "forever re-watchable" group. Shows like *The Office, Parks and Recreation, Modern Family, Friends*. Those comfort shows we could listen to, but still fall asleep. Shows that would help drown out any noise in our heads and let us fall asleep peacefully. It was something we bonded over when we first met. Neither of us could ever turn off our brains—something I'd learned later in life was simple anxiety and cured by medication—so we needed background noise to sleep. For years—decades even—I'd fallen asleep to music. It wasn't until I started crashing at Courtney's a few nights a week that listening to TV shows became the norm for me.

"I definitely don't think what I just had was a memory," I said after thinking about it. "That was something else, but I don't know what."

"Okay, mister, let's get you back to bed, then," she said, pulling my arm away from the dresser and toward our bed. Suddenly, I felt exhausted. My body felt drained and as if it could collapse at any moment. I did the only thing I could think of and flung myself back toward the bed, hoping I'd land there and not thud onto the floor.

I'd fallen asleep before I even remember hitting my pillow.

* * *

THE REST of that night was less dramatic, though. Once I'd fallen asleep so hard, I went right into a peaceful dream.

Again, I was at Gramps's house, but we were outside. This time, it was a memory—a memory that I was incredibly fond of. It was Gramps teaching me to ride a bike. I was five years old. My parents were away on some trip, somewhere.

Despite not getting it the first handful of times, Gramps didn't give up. Every time I fell, he'd dust me off—literally—bandage up whatever cut or scrape I had gotten and plop me right back on the bicycle. He'd right the training wheels if they'd gotten askew, tighten my helmet, and begin the trek down the long driveway, getting further away from the house.

Through my dream, I felt that peace that I'd had on that day.

I felt the utmost love that he'd had for me. I felt him protecting me from those falls, even when he wasn't quick enough to catch me. I knew somewhere inside me that he'd always protect me. It was a sense I'd had since I was a small child, going all the way back to my first memories of him and me together.

It was almost an out-of-body experience. I, as an adult, watching myself as a child from a distance. There I stood, off behind the lollipop trees, watching Gramps and me. Observing.

Then I noticed something I didn't have a memory of noticing at the time. I noticed something that I didn't recall happening, and I don't remember Gramps talking about it with my parents or me.

He let go of the bike for a moment, and I coasted away of my own free will and under my own power. Child me felt fearless. He felt powerful. He felt like he could rule the world someday. But adult me was suddenly full of confusion. From my perch behind the lollipop trees, I saw Gramps stop in his tracks and stare back at the house. His eyes glazed over, and I could see his left hand trembling ever so slightly. Dream me looked up at the giant house, trying to place what he was looking at. I scanned the brick facade, looking in each window and on the second-story porch on the left-hand side of the house. I checked the massive front doors. I had a fleeting memory of how hard it was to push those doors open when I was young. They had to be ten feet tall and weigh at least a hundred pounds each.

I darted my eyes around the entire house, but didn't see what had caught his attention.

Before I knew it, Gramps bounced back and jogged down the driveway to catch up to child me, just in time to catch me from my fiftieth fall of the day. His still-capable hands caught me just before I hit the ground.

He laughed as he caught me, swinging me up into the air before putting me down.

Child me didn't see any of what had just happened. All I knew as a kid, and the memory I have of that day, as an adult, was just Gramps letting me go and me riding my first time on the bike, unassisted, even if just for a few short feet.

* * *

"I THINK WE SHOULD DO IT," I said as soon as Courtney woke up the following morning. I'd been awake for an hour or so, quietly sitting and waiting for her to wake up. I'd been reading over the digital copy of Gramps's will that the lawyer had emailed to all of us who were left something in it. I'd also looked at the Zillow listing of Gramps's house—sorry, *our* house—a few times that morning, as well.

"Good morning," she said, kissing me on the cheek, as she'd done every other morning for the last twenty years or so. "Do what?"

"We should move into Gramps's house."

"What made you come to that decision?" she asked.

"Something about the dream I had last night."

"The one where you were groping the dresser?" she joked.

"No," I laughed, trying to brush off the weird experience I'd had before going to sleep. "The dream I had once I'd finally gone to bed."

"Do you want to tell me about it?"

"Not now," I said. "But listen, there's some weird stuff in Gramps's will that the lawyer didn't tell us about."

"Oh?" she asked, sitting up and leaning on my shoulder. "Like what?"

"Well, we now know about the four houses and the occupants of two of them. We know about the trust that'll pay for those employees. But the lawyer spent so much time focusing on the house Gramps had left us, he didn't talk about any of Gramps's other wishes."

"For us?"

"For everyone," I said, grabbing my phone from the nightstand and unlocking it to the document I'd left open earlier. "The will is like three hundred pages long, but I'll summarize the bits I was able to read through this morning. Gramps left us the property; we know that. The wording of it is a little weird, but I'm not an expert on wills, so maybe it's totally normal. But the will says 'the contents of the property' as well. As if there's something on the property that he didn't want to specifically call out, but wanted us to know was ours."

"Okay, so what else?"

"He specifically left my parents some money. Just money. No possessions. No property. No art. Just money. He left them just over two million dollars. I only remember that specifically because…" I searched the document for $2, figuring it'd bring up the amount. "I remember that because it's such an oddly specific amount. Two million, three hundred fifty-one thousand, seven dollars. That's a weird number, right?"

"Maybe not weird," she said. "But definitely specific."

"Uncle Matthew and Jennifer got two million exactly. Uncles Joey and David each got one million. I guess Matthew got an extra million because he's married."

"I guess that makes sense. But why the specific amount for your parents?"

"I don't know," I said, switching over to the Messages app on my phone.

Hey, Dad, hope you and Mom are enjoying your trip. Did you get a copy of Gramps's will and review it yet?

He read the message immediately, but didn't respond right away.

"I guess I'll find out if he knows anything soon," I said.

"What else?" Courtney asked. "You said there were other wishes."

"Right, yes. So I mentioned the money he left my dad and his brothers. I mentioned the property that goes to us and whatever else is on the property. He left his prized Rolls-Royce to his assistant, Geoffrey." I never thought much of their working relationship, but I sure got a kick out of it when *The Fresh Prince of Bel-Air* started airing on TV, and the butler on that show was named Geoffrey, too. Coincidence, I guess.

"That's nice of him," Courtney said.

"It is. Geoffrey has been with Gramps for as long as I can remember. I think he hired him when I was four or five. He's been a staple of that house for as long as I can remember, always acting more like a friend or confidant than an assistant. Gramps would have been lost without him, I'm sure."

"Anything else?"

"There's more money left over," I said. "A lot more. He left a bunch to different charities. A lot of it is in the trust, specifically called out to any future relatives that might pop up. A call out to great-grandchildren as well. Not that there are any." Like Uncle Matthew and Aunt Jennifer, Courtney and I had some trouble getting pregnant. Though unlike them, we didn't keep trying until it almost bankrupted us. We had one close call, which we lost in a miscarriage, but then we gave up. And we never really discussed it again. That was a really hard point in our lives, and one that I'd tried to lean on my dad for, but didn't get the support I'd hoped for.

Yes. Received. Reviewing with my lawyer today.

Dad had responded to my text. Brief and to the point, like always. I noticed Courtney reading over my shoulder as I switched apps, so I didn't feel it necessary to read his message out loud to her.

"Gramps sure was an interesting guy," she said.

"He sure was," I said, thinking a little out loud to myself.

"Anything else in the will a surprise?"

"Not really. But I didn't read the whole thing. It's very long."

"So what has your mind made up that you want to move into the house?"

"I can't put my finger on it," I said. "But something about the dream I had last night. Something about this memory just put me at peace. Without doing it intentionally, the dream told me it's what Gramps wanted, even though he didn't specifically say so in the will. I feel like he wants us to move there and take care of the house and all of its surprises."

"I don't want to be a Debbie Downer," she said. "But can we afford to live there? It has to cost a fortune to upkeep, doesn't it?"

"I'm sure it does," I said, snapping back to reality. "Maybe there's something in the will that'll explain that part of it."

I scrolled back through some pages of the will, doing my best to pay attention to what I was seeing and not daydream of living in the big house with the massive kitchen and giant dining room. I did my best to focus on the words on my phone's screen and not try to remember what it was like upstairs. A place I was only allowed to go to once in a very rare situation where, at a dinner party, all the downstairs bathrooms happened to be occupied at the same time, and twelve-year-old me couldn't wait any longer. I remember Geoffrey walking me through the kitchen to the back of the house and up the back staircase. I always thought it was so cool that Gramps had multiple staircases in his home. The one at the front was sweeping and rose to the second floor from both sides of the foyer. Each staircase, almost a half circle, meets at the top of the landing, as if closing the loop. I often dreamed of running up and down those stairs when I was a kid, pretending I was scaling a mountain.

Geoffrey walked me to the top of the back stairs, the ones the housekeepers usually used, and down a long hallway to the bathroom that was outside of a bedroom that I had assumed to be Gramps'. Geoffrey stood by the door, waiting, while I went inside and closed myself in. I turned the light on to find my reflection staring back at me in the largest mirror I'd ever seen. It spanned the entire wall along the backside of the toilet, which felt like it was in another zip code from where I stood. My reflection caught me by surprise for a moment, but didn't distract me from the job at hand. I had to pee like I've never had to pee before in my lifetime.

I walked the few paces to the toilet and was thankful to relieve myself.

By the time I was done peeing and walking back toward the door, I heard Geoffrey. "Wash your hands, Maxwell." I hadn't even opened the door, but he knew I was planning to skip that part of my bathroom visit.

"Ow!" I yelled as the scalding water rushed over my hands. As I jumped back, I thought I heard him talking to someone else in a hushed tone.

"Are you all right in there?" he called back.

"I'm fine," I said, grabbing the towel from the rack and

drying my hands, which were now red from the hot water. As I opened the door, I peeked out briefly to see if I could see anyone other than Geoffrey.

"Were you talking to someone?" I asked.

"No, sir. Everything is fine, Max. Let's get back downstairs."

He rushed me off down the back staircase and to the dinner party, where my parents were chatting it up with some of Gramps's friends. Gramps was sitting at the head of the table, like always. His good friend and fellow video game creator, David, was by his side, as was the custom at these types of dinner parties. I liked to pretend they treated the parties like business meetings, inviting important people that they wanted to impress with Gramps's massive house. "Look at how good I am at video games," he'd joke. "I have this massive house. I must be so great at the games."

My adolescent mind was wild.

"There," Courtney said, "go back a page."

I scrolled up and there it was. **The estate's trust will pay all expenses for 1 Stone Way for its inhabitants, provided the inhabitants are direct descendants of the deceased.**

"What does that mean?" I asked.

"It means that as long as we live there and the trust has money, the trust will pay for the house."

"Is this real life?" I asked. "Like, is this real?"

"It sure seems like a dream," she said, nuzzling into the space between my arm and my body. "If it is a dream, I don't want to wake up."

CHAPTER 5
DAD'S RESPONSE

WOW

That was all the response my father gave, at least initially.

"What do you think he means by that?" Courtney asked after I held up my phone to show her the message.

Deciphering my father's thoughts or meanings behind things over the years had become somewhat of a specialized skill set. Reading between the lines to figure out what he meant based on what he said was something I sometimes wished I'd had a sibling to commiserate with. He was often cryptic, somewhat terse, and usually blunt in how he spoke, especially in digital communication.

I could often figure out the subtext of what he said, but those three little letters stared back at me from the screen of my phone, elusive whether he was pleased with the will or appalled by it.

"The lack of punctuation would indicate displeasure, based on previous messages, I'd think," I said after thinking about it for another minute.

"Oh, yeah. You're right," Courtney agreed. "Like when we

told him about losing the baby. All he said was 'sorry'. He didn't even capitalize the word."

The truth was that my father and I didn't communicate much over text. In fact, I only had to scroll up three times to see the aforementioned 'sorry' he'd sent eight years ago when we lost the baby. One of the most painful events of my entire life, and all he could muster was 'sorry'. At least my mother called me and had me put the phone on speaker while she wept with Courtney and me as if she had suffered a great loss herself.

I kept flipping back and forth between the wall and my phone. That tiny little word seemed to say too much and not enough at the same time.

"I'm just going to call him," I said aloud, more to reassure myself that it was the right path forward than to let Court know what I was doing.

He picked up on the fourth ring. "Yes?"

No matter what, that's how he always answered the phone. As if your call inconvenienced him. As if he were so busy that he painfully tore himself away from whatever he was doing to take your call. And as if he had no idea who was calling. I never specifically looked at his phone to see whether he ever saved anyone's phone number, but he had to have, right?

"Hey, Dad," I said, emphasizing the *dad* in case he needed a reminder of who was calling. As if he needed a reminder of what that number may have been that popped up on his phone. The same phone number I'd had for twenty-five years, at least.

"Hello, Maxwell."

I mouthed *Maxwell* to Courtney to show he'd full named me —a clear sign of distress in my father's world.

"I wasn't sure how to take your response," I dove right in. "How are you feeling after reviewing Gramps's will?"

"I'm taken aback," he said. Even now, on the phone, he was still his cryptic self.

"In what way?" I pulled the phone away from my head quickly and pressed the speaker button.

"I'm surprised by a lot of it. Geoffrey? Really?"

"Dad, Geoffrey was Gramps's assistant for decades."

"Did you put me on speaker? Hello Courtney." He didn't wait for either of us to reply. "Yes, Geoffrey was my father's assistant for decades. I was his son for my entire life."

I was surprised by this response. And honestly, it was a little more hostile than I had expected it to be. My brain immediately thought, "You just got two million bucks, you jerk" and "Your father just died", but I didn't say either of those things. I flashed back to Gramps, reminding me that money could not and will not buy happiness, and I pictured the sourpuss on my father's face.

I'm sure Mom wouldn't have been so upset. I didn't hear her in the background, so I assumed that he'd gone to meet with the lawyer without her, telling her he'd fill her in when he got back. He often did things like that. I wouldn't call him a full-blown chauvinist, but he was the closest thing to one that I knew.

"Dad," I started, thinking I could reason with him, but he cut me off.

"And he left you his home? You and not me?"

"Whoa, hang on a minute, Dad." Will and Marcus from *About a Boy* popped into my head. Their complicated relationship reminded me a lot of that of my father and me.

"Don't you hang on a minute dad me." He raised his voice, and I immediately remembered why we had such a fractured relationship once I became an adult, and realized I didn't just have to take everything he fired off at me when he was upset.

"Gramps left me his house because I was there for him," I shot back. "I spent a lot of time with him throughout my lifetime. Time when you and Mom would fly off to wherever and leave me for weeks at a time."

Wow, Courtney mouthed. At first, I didn't understand why, but then it hit me she'd probably not heard me talk to my father like that before. I usually just let him get away with whatever behavior he wanted because I knew our interactions were limited. If I only spoke to him once a month and saw him even less frequently than that, why should I let him occupy space in my brain with his antics?

"I was there for him, too!" He yelled. "Even when..." he trailed off.

"You weren't there for him like I was," I found myself starting to shout back.

Calm down, Courtney mouthed, motioning with her hands like Ross Gellar telling others to lower their voice on *Friends*. *It's okay*.

She was right. It would be okay. Who knew what he'd try to pull or where he'd take things, but I would not let him make me feel bad about Gramps's decision to leave the house and property to Courtney and me.

"I'm just in shock. I'm his son," he said.

"And I'm his grandson," I retorted. "His only grandson. And not for nothing, Dad," I put a lot of spite into how I said *dad*. "He left you a boatload of money."

He was silent for a moment. Just a fleeting pause in time where I thought he was reconsidering his position, his attitude, and his response. "Congratulations on your new home," he said. "Best of luck with it."

Then he hung up on me.

I stared at the phone in disbelief. I couldn't remember another time in my life, even when we were at our worst, when he'd hung up on me.

"Wow," Courtney said.

"That seems to be the word of the day," I tried to joke and make light of what'd just happened.

"It's safe to say he's a little mad."

"Safe to say," I said.

"I get it," she said quietly. "His gravy train is over."

"What do you mean?" I asked, not sure whether she'd intended for me to hear her.

"Well, I never wanted to say anything because it's not my place. But your parents had it easy."

"How so?" I asked, scooting around to face her, my phone still in my hand, its screen now dark.

"We've known each other for a long time now, right?"

I nodded.

"Your dad never had to worry about money. He never worked, as far as I know. And he and your mom, who I love dearly, don't get me wrong, got to galavant all around the world, on your grandfather's dime. As far as we know, he paid for everything, including the lavish apartment they have in Manhattan and their house in Malibu, right?"

I nodded again.

"And now that's all over," she said. "Sure, he left them some money, but that money is finite. It'll run out eventually."

"Oh my God," I said, clasping my hand to my mouth. "You're absolutely right."

"And last night, after you went to bed, I read a good portion of the rest of your grandfather's will."

"Oh?"

"All the future money that his company makes? All the royalties from his inventions, and patents, and whatever? It all goes into the trust."

"I don't know what you mean," I said.

"I asked ChatGPT to analyze that part of the will," she said. She loved using artificial intelligence to decipher legalese and medical documents. It was one of her favorite things in recent times. "The trust is tied to the property, but you're not specifically called out as the beneficiary of the trust anywhere. Another of your grandfather's companies is."

"Still not following you," I said, furrowing my brow.

"All the money your grandfather's company will ever make goes into the trust. The beneficiary of the trust—who can benefit from it—is a business."

"Okay. So what?"

"The name of the company is MJW Enterprises. Your initials."

It suddenly hit me like a ton of bricks. MJW Enterprises. My initials tied to a company that I'd never heard of. All the inventions Gramps had created were attributed to his main business, the Stone Washington Company. Stone, because it's the name of the road he named once he built the estate. It was my Gram's maiden name. Washington, which was our family name. Everything he ever invented was tied to that company. It held all of his income, his assets, and his money. It'd continue to be run by the board of directors, which was headed up by David's grandson, who was a little older than me. The will explicitly called out that nothing would change with that company.

"What does this mean?" Courtney asked.

"I have no idea," I said. "But I think we need to scrape up some money and talk to a lawyer. Just in case."

"Just in case," she parroted back to me.

CHAPTER 6
BEADS OF SWEAT
& NIGHT TERRORS

COURTNEY WOKE ME UP, shaking me and yelling my name. "Max! Max!" she called out.

By the time I opened my eyes, I was sweating and freezing cold at the same time. The covers felt like the inside of a freezer. The room felt like the Arctic. I couldn't breathe. I was gasping for air and clutching at my chest. "What happened?" I managed to push up my dry throat, past my shivering lips.

"You were screaming," she said. "No, Gramps, no. Over and over again. It woke me up."

"Jesus," I said, not knowing what else to say, still struggling to force air into my burning lungs.

My feet somehow fell off the side of the bed, and I was able to sit up. My face lay in my hands, the sweat dripping through my partially open fingers onto the floor below me. Courtney had run to the bathroom down the hall to get a cold towel and was putting it on the back of my neck before I knew she was gone.

"What was the dream about?" she asked. But I had no idea. I couldn't recall any of it.

I shrugged.

"Are you okay?" she asked.

After running my hands down my torso and across my thighs, I felt physically all right. Nothing was missing or damaged. Nothing was out of sorts, other than my boxers being soaked through with sweat. "I just need to change," I said. "I think I'm okay now. Thank you."

"Of course," she said, downplaying what'd just happened. "I'm here if you need me." Then she lay back down on her side of the bed and closed her eyes. I was always jealous of how quickly she could fall back asleep after waking up. I, on the other hand, would be awake for hours. I'd normally listen to whatever TV show we'd put on before we went to bed. Often, I could picture what was happening in the scene, even though we'd turn the screen off when we went to sleep. But there I'd lie. For hours. Awake. Stewing in my own thoughts and anxieties.

Once I'd changed into dry boxers and tossed the soaked ones on the floor, I climbed back into bed. My blanket was soaked up near my head, so I flipped it around, putting the wet part down by my feet. It was still uncomfortable, but not nearly as bad as when it was the other way.

Closing my eyes felt like a chore. I have a weird thing where the longer I'm awake, the harder it is to fall back asleep. If I get up, go to the bathroom, and then get right back into bed, I can fall asleep pretty quickly. But if I do anything or anyone talks to me while I'm awake, forget about it. Falling back asleep was almost impossible some nights.

And that night was one of those nights. I sometimes felt like Christian Bale in *The Machinist*. Unable to sleep. Constantly awake, tossing and turning.

My eyes kept popping open, hearing sounds I'm sure weren't

there. Seeing the lights flicker across the ceiling from passing cars. The sounds of Michael and Dwight getting up to no good on the episode of *The Office* playing through the blank screen. Everything felt overwhelming.

But I forced myself to keep my eyes closed. I pressed them firmly together and told myself to breathe. Just in and out, one at a time. It was a method that my therapist had taught me in one of our earlier sessions. A technique of grounding myself when I felt I couldn't be grounded. A way to reconnect with my body and the place I was.

It'd never worked very well before, but that didn't stop me from trying. When I remembered to try, at least.

No sooner had I started thinking that what I was doing was stupid and wasn't working than I fell asleep.

Unfortunately for my brain and my body, I fell right back into the same dream I was having before Courtney woke me up.

"You have to believe me," Gramps said. His voice echoed through the empty dining room of a house I didn't recognize. The walls were covered in portraits of old men and their families, none of whom looked familiar to me. But the dining room was massive. The table must have seated a hundred people. Its end was so far away from me that I couldn't have thrown a football and hit it.

The echoing intensified as I looked Gramps in the eyes. His face just a foot or so from mine.

"You have to believe me," he said again. "They don't believe me," he added.

"I don't know what you're talking about, Gramps," I mustered. "Where are we?"

"Where we are isn't important," he said. "But it's safe here."

"Safe from what?"

I let my eyes look past him, almost through him, to the door at the far end of the dining room. It was open, slightly, with a bright light shining through it. The light flickered as if something passed between its source and the door, causing a dark shadow.

"Maybe it's not safe," Gramps said, motioning toward the door at the other end of the room. "Quickly."

"What's going on? Gramps, what's happening?"

"There's no time," he said, now forcefully pushing me toward the closed door.

"No time for what?"

"Just trust me," he said. "Believe what I've told you when you get back. It'll all make sense when you move into the house."

"Gramps, I'm confused."

Just then, the door at the other end of the room flung open. The light shining through it was entirely eclipsed. I was being forced in the opposite direction and wasn't able to fully turn to see what was in the doorway, which was now blocking the light. But it seemed to frighten Gramps, so he pushed me faster toward the other door.

"You have to go. Wake up, Maxwell. Go through the door and wake up!"

He pulled the door open in front of me. Warm air hit my face, and a whooshing sound swept over my body. I felt the force of both of his hands land on the small of my back, pushing me through the door to the other side. I instantly fell, clutching for the door or the frame to stop myself from falling. I couldn't see the ground below me.

I gasped myself awake, once again trying to force air into my lungs that weren't cooperating. My eyes burned, and my face felt like it was too close to a campfire. I felt an immense pressure on my chest, like a child was sitting on me.

"Max? Are you awake again?" It was Courtney's velvety voice.

"Yes. I am. I just had the most bizarre dream," I said.

"Do you want to talk about it?"

"It's late," I said, taking a quick look at my watch. "It's just after three. Go back to sleep. We'll talk about it in the morning."

As I closed my eyes again, something popped back into my head. Just as I was falling out of the door in my dream and about to wake up, I thought I heard something from the dining room. I swear, even if just for an instant, I heard a voice say, "I told you I'd find you."

I might have been imagining it. I could have been making it up. I had to have been. It was one of the weirdest dreams I'd ever had. Nothing like that had ever happened before, and the only other dreams I'd ever had of Gramps were happy ones. Dreams inspired by memories of things we'd actually done together. Like the day he took me to the dog track with him—he loved betting on dog races. Or when he took me to Disney World when I was ten, because my parents wanted to go to Fashion Week in Milan. Or when he took me to London as a gift when I got my Master's degree.

But every one of those dreams included fabrications, depending on how old I was when I had them. Like when I dreamed about Disney World after we'd just gotten back. Sure, we did all the things we did in real life, but in my dream I also got to have dinner with Mickey and Minnie, and was riding on a float in the parade. Things that my brain wanted to have happened but would have never actually happened in real life.

Those amazing fabrications that my brain filled into the dream to make the memory a life-changing experience.

Never once had I had a bad dream about Gramps. I had bad dreams as a child about my parents fighting. About being chased by a tiger. Or about my elementary school bully beating me up on the playground, and everyone laughing. I had typical bad dreams that kids have. But never once about Gramps. Never once like what had just happened.

And as I lay there, drifting back off to sleep, hoping I wouldn't land back in that dream, I thought I heard a creak come from the hallway. Just for a moment. Just a tiny blip in my brain while I was dozing off. A small creak that surely was just the floor moving or the apartment building settling. Something so quick and so minute that it couldn't possibly have been real, and if it was, it couldn't have possibly been anything to worry about.

CHAPTER 7
GOOD NEWS FROM THE LAWYER

"YOU'RE ABSOLUTELY SURE?" It's all I could ask, as Courtney and I sat across from the lawyer we'd sought to review Gramps's will on our behalf, not just deliver it to us, as Gramps's lawyer had.

"I'm absolutely sure," he said, pulling his glasses the rest of the way off his nose and plopping them onto his desk before pushing his chair back. "Listen, I've been a lawyer for a long time. But whoever your grandfather hired to write his will is a better lawyer than anyone I know. It's rock solid."

I looked to my left and made eye contact with Courtney. Honestly, what Mr. Decker was saying didn't surprise me. Gramps was always one to, as he'd say, "cross the Ts and dot the Is." His thoroughness with his last wishes was right in line with what I'd have expected from him.

"So there's no way that Bruce can do anything about it?" Courtney asked.

"My dad, Bruce," I began, "seemed a little upset when he read the will."

"Entitled is the word I'd use," Courtney added. "As if Max getting the estate was a mistake, and it should have gone to him."

"He didn't even say anything about his brothers," I added. "Sort of a one-track mind on him, I suppose."

"All he could do is contest the will," he said. "That'd possibly draw things out some in terms of finalizing the estate, but I don't see anything here that would ultimately cause a judge to over-turn the will. Especially with your grandfather's upstanding reputation."

"Your father's always rubbed me the wrong way," Courtney said.

"Try being his son," I said quickly, without thinking.

"Be that as it may," Mr. Decker said, "the will is solid. And you know the old saying is an old saying for a reason. Money is the root of all evil. And money brings out people's greed."

* * *

WE LEFT Mr. Decker's office that Friday afternoon excited, though a little worried. I knew, somewhere in the back of my mind, that my father would do everything he could to get more than his share of Gramps's wealth. More so, even that he'd already been left in the will.

As we walked down the little alleyway between Mr. Decker's office and where we'd parked, I couldn't help but think of Gramps. His smile popped into my head just as we were rounding the corner, and I felt like I could smell his cologne. Just for a brief second. Just as we passed an old Jewish bakery that I know he used to like to go to when he was in the city. "Ruben-stein's Bakery has the best fresh bagels on the planet," he'd once told me. And it was hard to argue with him. Their bagels were incredible. The size of a child's basketball. Somehow, they were always hot, right from the oven. Always crisp on the outside, but soft as a pillow on the inside.

The memory made me smile. But the smell of his cologne brought an even bigger smile to my face. It wasn't until that moment that it really hit me how much I missed him.

It'd been a little less than three weeks since he'd passed. We'd had the funeral. We'd had three consecutive nights of wakes where hundreds—maybe thousands—of people showed up to pay their respects. People I'd never heard of, let alone met. Old people. Young people. Plenty of in-between people. The lines stretched all the way around the funeral home and out the front door, down the stairs, and onto the sidewalk. I heard stories about Gramps from strangers. How he touched them in some way. How he helped them. One younger woman told me she'd gotten into video game programming because she loved playing the "old school" video games that Gramps had his hands in. She gushed about how much more she fell in love with programming once she'd learned about all the techniques Gramps had invented. One older man told me how Gramps had invested in a company he founded when it was on the brink of bankruptcy, and how the business was flourishing because of Gramps's investment and the business knowledge he shared with him after investing.

I went through the entire process with my family there. My parents. My wife. My Uncles and Uncle Matthew's wife. We all seemed to get through it together just fine. Dad and my uncles handled the arrangements, which felt like some top-secret government project. There were whispers and "shush shush, quiet quiet" proclaimed sometimes when I'd walk into the room.

We met at Gramps's to plan. Or at least that's what Dad had said. I think, secretly, he wanted to be at Gramps's house unsupervised. I don't know what for, though. At the time, I thought perhaps he wanted to snoop around in Gramps's things. I suppose I couldn't blame him. But knowing how he reacted to the will, I wondered if he'd taken anything he wasn't supposed to.

"It wouldn't surprise me," Courtney said out of the blue, just after we got into our car.

"What's that?"

"You were just mumbling a little. About your dad."

"Oh," I paused a moment to try to remember what I was saying. "Was I?"

"You were. It's okay. It's a lot. I get it." She'd always been one of the most understanding people. It was one of the reasons I fell in love with her. She didn't just understand situations; she also had empathy and sympathy at the right times. Did that, but she also really just understood me. On a level others never had before. She understood how I thought and felt and acted. I knew she was my match very early in our relationship.

"Mr. Decker's right. I know the will is solid, but I also know my father."

"You must have heard the whispering the second night of the wake, right?"

"I don't think so," I said. "Tell me."

"Oh, I thought you were with me. I must have misremembered. I was walking down the hallway toward the bathroom. Not the one at the front of the funeral home, but the second one, near the back."

"Mhmm." I had a habit of nodding or making an audible sound to let people know I was listening to them, even when I wasn't. It was something I'd told myself to work on a number of times throughout my adult life. But with Courtney, I was usually listening.

"I was approaching the door of the funeral home director's office. I forgot his name. Mr. Jacobs? Mr. Jackson? Something with a J. Anyway, as I approached the door, I heard men talking quietly, just above a whisper. I couldn't tell what they were saying, but I also didn't really try to. It just seemed odd that they were talking so quietly."

"Well, it was a wake. Some people do that because they feel it's more respectful to the deceased."

"You're right. I'd agree with you there. But when I stepped on a squeaky part of the floor, right before I got to the door, the door started closing. I caught only a quick glimpse inside."

"Who was in there?"

"Mr. J-whatever and your father. And I think I saw one of your uncles in there, too."

"That's weird. But maybe nothing nefarious."

"You're right. They could have been settling a bill or something else."

"More than likely."

I put the car in drive and headed back to our apartment. I think both of us were feeling a little better about all the moving boxes and rolls of packing tape that Amazon had delivered earlier in the day. My mind raced about how much packing we'd have to do. We'd had two storage units in the basement of our apartment building that we hadn't been to in years. They were both full of things we knew we couldn't let go of—old family photographs, records that I'd collected over the years but never listened to, my Nintendo from childhood, Courtney's Aunt's wedding dress that she'd left her when she passed—but would now have an abundance of space for.

"When are the movers coming?" I asked, forever the forgetful one in our marriage.

"Three days," she said. I couldn't turn my head to look at her at that moment, but I sensed she was smiling.

It seems like such a typical cliché, doesn't it? Someone's rich grandfather dies and leaves them a fortune, changing their lives forever. And it is. I know it is. I also know that I led a pretty privileged life leading up to that point. Gramps had taken as much care of me as I'd let him, Courtney, too. He'd never outright offered us money, even when we struggled. And I'd never asked. But periodically, when we'd leave his house after a Sunday dinner, I'd find money in my wallet, somehow, that I knew I didn't have before going there. A few crisp hundred-dollar bills I felt Gramps had somehow snuck into my wallet. The weird part was that I'd never—in all the times I'd gone to Gramp's for dinner—taken my wallet out of my back pocket.

But, like many things in my life, I never questioned it. I was thankful when it happened, and I think it made Gramps feel like he was helping without any recognition. That was something I learned about him at the wake. He often helped people, but made them keep it a secret. I don't know why. Maybe he didn't want people knowing how generous he was, so they wouldn't come to him asking for a handout. Perhaps he liked the anonymity. I don't know. And it's not like I can ask him now.

CHAPTER 8
MOVING DAY

THERE I SAT in my living room for the last time, surrounded by literal walls of boxes. Courtney's muffled singing came from the bedroom; her excitement was palpable. A small smile came across my face. I realized then and there that life truly was about to change.

Sure, I had worries about lots of things. How we'd upkeep the house. How we'd get along with the housekeepers and Geoffrey. How we'd maintain our marriage with such an enormous change to our financial status. Whether my father would try to squeeze the estate for something Gramps didn't want him to have. And speaking of that, why didn't Gramps leave his estate to his sons? Why me?

It's not survivor's guilt I felt, but it's something like it. My Dad and uncles weren't dead, so I didn't survive anything. But I had this queasy, guilty feeling in my stomach for a week or so, absolutely confounded as to why Gramps didn't do more for his sons but left the bulk of his estate to me.

Courtney came bounding into the living room, sliding a

stack of boxes out of the path between her and I, literally lighting up the room, as those boxes were blocking the window. "The movers just texted me. They'll be here in an hour. How are you doing?"

I half-motioned to the boxes around me and the tape gun by my feet. "I think we're ready," I said, trying to force myself to believe we were ready. Yes, we were ready for the movers. Physically ready with all our things packed, labeled, and stacked up. We were ready to move, but I kept questioning if we were ready or not. Were we mentally ready for what was ahead?

Until that moment, it'd never even crossed my mind how weird it'd be to live in Gramp's house. To live there full-time. I'd spent plenty of time there growing up, even into my twenties. My parents would galavant off to wherever, and Gramps would welcome me at the door with a glass of lemonade and a smile. When Ginger was alive, she'd make fresh bread, and we'd eat enough pasta for ten people. But even being there without him at that one time when we were all planning his services was odd. It felt different. It felt unfamiliar.

My father and his brothers had never lived in that house. They'd visited plenty, and I'm sure they'd had the occasional sleepover sometimes. There were plenty of bedrooms that they could have picked from, after all. But other than Gramps—and maybe Geoffrey—I'd spent more time in the house than anyone else. Yet something still felt unfamiliar that day when I sat in the massive dining room across the length of the table from my father. He'd shuffled papers around and sometimes raised his voice at his brothers. "That's not what Dad would have wanted," he's said on a number of occasions in response to some of my uncles' suggestions.

"Does it feel weird to you?" I'd finally vocalized what I'd been feeling since we started packing.

"What?" She did that thing she does when she pushes my knees apart and kneels in front of me, looking up at me with those big, beautiful eyes.

"The whole thing. Gramps dying. He left everything to me, not to my father. Our moving into his house. Our having house-keepers and a butler."

"Geoffrey's not a butler." She choked back a laugh.

"You know what I mean; he might as well be."

When she and I sat down with the handful of housekeepers, Geoffrey, and a man they called Otto, who didn't speak, to talk about what the future looked like, Geoffrey was very insistent that "anything you need, I will be glad to assist you." It stuck in my head because it sounded like something a butler would say, not a personal assistant. Although who am I to judge, right? It's not like I'm an expert on butlers.

"We have a staff," Courtney said. "Imagine that?"

She batted her eyes up at me, and I, like always, released the stress I'd been holding in my shoulders and neck. She had a magical way of making me feel better just by saying something silly.

"I'd never have imagined it," I said.

"Did it feel weird growing up?"

"What do you mean?"

"Well, *my* grandpa wasn't filthy rich. So I don't know what that was like as a kid."

"I guess I never really thought about it. It wasn't anything. He was just always Gramps. Yeah, he had a huge house, and we never wondered who'd pick up the bill when we went out for dinner. Come to think of it, I can't even remember ever seeing anyone bring a bill to our table. Weird."

"You never wondered how much money he had?"

"Oh, of course I did," I said. "I don't know why people don't talk about money like it's some taboo subject."

"I never knew how much money my parents made," she said. "I think, for the same reason. Our parents' generation, and I think their parents, too, were so caught up in money that they never talked about it."

"I think there's probably a point where you stop telling people how much money you have."

"Beggars," she said. "And leeches."

"Exactly. The more money you have, the more people want it."

"Speaking of," she said, her voice trailing off. "Have you told anyone about this?" She motioned around the room to indicate *everything*.

"Other than my immediate family, the only person I told was Taylor." Taylor was our landlord. She and her husband owned all eight apartments in the building we lived in, as well as the building next door. I told her only because she had to know we weren't renewing our lease.

"How'd she take it?"

"Good. I told her we'd keep paying rent through the end of our lease." Courtney looked at me with a bit of a side-eye.

"Can we afford that?"

"Hopefully," I said immediately. "But since our cost of living won't be much at Stone Way... I didn't want to leave her in a bind."

"Max, she owns two buildings. I think she'll be okay."

"You're right," I said. "You're always right. You know me. Ever the people pleaser."

* * *

ON THE RIDE to Stone Way—about forty-five minutes from our apartment, on the other side of the city—the movers texted Courtney to tell her they'd be there tomorrow morning with all of our stuff. That felt off to me, but she assured me they did this sort of thing all the time. One truck, one crew: they'd load up a handful of families to move, then drop off all their stuff the next day or so.

It gave me anxiety to think that strangers had literally every single one of our Earthly possessions in their truck, save for my wallet, phone, and Courtney's purse. And the toothbrush, she reminded me, she hadn't packed, so we "didn't get icky" in the morning.

As we approached the driveway gate, it opened automatically. It had always reminded me of the one at Buckingham Palace that I'd seen on a family trip to England as a child. Big, wrought iron bars embossed with gold. A giant W in the middle of Gramps's gate. It squeaked and almost cried as its two individual gate doors swung open. It felt so slow that I felt like there was a tiny man somewhere cranking a handle as fast as he could, but unable to open the doors at a speed fast enough.

"Note to self: get some WD-40," I said, rolling the window up to hopefully dull the sound coming from just in front of us.

"Hello, sir, ma'am." It was Geoffrey's voice, coming from the small security system to my left. I looked through the now-closed window and saw his face on a tiny screen. He waved, so I rolled the window down, thankfully, just as the doors of the gate reached their fully open position.

"Hello, Geoffrey," I said, waving back.

"If you please, drive up to the house. We've arranged a welcoming for you." He smiled and reached off-screen to his left just before the video feed cut off.

Just as we finished pulling through the gate, its doors closed behind us. This has happened plenty of times before in my life, but this time felt different. It felt like the gate was closing to keep us in, not to keep anyone else out.

* * *

WE APPROACHED the end of the driveway the same way we always had. Our car was making more noise than I felt comfortable with, but I couldn't afford to do anything about it. I could sense Courtney's excitement from the passenger seat. The excitement seeped across the console to me, but seemed to stop. I couldn't feel excited for some reason.

I knew what we were doing and where we were about to live. I also knew the circumstances that led us there. I knew Gramps was gone. I knew my father was mad, but what else was new? I think what I was feeling was anxiety. I truly hate the unknown, and there was a lot of it in my immediate future.

No sooner had I stopped the car than Geoffrey approached the passenger side and opened Courtney's door for her. A woman whom I vaguely remembered from the meeting with the staff appeared on my side of the car and opened my door.

I shook the cobwebs from my head and took a step away from the car to look up at the house. Its brick facade stared back at me as if it were its own being. The windows were eyes: the door, a mouth. The house, it felt in that moment, was alive.

"Welcome home," Geoffrey said from across the roof of the car. "We're most pleased to have you here with us."

"Thank you, Geoffrey," Courtney said, sidestepping him to get around the car door that still stood open.

"Your grandfather would be so happy that you're here," he said. A slight reflection in his eye caught my attention, but he blinked it away before it became a full-blown tear.

"I miss him, too," I said, letting him know I saw what he tried to hide.

The rest of the staff—our staff—had gathered on the front porch. Had we not known who they were, it would have just looked like a group of people standing there. Geoffrey did not wear a tuxedo. The housekeepers did not wear maids' outfits. The groundskeeper didn't wear coveralls with his name on a white oval emblazoned over his heart. They just looked like seven ordinary people. They just happened to work for us and live on our property.

No matter how many times I thought it, said it, or now having written it down, it still didn't feel correct to call it "our" property. Even though it was. Even though the paperwork had all been filed and signed off on. Even though the judge who had finalized it all assured us we were the rightful owners, as Mr. Decker had, and Mr. Statler had back when this all started. It didn't feel right.

"Welcome," one housekeeper, who I'd later learn was named Joy, said as I approached the bottom step. The six of them looked down at us as Geoffrey joined us from the back of the car.

"Sir," he said, "I can't help but notice you've brought no suit-cases or boxes."

"The movers will be here tomorrow," Courtney interjected.

"Excellent. We'll be fine until then," he said, gesturing for us to climb the stairs.

The staff parted like the Red Sea as we made it to the top, stepping aside for Courtney and I to become face-to-face with the giant oak door that I'd spent so much of my childhood trying to move on my own but never able to until my teenage years. Either it was too heavy, the hinges were too rusted, or I wasn't strong enough. I never gave it much thought, as Gramps or Geoffrey would always be there to help me in or out of the house.

"Are you ready?" I asked Courtney.

She smiled and reached for the doorknob. The door swung open wide, a faint cry from its hinges.

She stepped inside, and as I followed her, the staff clapped. "Oh, stop that, you all," I said, feeling embarrassed and awkward.

The foyer was covered with balloons. Pink, and purple, and blue, and white. A banner bigger than I'd ever thought a banner in someone's house could ever possibly be read, "Welcome Home" in a beautiful red font. It hung between the two staircases that flanked the far sides of the room.

A small table sat in the middle of the marble-tiled floor, and the vase of flowers sitting atop it looked fresh. They filled the room with a wonderful aroma that reminded me of summers in the yard with Gramps. Next to the flowers was a small wooden bowl. Etched on the side of the bowl was the word "keys". I instinctively approached it and picked it up, not recognizing it, having never been there previously.

"Do you remember that, Max?" It was Otto. It startled me, as it was the first time I'd heard him speak.

"No," I thought about it for a moment. "Should I?"

"You were six," he said. "I don't know how I remember that, but I do. Mr. Washington had asked me if I could cut up a piece of a tree limb that had fallen at the back of the property so that he could make that there bowl."

"Gramps made this?" I asked.

Otto nodded. "Nineteen eighty-five, if memory serves. He kept it on his dresser in his room. You carved the word 'keys' in it on the side there."

I looked at Courtney, devoid of memory of this day.

"It was a long time ago," she said.

"And likely just another day of you and your grandfather," Geoffrey added. "Nothing memorable to remember. Lots of things happened in this house over the years."

"We thought it would be a fitting welcome for you if we placed it there," Joy said. I looked over to find her and the rest of the housekeepers smiling. I was terrible with names, but it was never more obvious to me than at that moment. I'd met them all before, but couldn't remember any of their names to save my life. I'm sure socked away somewhere in her memory. Courtney knew all of their names, their birthdates, their social security numbers, their favorite movies… Well, you get the idea. She was always much better at that stuff than I could ever hope to be.

"That's very kind," she eventually said on my behalf.

Otto picked up the bowl and moved it in my direction, as if pleading for me to drop my key ring into it. I obliged and dropped my keys in, which echoed throughout the foyer. I immediately felt like a child who'd just sneezed in the library and someone would be along any moment to scold me.

But that moment never came. In fact, the staff all seemed pleased that we were there. In the back of my mind, I'd thought that they were probably happy to still have room and board and jobs. That they would be thankful that Gramps had ensured they were taken care of after he was gone.

"If you'd like, I can show you to the room we've made up for you," Joy said.

"Oh," Courtney said.

"It's not Gramps's room, is it?" I asked, nervous about having to sleep where Gramps had slept all those years.

"Heavens, no!" she said. "We've made up one of the other bedrooms for you and left your grandfather's room as it was."

"We can discuss what to do with his things when you're more settled," Geoffrey said. "It's getting late now. Why don't we hurry along?" He checked his watch and motioned toward the staircase on the right.

* * *

"THIS WILL DO JUST FINE," I said to both Joy and Geoffrey, who'd followed us up the stairs and guided us down the hall. The room was diagonally across from Gramps's room. I recognized it from having run around the second floor a million times as a rambunctious little boy.

Its walls were lined with sturdy-looking wooden panels. Not the cheap stuff you had in your basement as a kid. Good-quality wood, probably built on-site by hand by carpenters. The wall on the side of the house nearest the foyer we'd just come from had a fireplace that looked like it was from Game of Thrones. The house was fairly modern, but it reminded me of a castle fireplace. One so big you could stand up in, and also one that, according to the laws of thermodynamics, would never *actually* heat the room because the heat would just be swept right up the chimney.

Joy walked around the bed, toward the windows, and began pulling the curtains closed. "It's late," she said, echoing what Geoffrey had alluded to downstairs. "You're both probably exhausted from the move today."

"The bathroom is here," Geoffrey said, pushing in one of the wooden panels to the left of the fireplace to reveal a doorway. I'd never known it was there before, despite having been in this room at least a hundred times. "Just push on the right side of this panel, and the door will unlatch."

"Thank you, Geoffrey." I mouthed "wow" in Courtney's direction, but I don't think she saw me as she was distracted by the chandelier dangling from the center of the room. I noticed the light shining through the crystals, bouncing off the walls all around us, and felt, for a moment, like we were in some fairy tale or a dream.

"Geoffrey," Joy said, making her way toward the door, motioning to him to come with her.

"Ah, yes. The time," he said. "We'll be going now."

"We'll be back in the morning," Joy added.

"Oh," I said. Although I knew better, a part of me had expected them to stay in the house. I don't know why. I'd toured the property twice since inheriting it and had seen where they all lived. The five housekeepers—I know, I know, did we really need five?—lived in one house. Geoffrey lived in his own house, which I believe was technically the guest house, and Otto lived in the loft above the garage. When I say the word garage, I'm not adequately describing it to you. Imagine the biggest garage you've ever seen, and then add two or three more garage bays to it. Gramps loved his cars and kept adding on to the garage to accommodate his collection. The loft Otto lived in spanned the whole thing, so he probably had more space to himself than anyone else on staff.

"Fret not, Mr. Washington," Geoffrey caught himself. "Oh, my. I don't think I've ever called anyone other than your grandfather that." He smiled as if that made him proud. "Rest well. We're just there if you need us." He pointed toward the window, though we knew what he meant.

"It's time," Joy said.

"Good night," Geoffrey said. "Open or closed?" His hand hovered over the doorknob, waiting for one of us to respond.

"Open," I said.

"Good night," Courtney said, reaching for the comforter to pull it down.

We heard their footsteps move down the hallway and onto the stairs before losing track of them.

"I'm exhausted," I said, immediately lying down on the bed.

"What's up with Joy?" Courtney asked, sliding her pants off and slipping under the covers next to me.

"What do you mean?"

"She seemed a little pushy in getting Geoffrey out of here, didn't she?"

"I didn't notice," I said.

"Maybe she's off the clock at nine and wanted to get back to watch The Real Housewives of something or other," Courtney chuckled to herself.

I smiled and stared up at the ceiling. My body flinched as I tried to get up and shut the light off. A heavy weight felt as if it had suddenly settled on my chest.

"Court?" I asked, angling my head over and up to see her.

But she was already asleep. Passed out is probably a more accurate term for what happened to her.

I, too, was asleep before I knew it. The light was still on. My shoes and pants were still on me, where I'd put them twelve hours ago when I finished packing the living room.

CHAPTER 9
THE FIRST NIGHT

I JOLTED UPRIGHT IN BED, as if a bolt of lightning had just struck me. My entire body was tingling, and my eyes struggled to focus. Confusion clouded my mind, leaving me disoriented about my whereabouts and the current situation. The room, shrouded in unfamiliarity, seemed to spin around me. The only light source was a faint glow seeping from what appeared to be an invisible door across from the foot of the bed. I must have turned the light off at some point. I recalled leaving it on when I'd fallen asleep.

To my left, my wandering hands felt Courtney. Her body was warm and motionless, still sound asleep. Certainly, my incessant panting would wake her up at any moment. I closed my eyes and shook my head, silently telling myself to calm down. That everything was fine. The vision of Ted Lasso having a panic attack flashed before my eyes a number of times.

My night vision kicked in as soon as my eyes were able to focus, and it all came flooding back to me. I was in our new bedroom at Gramps's house. No, not Gramp's house. Our house.

Even in my half-awake state, my mind knew it felt wrong to call it *our* house. Stone Way. The mansion? The estate? I didn't know what I'd call it, but I'd find something that felt more natural.

Courtney stirred, rolling from her right side to her left, now facing away from me. The row of windows facing the side of the property where the housekeepers and Geoffrey were undoubtedly sound asleep stared back at her.

I shook my wrist a few times to wake my watch up. Three fifty-three. It was still the wee hours of the morning. Approximately an hour after my body would normally wake me to use the bathroom. A habit Courtney often joked she could set her watch to.

No sooner had I found my bearings and surveyed the room than I heard a thump in the hallway. Not overtly loud. Not even loud enough to cause Courtney to jostle in her sleep. But loud enough for me to hear it. Loud enough that it caused me to turn my head to the right and stare out the open door. A sound so foreign yet so distinctive that it was unmistakable. A single footstep from the far end of the hallway, back toward the front staircase. The one we'd come up earlier in the evening with Joy and Geoffrey.

I saw nothing through the open doorway. I squinted to be sure I wasn't missing something. I listened intently while I held my breath. I knew what I'd heard. I knew the exact sound of a footstep in that hallway. I knew how a child's footsteps sounded and how an adult's sounded. The one I heard sounded like neither. It was a longer thud, with more force behind it. A sound that was unmistakable but completely different from the footsteps I'd heard in that hallway a million times over the course of my life.

Courtney tossed and turned for a moment, causing me to

turn and focus on her, distracting me from the doorway. She settled a moment later, letting out a very faint sigh. I envied her in that moment. So calm. So content. So at peace in whatever she was dreaming. She seemed genuinely happy.

No sooner had I started breathing again than I heard another footstep. A louder, closer thud. One that was absolutely coming toward our room. I panicked. A complete sense of terror struck over my body, taking the place of the tingling that'd woken me up just a few short minutes ago.

Three fifty-seven now. My watch beamed up at me, causing me to squint against its light. The room suddenly fell dark again. The sole source of light flickered under the bathroom door. It must have been the little nightlight Courtney plugged in above the sink, I told myself. She'd always been good at making herself feel more comfortable in unknown places. And her little mermaid nightlight—that she'd had since childhood—always made her feel better. It was always too bright for me, so it always ended up in the bathroom wherever we'd visit. Wherever we slept, that nightlight came with us, and Courtney always slept like a rock.

When I looked back at the door, it seemed to move into the bedroom. A trick my mind was clearly playing on me. "Doors don't move," I told myself. "You're imagining it." The wall on the far side of the hallway seemed to pulse. Faint at first, and then more rapidly, as if it had a heartbeat of its own. A silent heartbeat that I could only see but not hear.

I slid my legs over the right side of the bed, feeling around on the floor for slippers that I hadn't yet realized were still in a box on the moving truck, somewhere away from where I was.

Despite my best efforts, my first attempt to stand up failed. My legs buckled under me, and I collapsed back down on the bed. I fell hard enough to wake Courtney up, even if just for a second.

"You okay?" she asked. Her eyes were closed again, and her sleep returned before I could even turn around to answer her.

I tried again to stand. The second time, I was able to plant my feet firmly and heave myself up to a standing position. The tingling that woke me up returned, replacing the nausea that the room's spinning had caused just a moment ago.

Three fifty-nine.

I re-squinted across the hallway. The photograph of my great-grandfather that hung on the wall was askew. Not enough for most people to notice, or perhaps just slight enough that anyone else might have thought it was like that all along. But not me. I'd studied that picture a thousand times, often hearing stories from Gramps about his father. How he'd fought in the war and killed many men for his country. How great-Gramps had been one of the first people in the family to have his photograph taken. Gramps still had that old photograph somewhere in the house, packed away in a box. But the one that hung in the hallway was from right before Great-Gramps had passed away. I know Gramps had told me the year it was taken at some point in my childhood, but the tingling and rising sensation of fear was preventing me from being able to think straight.

Another thud. Closer. Louder.

In turn, I took a step toward the door. My body was on autopilot, though my brain had no idea why. "What's driving me to go out there?" I whispered to myself.

Curiosity? Fear? A little of both.

"Hello?" I whispered toward the door, but still fifteen feet or so away from it. "Is someone there?"

A cloud must have moved out of the way of the moon

because, suddenly, the hallway became illuminated. A soft, gray light shone in from the skylight over the top of the landing where the staircases met, just twenty feet away from the door to our room.

"Hello?" I said again, slightly louder.

Courtney stirred in the bed behind me. Her motion caused me to turn briefly, just as I filled with a sense of dread.

I quickly turned back toward the door, making sure not to take my eyes off of it, and quickly shuffled my bare feet across the hardwood floor. I closed the gap between the bed and the door much faster than I'd intended to. My body now stood in the doorway, but I was too afraid to poke my head out and look in the direction I was sure the sound was coming from.

My lungs filled quickly as I took a deep breath in, pausing long enough to psych myself up to jump out into the hallway and confront whoever was creeping around. It could have been anyone. I tried to tell myself it was just Geoffrey coming in to check on us. He couldn't sleep or something, and felt obligated to make sure we were okay. But he crept down the hallway not to wake us. I told myself it was just one of the housekeepers or Otto coming in because they'd heard a noise or had forgotten they'd left a light on somewhere, and they couldn't sleep, worried about it.

I told myself a lot of things. I convinced myself it was nothing, just someone in the house.

My lungs burned as I'd been unintentionally holding my breath.

My left foot took the first step out, and I pivoted my body immediately to face down the hall where the sounds had come from.

As I turned, I checked the picture of great-Gramps. It wasn't pulsating anymore. I'd imagined that. A lack of sleep and total exhaustion from a very long day, I'm sure. Nothing more than my overactive imagination. Something that I was proud of as a child.

I couldn't help but close my eyes as I finished turning ninety degrees to my left. Only for a brief second. Just long enough to finish my pivot.

When I opened my eyes, there was nothing. No personal assistant coming to check on us. No housekeeper getting a very, *very* early start on her day. No groundskeeper checking a fuse in a mysterious fuse box that was hidden behind Great-Gramp's very old photograph. Nobody at all.

For two solid minutes, I stood there waiting, motionless. My eyes darted around the hallway, up through the skylight, trying to peer around the corner and, somehow, down the stairs into the foyer.

"You did it!" my watch buzzed, scaring the hell out of me, and lighting up the wall to my left. The hourly reminder that I needed to stand up and move. Thanks, Apple. That mini heart attack was a perfect end to my first night in our new house.

I took a deep breath, forcing fresh air into my lungs. I forced myself to do it three more times before moving. A cool breeze from the bedroom door behind me startled me.

"What are you doing?" It was Courtney. She, like my watch just a moment before, scared the hell out of me, too.

"Jesus!" My yell echoed down the hallway, down the stairs, and died in the foyer. If anyone had been anywhere down there, out of eyesight, I'd likely have just scared them as much as they scared me.

"Are you okay?" She reached out as she approached me, still a few feet away.

"I am, yes. I'm sorry. Did I wake you?"

"No," she said. "It's almost four. I have to pee." Much like my three in the morning bathroom visit, her time was at four. And much like mine, her visit was like clockwork, too.

"I thought I heard something," I confessed. "In the hallway."

"Are you sure it wasn't just you?"

"No, no. I heard footsteps. Slowly, but loud and distinct."

"Like someone was trying to sneak up on you?" She made a pretend ghost noise and tried to tickle me.

"I'm serious," I said.

"I'm sure it's nothing," she reassured me. "It's a big house. I'm sure it's just settling or something."

"I've slept here a lot in my lifetime," I said, sliding by her back into the bedroom. "I've never heard anything like that before."

She followed me back into the bedroom. "Do you want me to close the door? Would that help?"

"I don't even know," I said, falling back onto the bed.

"It's okay. Don't worry about it. It's a new house, a new environment," she said, making her way to the wall where the door to the bathroom was. "Where'd Geoffrey say the door was?" She frantically tapped on the wall, trying to find the right spot where she could press and have the door open.

"Step back," I said. "Look for the light underneath it."

She did. As soon as she saw the glow from her beloved mermaid nightlight, she was able to locate the door and open it. She left it open while she went inside to find the toilet, which was just out of my sight.

"I'm sure I heard something," I called out, no longer worrying about how loud I was being.

"I'm sure you did, too, honey," she called back. The toilet

flushed, and she appeared in the doorway, silhouetted by the nightlight. "Do you want me to leave this door open so that the mermaid can protect you?"

"No. I'm fine," I said, more telling myself than telling Courtney. "I'm fine."

I repeated it in my head a few more times as she made her way from the bathroom back to her side of the bed, climbing in behind me. I sat with my back to her for another minute, looking out into the hallway, before she wrapped her arms around me and pulled me back into her.

"We have plenty more time for sleep," she said. She knew me well enough that, in most cases, if I woke up at four in the morning, my anxiety would have kept me awake, and I would have just gotten up and started my day. My brain wouldn't shut off sometimes, so I'd get up and read the news on my phone, check social media, read my email, or do whatever else I could do to occupy myself until the sun came up. "Plenty of time," she repeated, pulling me back into her until I had no choice but to lie down.

She nuzzled her head into my chest and shrugged her shoulders in this way she always did, which caused my arms to flop over her back. The "Maxney" she called it—a cute nickname for when we were intertwined like a pretzel.

Her body tensed a little at first, but relaxed a moment later when she fell back asleep. I was jealous of how quickly she could fall back asleep after waking up in the middle of the night.

I looked at my watch one final time. Four seventeen. I tapped the watch face behind Courtney's head with my free hand to shut it off and closed my eyes. I tried to free my brain of all the anxious thoughts running through it. I tried not to worry about the movers not showing up tomorrow. I tried not to worry about the movers showing up, but telling us they'd lost all our belongings. I tried not to worry about the sounds I'd heard or the big, empty house surrounding us. I tried not to worry at all.

But that's not how my brain works. So I worried. For what felt like hours but was likely only minutes.

Just as I'd drifted back to sleep, right as I was at that point where you can't wake yourself up, even if you wanted to. Right at the perfect moment, as I drifted off, I felt Courtney's breath on the back of my neck.

And then, as if by some sort of magic, I was asleep.

CHAPTER 10
THE NEXT MORNING

"GOOD MORNING," Courtney called out from the bed once she'd woken up. I had done my best to be quiet as I fumbled my way across the room to find the door to the bathroom that was hidden for no reason whatsoever. I had made it into the bathroom and showered without waking her up, but something about the sound of the electric toothbrush must have broken through her deep, otherwise impenetrable sleep.

"Did I wake you?" I instinctively called out.

"No. Well, maybe," she called back. I could hear her starting to stir in the bedroom, likely wanting to come in and take a shower of her own.

"Sorry, I tried to be quiet," I said. "I woke up about an hour ago."

"What time is it?" she asked, presumably unable to find her iPhone to look for herself.

"It's a little after seven."

"That's late! We're usually up and about by now," she said, noting the change in our routine.

"I figured you needed the sleep," I yelled back over the sound of the running water as I brushed my teeth.

"You doing okay?" I think she could sense something was bothering me, perhaps because of my lack of our usual morning conversation, or because she understood me on every level.

"I'm a little weirded out by last night," I said. "Do you remember?"

"Not very clearly. What happened last night?"

Just as I was about to recall the story of the previous evening, I heard footsteps coming up the main stairway. "Do you hear that?" I asked.

"What a weird thing to ask. Of course I hear that," she said. "Hello?"

"Ah, Mrs. Washington. Good morning to you." Geoffrey had suddenly appeared at the door to the room. I caught a tiny sliver of him in the bathroom mirror just as I'd finished flossing.

"Good morning, Geoffrey," Courtney replied.

"Morning," I added.

"It would appear your movers got an early start," he said. "The truck arrived half an hour ago."

"Did they wake you?" Courtney asked. "I told them not to come too early because the gate would need to be opened for them."

"Not at all, ma'am. I'm an early riser."

"Thank goodness," Courtney said, ever the people pleaser. "I'll run down and meet them."

Off she ran, down the hallway and down the front stairs, still in her clothes from the night before.

"Geoffrey?"

"Yes, sir? How can I be of service?"

"Well, for one, you don't need to call me sir. Max is fine. Or Mr. Washington, if you must. But sir feels very out of place."

"As you wish. How can I help?"

"Were you in the house early this morning? A little before four?"

"Oh, heavens no, sir." No matter how many times I'd ask him not to call me 'sir,' he would. Old habits, I suppose.

"You're sure? Maybe another member of the staff?"

"I wouldn't think so, sir, but I'm happy to ask. We rarely come into the main house after nine in the evening."

"Was that Gramps's rule?"

"Sort of," he said. "It's just something the house staff told me about when I first joined your grandfather's employ."

"I thought I heard something," I said. "It sounded like footsteps. Big footsteps."

"Well, I assure you, sir. It wasn't me, and I'm fairly confident I can speak for the rest of the staff as well."

"Weird," I said, not knowing what else to say.

"Max?" Courtney yelled. "Can you come down? They have some questions about where to put some things, and I'm unsure."

"Be right there," I said, tossing the hand towel back into the bathroom from where I'd stood by the fireplace. "I guess that's that, then."

I nodded to Geoffrey as I brushed past him, still standing in the doorway, and headed down the hall toward the stairs. I took a moment to survey the contents of the hallway as I walked down it. I don't know what I was looking for. Footprints? Someone hiding beside the waist-high potted plant that had been there for as long as I could recall? The only thing that caught my eye was that the photograph of great-Gramps was once again straight on the wall.

* * *

"GOOD MORNING," I called out in the general direction of the front door, where several men in matching "Great Movers" t-shirts stood, waiting for my direction.

"Good morning, sir," one of them responded, taking a few steps toward me.

It was at that moment that I felt like kicking myself for not doing a better job of surveying the house the night before. We hadn't walked through any of the rooms to make decisions about where things would go. I knew we had lots of stuff from our storage units that we hadn't seen in a number of years, but I had no mental inventory of what it was or where it should go.

"I suppose anything labeled master can go to the first door on the right, up the stairs there," I said, pointing. "And anything labeled kitchen can go through there," again pointing toward the hallway at the back of the foyer that connected the formal living room to the dining room and eventually into the kitchen. "Sort of around the corner," I added, bending my arms as if that made it any less confusing.

He turned back to the crew and yelled out the directions I'd just given, but in Spanish. The rest of the men began scurrying about. Some picked up boxes that'd been left in the foyer while they waited for me. Some went out through the front door to bring more boxes in from the truck they'd parked just out front.

"What about anything else?" he asked.

"Sorry?" I replied, not understanding his question.

"Any other boxes? Not master or kitchen?"

I turned to look to see if Courtney had any ideas and noticed Geoffrey at the top of the left-hand staircase. "Geoffrey, do you have any thoughts?" I called up to him, feeling like he was too far away to have possibly heard what I'd said.

"I apologize, sir, ma'am. I didn't mean to eavesdrop," he said as he started descending the stairway.

"No apology necessary," I said as he hit the last step. "Do you have any thoughts about where they should put things? I'm afraid Courtney and I didn't do a great job of planning out where things would go."

"Ah, yes. Of course." He turned his back to the front door and pointed down a hallway to the left of the one I'd sent the guys with the boxes marked kitchen down. "Down that hallway there, on the left, is an unused room. You can stack any boxes in there for the time being."

"Gracias," the man said.

"Once we have time to survey the property in detail," Geoffrey said, "we'll figure out where everything should go. There's plenty of room."

"Is there a basement?" I asked, realizing I never knew whether there was one or not. I had always assumed, but something sparked in me, making me realize I didn't know.

"Yes, sir. There is. Just some dust and cobwebs down there, though. The electric and gas panels, as well as the HVAC system, of course. No reason for any of us to go down there."

The way he'd said it must have been off, because as soon as I turned to look at Courtney to see if she'd noticed it, she turned to look at me. We made eye contact for a second and had one of those we've-been-together-too-long telepathic couples moments where we both thought the same thing: "That was weird, wasn't it?"

"Is there anything else for now, sir?" Geoffrey asked.

"I think that's all," I said. "Court?"

"I'm good. Thank you, Geoffrey."

"Very well," he said. "I'll go check in with the housekeepers and ask if anyone was in the house early this morning. Though, as I said, we don't come in here after nine. We much prefer the daytime, anyway."

Courtney and I again made a telepathic connection for a moment.

"All right, then. Thank you, Geoffrey. And if you could, please ask them if any rooms are cleaned out enough for us to move our things into."

"As you wish," he said and sauntered off out the open front door, sliding past two movers carrying in our couch, which immediately felt too small to even be in the house, let alone be our only piece of furniture in the living room.

"You ever notice how everything he says sounds British?" Courtney asked. "But without the accent?"

"Huh?" I asked, genuinely confused.

"All the sirs and ma'ams. Very well. As you wish. It sounds like he's from Robin Hood or something, but his accent is from somewhere up north. Vermont, maybe? New Hampshire? I can't place it."

"Huh. I guess I hadn't given it much thought."

"You usually notice those things," she said. "Oh, well."

We did our best to stay out of the way of the movers, but we were still in the foyer in case they had questions about where to put some furniture or a box we'd missed labeling.

The few times an unlabeled box made its way to us, one of us would pop it open and take a quick look inside to inventory it before directing the mover to the unused room Geoffrey had said to stack everything in.

"I can't believe this is ours," Courtney said, doing a little twirl in the foyer, looking up at the arch and post ceiling overhead.

"Me either," I said. "I'm still waiting for the other shoe to drop."

CHAPTER 11
THE HISTORY OF OUR TRAINS

ONE THING I loved most about my upbringing was spending so much time with Gramps. As I got older, days turned into weeks, weeks turned into months, and months turned into entire summers. All while my parents were off around the world, enjoying living in the lap of luxury on Gramps's dime.

I didn't mind, to be honest. Maybe at first, when I was really young. When I was of that age, where I felt like I needed my parents around. I was resentful. I was angry. I was annoyed. But most of all, I was lonely. I felt abandoned. At least until one day —I'll never forget the tone in his voice—he asked me something that would change the dynamic of our relationship. "Do you want to see my train set?"

I was eight. I had just turned eight and had the first of many birthday parties at Gramps's house. With just a few of my friends, who begged their parents to drive them from where we all lived up to Gramps's estate. I loved that they came. Part of me felt it was showy, braggy, almost. Part of me felt embarrassed, purely by the sheer size of Gramps's house.

"Train set?" I asked quizzically.

"Yes, my dear Maxwell. I've recently gotten into building a train set. One day, I hope to have an entire city in the attic or the basement."

He took me by the hand and tugged me in the direction of the back staircase. My tiny hand began sweating with anticipation. It wasn't uncommon for Gramps to share his love of things with me. He taught me billiards at a young age. He showed me the best movies and the most incredible symphonies. He taught me everything I knew about being sophisticated. Or to pretend, anyway.

I followed him up the stairs and down the hallway on the second floor to the closed door of a bedroom I couldn't remember ever having gone in before.

"This is it," he said, reaching for the doorknob.

"Not again," I heard Grandma call from down the hallway. I couldn't see her, but I sensed she was close, and she must have heard the floorboards in the hallway creak as we got close to the door. It certainly made a noise that made me jump back a bit.

As he opened the door, I remember being immediately overwhelmed by the spectacle in front of me. The entire bedroom was devoid of any furniture. Where what once likely stood a bed and dresser now stood piles and stacks of boxes. In the center of the room was a crude structure built from what looked like scrap wood. Some two-by-fours, sheets of plywood. It looked like any piece of wood he'd had lying around was nailed, glued, and propped together. On top of it was one of those monster train tracks you'd see at Macy's for Christmas, or on television in a commercial for some toy company. It was monstrous. Enormous. Eight tracks were running this way and that. There were houses and buildings and cars. There were working street lamps and railroad crossing signals. There was a frozen pond with people ice skating on it. There were different scenes set around the town he'd built.

It was the first time I had ever uttered a profane word in front of Gramps. "Holy shit," I said, immediately throwing my hand over my mouth, as if that would undo the words I'd just said.

He laughed a laugh that would rival Santa's. My profanity amused him.

"You just wait," he said, scurrying around to the far side of the structure. He stood for a moment, smiling at me, as if a grand reveal was about to happen.

And happen it did.

Gramps reached under the table and flipped what looked like a lever I couldn't see. A small hum became audible, and Gramps smiled. No sooner did I notice the hum than I saw the tiniest plume of smoke rise from the top of the structure. I couldn't see the train from my vantage point, as the train making the smoke was behind a mountain, but I knew that's what was happening. The sound of trains running around the track filled the room. An artificial yet familiar sound reached my ears. The chugga chug that you hear from an actual train sped up as the various trains began making their way around the tracks.

I moved closer, trying to get a better view.

"Here. Here," he said, motioning for me to come closer to him. "There's a step here. For you."

I smiled. Gramps thought of everything. And he always thought of me. A little part of me felt like he'd built that step just for me. So I could eventually see his creation.

When I stepped atop the step and became eye to eye with the

city he'd created, I was even more excited. The frozen lake I could see had sprung to life. The tiny skaters—no taller than an inch—zipped around the ice. They twisted and spun; they pirouetted. They turned and skated. They moved around the frozen pond like professional ice skaters. The attention to detail was incredible. To the side of the pond, benches were full of other people. Some bent over, tying their teeny-tiny ice skates. Some were standing with little cameras, complete with periodic flashes here and there.

The lights started flashing as trains approached the crossings. The cars that had been driving stopped. The people who walked along the roads paused as the gates came down.

"Wow." It was all I could think to say. It was all I could muster because I was so overwhelmed.

"This is just the start," he said. "I only just began a few months ago!"

He seemed giddy. Happier than I could ever remember seeing him before. He even clapped his hands together once or twice. For a brief, quick moment, he looked like a mad scientist.

"What else will you do?" I asked.

"I have plans to make it much bigger. I want to add train stations, an amphitheater, and a movie theater. I want it to be its own town!"

"Gramps, this is so cool!"

I felt that same level of excitement every time I entered that room. I felt the same level of happiness that Gramps felt every time we went in there and built something together. Every time he bought something new. Every time he shared it with me. I felt a tingle in my hands and a warmth in my stomach.

After a few years, it felt like *our* town. It felt like something we'd created together. Like something we'd crafted and spent hours making decisions on. We had our own little democracy together. And we built it up quite a bit.

He'd order additional parts and things from a store in the city. Every time they got a new catalog, he'd rifle through it, picking out everything he wanted for our town, checking with me first. Did I like something? Did I think it fit with the town? Did I think it made sense to put it next to the harbor? He always asked me what I thought, and it made me feel like an adult, even when I was many years from actually being one.

Over the years, we built it up so much that it no longer fit in that room. We'd filled up all the space we would use to stand around the outside. We built the structure out to every corner of the room, having to relocate the electronic controls to a small hole we'd cut in the middle. That, in and of itself, required us to relocate the frozen pond to a new area we built specifically for it. The hole in the middle was just big enough for one of us to stand in, getting a three-hundred-sixty-degree view of the entire structure in all its glory. *Like Ron Swanson's swivel desk,* I'd tell myself when I had gotten older and had seen *Parks & Rec.*

Eventually, we had to dismantle the entire thing. Which, to some extent, was a good thing. It allowed us to rebuild the structure that held it all together and off the ground. It let us rethink how it was all put together and optimize a lot. Which at the time felt like very important work, though, in reality, was just something silly that Gramps and I did together. It bonded us, which I loved. But in the grand scheme of things, it wasn't exactly curing cancer.

We moved it to the only place large enough to support it in its current form. The attic. The up-upstairs, as I called it when I was younger. A place that, prior to moving the train set to, I was never allowed. I couldn't recall ever being explicitly told not to go up there, but the door was always closed, and there was one of those low-tech slide locks that was just out of my reach near the top hinge. So, perhaps I wasn't disallowed from going up there; I just physically wasn't able to reach that lock.

When we finished rebuilding the structure, it was glorious. It was amazing to see it all put back together, including the things Gramps had bought that were new to us. He got the movie theater he wanted. He got all the bus stations and auto shops he wanted. He even built a car dealership near the back.

It was perfect. It was exactly what he wanted, which made him happy, which made me happy. I loved that he and I had that to share.

I eventually outgrew the train set. Or perhaps I just outgrew spending that much time with Gramps up there, fiddling with things and poking at the trains.

But on the second day in the house, without Gramps, I went up to the attic. The trains were exactly as I remembered them. Pristine. Immaculate. Perfect. The sweet, familiar smell of cinnamon from the fake smoke from trains hung in the air. It brought me back to childhood almost immediately.

I had envisioned climbing those stairs to the attic and finding the train set in disrepair, covered in a series of massive sheets or tarps. I imagined yanking the sheets off the set, kicking up years of dust into the air, which would make me cough. I had pictured it abandoned. Especially as Gramps had aged. I pictured him unable to climb all those stairs to get up there and be with the train set.

But he was able to do so. He must have had no problem getting up there. There was no dust. There were plenty of signs of use throughout. Entire regions of the town had sprung up since I had last seen it. Whole parts of the town that I either had forgotten about or had never seen were before my eyes again, or for the first time.

I gasped quietly. I felt, just for a moment, Gramps was there with me. I felt him standing next to me, his hand on my shoulder—just like always—and a sense of pride over this massive, monstrous thing we'd created together over the years.

Though I had wanted to turn it on, I didn't. I told myself it might not be safe, that I could electrocute myself or burn the house down, or worse. There might be a problem with the electricity, even though I was mostly certain there wasn't.

I decided that day that in honor of Gramps, I'd keep building his town. I couldn't recall if we'd ever named it before, but I decided in that moment that it would be called "Williamstown", after Gramps. I decided I'd keep adding to it. That I'd keep building it until the massive attic had no more space. Until I had to crawl under the structure like we'd had to do in the bedroom on the second floor when we outgrew it. Until I felt Gramps would be proud of the legacy I'd carried on for him.

In my head, I made a million plans in the blink of an eye. Instantly putting together lists of things I'd need. I couldn't wait to show Courtney when she got home. Though I knew she would show interest, it'd be a pretend interest. That, even though she would be happy for me and supportive of the train set, she'd ultimately let it be a thing just I did. Maybe she'd come up and check on me from time to time while I built. Perhaps she'd let me show her all the things I added to it. Maybe she'd even express interest. But ultimately, I knew she'd let me have it to myself.

CHAPTER 12

TIME TO MYSELF

I SAT on the floor of the attic one morning. The massive room lay in front of me, with only the underside of the train set—set didn't feel like the right word anymore. Village? Town? City? Whatever it was now, it was massive—in front of me. The lights dim, the people still, the trains stationary. The town was asleep. But there it lay, just in front of me.

The closeness to it made me feel close to Gramps. It brought me some peace knowing that, although he was gone, we had this in common. And while I never particularly loved the trains or building the town, I cherished the time I got to spend with Gramps while he built it. It was time that we had together, alone, where we could shut out the world and forget about anything and everything.

When I was a child, I never really understood how stressed he was. I never felt his temperament change or his personality waver, but he must have been under immense pressure from work. And I, being just a child, didn't know the difference. Though, as I got older and became a pre-teen and eventually a teenager, I felt my own worries slip away when we were in the attic. When Gramps would put together a new building or slide in a new locomotive, I felt calm. My worries—though I didn't even know they were worries yet—slipped away.

Being up in the attic for the first time in a long time, I felt that same level of calm come over me. I felt at peace with everything that was happening around me and to me. I didn't worry about my parents. I didn't think about what my father was thinking or what he wanted to do. I didn't think about how that pain in my back wouldn't go away. I hadn't worried about the headache I'd had for a few days. Nothing bothered me when I was in the attic.

When the town was powered off, the silence in the attic brought me calm. It brought me solace from the world. And I loved it. It was one of the few times that I had gotten to myself in recent years.

The first time I powered the town up, it all came rushing back to me. I'll be honest: I wasn't sure I'd remember how it all worked. It'd been decades since I'd spent time up there with Gramps. But as soon as I grabbed the lever for the first time, pulling it from left to right and feeling that satisfactory click when it engaged, I knew I would soon feel that peace again.

The main locomotive—the very first one Gramps had gotten, the one he'd nicknamed Chet for some reason unknown to me— roared to life. I never knew much about its history, but I was pretty sure it'd been around on planet Earth longer than I had. Though faded in time, its dual red lights still lit up the track in front of it, and although there was plenty of chemical left in the bottle labeled "smoke" near the controls, it was clear that I didn't need to remember where that tiny hatch was to open it and add more. The smoke started puffing as soon as the train started moving. It gave off a nostalgic cinnamon aroma that immediately brought me back to my childhood. I think I recall Gramps telling me they added the cinnamon smell so people would know the smoke was safe, not actual smoke.

As Chet made his first lap around the track—at the slowest speed I could get it to go—I breathed in deeply. I felt like I was eight again. I felt like Gramps was right there with me, watching his favorite car pull its load around the track.

I gave Chet a little power and let him zip around the room. From where I stood, it took a few minutes for the train to make a full spin around the town. Longer if any of the railroad crossings took longer than usual to come down, and I had to slow the train down. Gramps had taught me that, sometimes, the signal from the train to the crossings was slow, so you had to monitor the train to not run over any pedestrians or cars that might be crossing.

"It's weird," I thought aloud. "The things that stick with you."

Just then, my phone rang, startling me.

I simultaneously pulled my iPhone from my pocket and slowed Chet to a stop, but didn't power down the town.

It was Courtney. "Hi, honey," I said, letting my free hand slide down Chet's spine onto the fake car of coal that had always been right behind the locomotive.

"Where are you?"

"I'm in the attic. Where are you?"

"The attic? Oh, what are you doing up there? I've been walking around the house looking for you," she said.

"Oh. I'm sorry. I didn't know. I guess I've been up here for a while. The trains Gramps and I built together are up here. The entire town."

Chet blew out a new puff of cinnamon-smelling smoke, and

it flew up my nose with ease. It felt like a warm summer morning when Gramps and I would have breakfast in the train room, plotting our next move or purchase.

"That's lovely. When are you coming down?" She asked. She sounded annoyed. A hint in her voice of something I hadn't heard since our lives had been turned virtually upside down.

"Are you upset?" I asked.

"No. I didn't know where you were," she said. "I woke up this morning, and you were already gone."

"I'm sorry," I said. "I'll be down in a bit."

"Love you," she said.

"Love you."

As I hung up, I flicked the power back on, letting Chet take off toward the frozen pond—his usual cargo in tow.

As Chet sped away, I flicked another control and let a few of the other trains take off on the various other tracks, as well. Some would fly through the tunnel in the mountain. Some would make their way through downtown. Some would get pulled off to the side of the track so that Chet could pass in the other direction.

Each loop around the track took me back. Each chugga-chug of the various locomotives made me feel Gramps's presence. Each horn, each crossing coming down, each tiny little person moving around on their predefined track. It all made me feel like Gramps was there with me, watching over me.

It made me happy, but also incredibly sad. Gramps was so special to me, and I couldn't hug him again. I couldn't bring my problems to him. I couldn't rely on him to give me the best advice. He was gone. And although I was so happy with everything he did for Court and me, I'd give it all up to spend more time with him.

My phone dinged and buzzed from the edge of the table. I looked down and saw a message from Courtney. *Soon?*

I ignored it, trying to enjoy my time alone with the trains and the memories of Gramps. As it did when I ignored it, it buzzed again a minute later to remind me I had a *thing* I hadn't paid attention to yet. It buzzed itself right off the edge, onto the floor.

Normally, I'd have bent over and picked it up immediately, worried about its safety, Worried it'd broken. But I let it sit there.

In the attic, nothing was urgent—even Courtney.

A few minutes later, I felt it buzz again—this time against the side of my foot. I found myself literally huffing out loud at the air. "Fine, I'm done," I finally said.

The entire town went dark and silent as I killed the master power switch. The trains slowed to a stop. The lights went out. The people stilled. The cars and trucks and vans all froze in place. When I thought about it, it was the longest I'd ever been up in the attic. As a child, Gramps would always have us "take breaks", where we'd go downstairs for a meal, or go outside to get some "much-needed fresh air."

Be right down. I texted Courtney after picking my phone up from the ground. It hadn't broken. But a tiny part of me wished, even if just for a second, that it had.

CHAPTER 13

AN UNWELCOME VISITOR

COURTNEY AND I, along with Geoffrey, Sadie, and Nicola—two of the other housekeepers on staff—were in the unused room, which looked to have been a study at some point, when a loud thumping seemed to come from within the house.

"Did you hear that?" I asked, not sure if I was hearing things.

"Yes," Courtney responded immediately.

I turned to look at the members of our staff who'd been helping us organize and arrange the stacks of boxes to prepare for when the house would be ready for our belongings.

"I heard it," Sadie said.

"I, as well," Nicola added.

"That makes three of us," Geoffrey said. He pulled out his phone and swiped a few times. "No one buzzed the gate," he said. "I haven't set you both up with that yet, so I'd have had to buzz in someone who came." He swiped again. "Ah, there's someone at the door."

I followed Geoffrey out of the room and down the hallway leading to the foyer.

We immediately heard muffled yelling from the other side of the door.

"Is that…" I said, mostly asking myself if what I was hearing was correct. "Is that my father?"

I rushed down the rest of the hallway and across the foyer, reaching for the doorknob to unlock the door and pull it open.

There he was, in the flesh. My father. It was the first time I'd seen him since the funeral a few weeks prior, and the first time I'd heard his voice since he'd hung up on me.

"Hello, Dad," I said, stepping aside and motioning for him to come in out of the sun.

"Yeah, yeah, hello," he said, clomping his way into the foyer and turning back to face me.

"Hello, Bruce," Geoffrey said. My father ignored him for a moment, then eventually turned to face him. "How did you get past the gate?" His question seemed a little pointed and somewhat accusatory.

"This is my father's house," my father immediately said. "Was. It was my father's house. Do you not remember when I was here with him every day, taking care of him when he was unwell?"

"William was sick," Geoffrey said. "He was never unwell."

"Dad was unwell, and we all know it," my father said, trying to hush the echoing sound of his voice. He took three steps toward Geoffrey before stopping, evidently rethinking his action.

"Opinions, Bruce," Geoffrey said.

"What are you doing here, Dad?" I asked. Just as I managed to get the words out, I noticed Courtney standing at the end of the hallway, with Sadie and Nicola flanking her on each side.

"How can you be such an ingrate?" he said, storming his way back across the foyer to get in my face.

He and I were the same height and had been since I was sixteen or so. I'd wager we were the same weight and undoubtedly had the same build. We could likely be mistaken for one another from behind, save for Dad's hair thinning on the top of his head. But something about how he got right in my face felt menacing. I couldn't remember the last time my father had made me flinch, but he did just then. Only for a fraction of a second, and only enough to make me lean backward for the blink of an eye.

Courtney stepped forward as if she was going to do something. She'd never been particularly fond of my father, but I couldn't think of what she was imagining doing at that moment.

"What are you talking about?" I spat out as I took a step back from his overwhelming presence.

"This," he said, spinning around and gesturing to the foyer, the staircases, the walls. "This. Everything. How can you be so ungrateful?"

"Again I ask," I said. "What are you talking about?"

"You've never appreciated anything. I raised you," he said. "You're the man you are now because of me." He turned back to face me, but didn't step into my personal space.

"Are you kidding me?" Courtney called out, now making her way across the foyer toward where we stood.

"No one's talking to you, little lady," my father snapped back.

"Don't speak to her that way!" I yelled a little louder than intended.

"Sadie, Nicola, let's head to the kitchen," Geoffrey said, scurrying across the foyer and swooping his arms around both women, disappearing down the hall before they could even respond.

"Can you calm down and tell me what's going on?" I asked.

"Dad left this all to you, and you don't deserve it," he said after thinking of the right words for a minute. "I was here for him every day when he got sick. He didn't even know who we were near the end, but I still came every day. I was here wiping his drool, carrying him to the bath, and changing his diaper. I was the one who was here every moment, making sure he didn't need anything."

"You opportunistic son of a bitch!" Courtney yelled.

"Hey!" I said, trying to calm her down while also understanding what she meant.

"You didn't give a damn about him. Let's stop pretending. We all know it. You never cared about any of your family," she said, stepping between Dad and I.

"How dare you!" he yelled. "I took care of him."

"The only person you've ever taken care of is yourself," she said, reaching behind her to find my hand. "We know why you were here, taking care of him." The way she'd said "taking care of" felt venomous and spiteful. "We know," she reiterated.

"What are you even talking about?" my father snapped back. "I took care of him, just like I took care of Maxwell!"

I couldn't help myself anymore and took the opportunity to speak up. "You're joking. Do you sincerely believe you took care of me? Throughout my childhood? You think you were there for me?"

"I was the best father!" he bellowed.

"You're delusional!" I yelled back, my voice echoing off the tile floor and oak-clad walls. "I spent more time at Gramps's or Uncle Matthew's than I did at my own house. You and Mom were always gone. Always off enjoying your lives while I was without parents!"

"You ungrateful little jerk!" he shouted.

"It's the truth," I continued. "I can count on one hand all the holidays I spent at our house with you and Mom. I can count on two fingers how many of my birthdays you were home for. Gramps took me to my first day of school almost every year. Uncle Matthew took me trick-or-treating. Uncle Joey taught me about girls and the birds and the bees! Uncle David picked me up from school the one time I got in trouble!" Once I started, it just kept flowing out of me. I felt a sudden rage flowing through my body and anger like I'd never felt before, all directed at my father. Years and years of things I'd wanted to say to him just came flowing out of my mouth, without much of a filter.

"Lies!" he yelled. "Sure, your mother and I traveled some, but we were always there for you!"

"You didn't even call on Christmas," I said. "You couldn't have at least done that from Milan or Saint-Tropez or wherever. You didn't even send a gift!"

"He doesn't care about you," Courtney said, now standing by my side, still holding my hand. "He's only in it for himself. He only does things that benefit him."

"This is family business!" he shouted at her, stepping closer.

"She's my family," I said. "She's more family than you've ever been." I knew those words would hurt him, but I didn't care. I couldn't stop saying the things I'd wanted to say. I had no control over what was coming out of my mouth.

"Tell him the truth," Courtney said. "Tell your son why."

"Tell him what?" my father asked, looking genuinely confused.

"Tell him why you were here with your father."

"I loved Dad," he said. "I loved him until the end!"

"No, you didn't," she said. "Tell Maxwell the truth."

"What are you talking about, Court? Dad, what is she talking about?"

"He won't tell you," she said. "He won't tell you the truth."

"I've told you the truth," he said. "That is the truth!"

"He hadn't seen your grandfather for a couple of years, prior to when he got sick. Isn't that right, Bruce?"

"How could you…"

"And when Gramps got sick, he showed up. He showed up because he thought, somewhere in his twisted, self-centered, egotistical, narcissistic brain, that if he came and stayed with his father and 'took care' of him. If he made the bed and took out the trash and helped Gramps eat, then Gramps would forget about all the terrible things that your father had done throughout his life. Things I don't even know about. That Gramps would leave everything to him."

I gasped and jumped back as if I'd been literally shocked. The look on my father's face said everything else I needed to know.

He was, for the first time I could ever remember, tongue-tied.

"You should go," I said, opening the door and moving out of the way. "You may think I'm an ingrate, but at least I'm not a monster."

"What she said isn't true," he said, calling back over his shoulder as he stomped down the front steps. "She's wrong. She's lying."

I slammed the massive door behind him. I couldn't help myself. The anger I'd felt had come to a boil, and what Courtney had said made so much sense to me that I didn't even need to wait for my father's response. I knew what she said was right. In the same way, I'd known for all those years that Gramps had funded the lifestyle my parents loved. That it was Gramps's money that took them all the places they went to and bought their cars and houses and anything else they'd wanted.

What I didn't understand was why Gramps would do that. Why, if my father was as terrible and selfish as it seemed he was, would Gramps help give him that lifestyle he had lived?

"Your grandfather was protecting you." It was Geoffrey, coming back down the hallway from the back of the house.

"I'm sorry?" I asked, unsure I'd heard him.

"What your wife has said is correct. Your father, Bruce, hadn't been here to see William for years. I believe somewhere around five years. As long as the money kept going into their account and funding their lifestyle, your father had no reason to come here and face your grandfather man to man."

"I can't believe it," I said, stunned.

"Your father only looks out for two people in this life," Geoffrey continued. "Himself and your mother."

"I'm sorry," Courtney said. "I don't know what came over me. I felt I had to say something. I got this gut feeling about what he was up to."

"I believe he came here to intimidate you," Geoffrey said. "Perhaps to entice you to hand your grandfather's estate over to him."

"Why would he think I'd do that?" I asked out loud, but to neither of them specifically.

"As we've learned, money corrupts. And he thought he could get more of it," Geoffrey said. "As I said, your grandfather was trying to protect you. That's why he sent your parents away so much."

"Sent them away?" I asked.

"Funded their trips. Their lifestyle. Call it what you want. But he was sending them away."

"Why?" Courtney asked.

"He'd confided in me once, a long time ago, that he knew Bruce wasn't fit to be a father. Your grandfather knew it even before your parents had you. He'd said that growing up, he'd always known your father was different. That something was 'off' about him. And when you came along, he knew he had to protect you. To not let whatever was wrong with your father affect who you'd become. So, very early on in your life, he started giving your parents money so they could travel. So they could buy the nice things they wanted. He told them it was because of how happy he was to have a grandson, a new person in his life, to love unconditionally. And because he knew your father wouldn't care about the reason, he knew your father would take the money and go."

"I..." I didn't know what to say. It felt like the weight of the world was falling on me, crushing my chest. I fell to the floor and put my hands out behind me, looking up at Geoffrey.

"He knew he could have hired someone to take care of you. He knew he could get you the best care there was. But instead, he had you come here as often as he could. Or stay with one of your uncles, who he didn't see the same qualities in that he'd seen in your father."

"So Gramps knew something was wrong with my dad, even all the way back then?"

"He did. And he did his best to keep that from you as much as possible. It was one of the reasons you went to boarding school so far from home, and the colleges he urged you to apply to were also far from your parents. He knew that if you were far enough away from them, they wouldn't visit you. Well, Bruce wouldn't. I'm sure Ellie, as lovely as she always is, would have. But I think we both know that she cannot do anything that your father does not approve of."

"I pointed that out the first time I met them," Courtney said. "I didn't want to ask if he was abusive toward her, but I certainly get that feeling from them whenever they're in the same room together."

"No, he can't..." I caught myself and really thought about it for a minute. Could he have? I never remembered seeing my mother hurt and never recalled hearing her tell any stories about him as anything other than a loving and caring husband. But I had also spent only a small fraction of my life with them. As soon as I was old enough to be shipped off to boarding school, I was. "All these years," I said, somewhat mumbling. "All these years, I thought *they'd* sent me away. I thought my mom and dad had been the ones to abandon me and dump me at that school. I thought *they* were the ones who didn't want me to come home during the summers because *they* wanted to gala-vant off to wherever they were headed next. But it was Gramps. Gramps was the one who'd kept me away."

"Please don't be upset with William," Geoffrey said, reaching down to grab my hand and help me up from the floor. "He had the best of intentions."

"No," I said. "I'm not mad at him. I think on some level I'm mad at myself for never putting this together on my own. How long have you known?" I asked Courtney.

"I've had my suspicions for a while," she said, avoiding eye contact. "But I didn't think it was my place. I've known your family life is complicated."

"All these years," I said. "All these years, I never pieced it together."

"Your grandfather loved you so much," Geoffrey said. "Though you were his only grandchild, he took great pride in the man you became and was so proud of you for everything you'd done. Who you are as a man is the reason he left you his estate."

"I wish I could have known him more as a person and not just my grandfather," I said, realizing he was never more than just Gramps to me, realizing that I didn't really know much about him.

"You'd have liked him," Geoffrey said. "He was a wonderful man."

I took a moment to bury my head in Courtney's shoulder, realizing the weight of the morning was weighing on me. All of it, so heavy, so sudden. So eye-opening. Prior to that morning, I'd had no idea who my father really was. And now, left in the wake of his stomping off, I knew he was only after one thing in his lifetime: money.

CHAPTER 14
GRAMPS' FAREWELL

IT'D BEEN A LONG WEEK. After the encounter with my father—which, in retrospect, felt weird because he didn't bring my mother—we'd spent the week dispersing our belongings throughout the house. Gramps had, well, old-person taste, so a lot of his furniture and decor was put into various piles in the foyer, with calls out to a number of charities to come and collect the items as donations in Gramps's name. The only item I'd kept was his credenza. The family crest adorned the front in vivid color.

Aside from his bedroom and the basement, which Geoffrey reminded us there was no reason to visit, we'd cleaned out the entire house. It felt weird to give away all of his things, but we had very different tastes. And while we didn't yet have access to the inheritance money to replace much of it, Courtney and I decided it made more sense to give that stuff to people who could benefit from it more than we needed to. And she reminded me that someday we'd be able to buy new stuff to fill all the space.

One item of disagreement, however, was Gramps's billiard tables. Yes, tables. He had three. One for what he called "regular" billiards, one for snooker, and one for 9-ball. I understood the difference between the snooker and pool tables because the snooker table has bumpers. But I never understood why Gramps had different tables for 8-ball versus 9-ball. I'm sure he had his reasons. Courtney said it was "braggy" not only to have a room big enough to fit three billiard tables—comfortably, I might add—and insisted we could eventually use the room for something more *us*. I didn't quite know what that meant, but I knew a couple of things about those tables. Gramps had sought them out, one by one, over the years. They were made by a master craftsman in the 1920s and 1930s, and Gramps had paid a fortune for them. They were also solid wood and slate, and likely weighed a ton. So, for the sake of Gramps's memory, combined with the memories I had *trying to* play 8-ball when I was growing up, and the sheer laziness of finding some moving company to get them, I talked her into keeping them. At least on an interim basis while we figured out if we'd use them and also agreed that if we didn't end up using them. Sorry if *I* didn't end up using them; we'd give them to literally anyone who came by and took them away.

"I think that's the last of it," Courtney said as she walked toward me in the formal living room. I'd just been on my way back from what we were calling the guest room, where we'd put all of our unnecessary bedroom furniture. The room we had been occupying all week had built-in closets, so our armoire was superfluous, and the bed was comfortable enough that we didn't need ours.

"I'll do one final sweep," I said. "Just in case."

"You and your final sweeps," she said jokingly. "You forgot

the remote control for the Roku at a hotel once, and you've been worried about forgetting something ever since!"

"You can never be too careful," I said, knowing she was joking, but that part of her joke hurt because she was right.

When I first walked into the study, I realized it was now empty of just about everything. There was one office chair on wheels we'd left in there, specifically for someone to sit down while they dug through boxes, should they need a break from standing. The built-in bookcases at the back of the room, along with the matching credenza, were still stacked with Gramps's things that I'm sure he'd long since forgotten. I could see old books he may or may not have read. Drawings that looked like early sketches of video games he may or may not have ever made. A framed picture of him and me when I was six or seven. Sentimental knick-knacks that I didn't feel like dealing with just yet.

Now that all our boxes were out of the way, I noticed the bottom of the credenza had two cabinets on opposite sides. Their handles were recessed into the door, making them barely noticeable from a distance.

When I bent down to open the cabinet on the right, closest to the formal living room entryway, I noticed a bit of dust on it. I brushed it off and yanked it open. Inside sat a few more collectibles that Gramps had at some point put in there. A copy of a patent for one of his technologies, what looked like the original artwork for the *Pitfall* game with the artist's signature on the reverse, and a number of old-looking documents I didn't have the physical or emotional strength to deal with at that moment.

After having to shove the falling stack of papers back inside, I was able to close the door and felt the magnet engage, which, thankfully, held it shut.

As I approached the left-side cabinet, I couldn't help but notice the lack of dust on its handle. It seemed disturbed recently. I shrugged it off, thinking maybe one of us had bumped into it while moving boxes. Or possibly one of the movers slid against it when they were loading our belongings into the room last week.

I pulled at the handle, but the door was stuck. I peeked my head around the far side closest to the built-in bookshelf to see if I could spot a lock or latch of some kind, but there wasn't one.

"Hmm," I thought out loud. "That's unusual."

Without worrying too much about breaking it since it was mine, after all, I grabbed the handle again and pulled it with all my might. It took most of my body weight, but the door popped open.

Inside was a medium-sized wooden box. At first glance, it seemed to be a cigar box, but when I lifted it, it felt too heavy to be a cigar box. It had something of heft inside.

As I pulled it out, I used my sleeve to dust it off, and there, staring back at me, were my initials. They were inlaid into the top of the wooden box and appeared to be made of ornate woods and pieces of Abalone. But there it was, staring up at me, MJW.

I flipped the box over as carefully as I could and found that the whole box seemed to be one solid piece of wood. There was no lock or clasp holding it shut; only the weight of the lid held it closed when upright.

"Geoffrey, can you come in here?" I called out, hoping he was close enough to have heard me.

"Coming, sir," I faintly heard him call back from the direction of the kitchen, or possibly from the billiards room beyond.

A moment later, he joined me in the study, my back against

the bookcase, facing him as he entered. "Do you know what this box is?" I asked.

He came closer and looked it over, running his fingers along the top. "I haven't seen this before, sir. Where did you find it?"

"Just there." I pointed to the cabinet in the credenza that I'd left open. "I was making sure we didn't leave anything behind when we cleared out the room."

"I'll give you some privacy," he said. "Whatever's in that box was meant for you and not for me." He quickly exited the room.

I waited for the sound of his footsteps to shift from thuds to clacks and back to thuds, indicating he'd gone through the formal living room into the kitchen, then into the billiards room. There was no need to be secretive, but I wanted some privacy before opening the box. I hadn't even thought of calling out to Courtney. I wanted to see what was in the box before telling her about it. I'm not sure why, though.

Much like Geoffrey had done moments earlier, I ran my fingers across the lid of the box, brushing off the remainder of the dust I'd missed with my sleeve. "There's no time like the present," I told myself and cracked open the lid.

As soon as I opened the lid, an envelope flew up into the air. The motion of its opening, combined with the air current, caused a sort of updraft. I scrambled to catch the letter, trying to gently place the box down on the floor next to me. It fell a little harder than I'd intended, but it seemed unharmed upon inspection.

The envelope I held felt hefty. On its front was my name, written out in Gramps's unmistakable handwriting. The back of it was sealed with a single piece of Scotch tape with Gramps's initials written over it in what looked like black Sharpie. "You clever old man," I thought. It was his way of letting me know if someone had already opened the letter, I guess. If someone had opened it, his initials would be damaged, and it'd be impossible to put it back together correctly. Kind of like those "void if removed" stickers on the bottom of electronics that the manufacturer doesn't want you tinkering with.

I couldn't help myself, and I tore open the letter. Two pages came out. I flipped them over to examine them, finding Gramp's signature at the bottom of the second page.

The wheels of the office chair squeaked as I pulled it closer to me, just under the overhead light, and plopped myself down.

My dearest Maxwell,

If you're reading this, then I am gone. Don't worry, and please don't be sad. As I'm sure people have said to you many times during my funeral, I lived a very long and very happy life. I got to be in love with two amazing women in my life, and that's not something many people can say.

You've likely found this letter among the box I hid in an old study I haven't used in decades. You're likely in that study because you and your lovely wife are moving in or have moved into my home.

I'm leaving this letter for you for several reasons. By now, you know my will is ironclad, and you are the rightful owner of this property and everything in it. You also know that I've set it up so that all of my money for the rest of my life —or at least while my company makes money—will funnel into an account that will benefit you. That may raise some red flags, especially since I know your father. I've prepared for his imminent poking and prodding.

You may be surprised to learn that there are several secret rooms around this house. If you've found the hidden bathroom in the bedroom, I'm sure Geoffrey will steer you into sleeping in; you know what I'm talking about.

Geoffrey knows many of the hidden rooms. He helped me design this house when I built it. But he may have forgotten about some of them by now. My point is, Maxwell, within those rooms, you'll find great treasure. I mean this both figuratively and literally. Those rooms contain enough fortune to take care of your family for the rest of their lives, even if your father or his brothers hold you up in court over my company. I mean this literally, Max. There is money hidden throughout this house. Some of it starts right where this letter is, in my old study. I had this box made especially for you, and if everything's stayed the same since I left it here, there should be three hundred thousand dollars in one hundred-dollar bills in the box.

The most important reason I've left you this letter is that you must know the truth. You must understand that your father will try to disparage me now that I'm gone. He'll tell you many terrible things about me to get you to give him whatever he wants.

None of it is true. I am not crazy.

I tried to tell them for years. There's something wrong with this house. If you've been here long enough, by the time you're reading this, you'll have heard the noises. If you're unlucky enough, you've seen it, too. I don't know what it is, but I know it lives in the attic. I know what I've heard, and I know what I've seen. No one believed me, not even Geoffrey, my closest friend for decades. They all think I'm crazy. I'm not, Max. I'm not crazy. I know that you'll find the truth and you'll tell them all. You'll make sure they know I am not crazy.

Please be careful. Take care of Courtney. Protect her and protect yourself. The staff knows to stay away at night. They'll tell you it's because of professionalism or some other story. But I think they know, and they're scared to be in the house when it might show up.

Whatever it is, know it never hurt me. It never even tried to. But over the years, I felt it get angrier and angrier. Please, Maxwell, be careful. Whatever you do, don't leave your room after dark.

And please remember that I'm not crazy.

I never was.

With all my love,
Gramps
December 17th, 2019

"Courtney," I yelled out. "You're going to need to see this. In the study."

She came racing into the room just as I'd pulled out handfuls of hundred-dollar bills, the excess spilling out of the box and onto my lap.

"What the…" she asked.

"You need to read that," I said, gesturing to the letter I'd let fall to the floor.

CHAPTER 15

WHAT WAS THAT?

"COURT?" I whispered.

It was just after three in the morning, according to the dim glow of my watch, which, as usual, caused my night vision to disappear as soon as I flicked my wrist to turn it on.

"Court? Are you awake? Did you hear that?"

I found my eyes drawing themselves toward the door to our bedroom. It'd been a few weeks since I heard whatever I'd heard that first night, and just earlier, I had read Gramps's cryptic note about something being in the house's upstairs. Don't ask me how we could fall asleep that night. It might have been sheer exhaustion from moving everything we owned into different parts of the house, or it could have been the twenty milligrams of melatonin we'd taken on top of the Sleepy Time tea we'd drunk. It must have been around one in the morning when I'd fallen asleep. Just long enough ago that I'd dropped into REM sleep, dreaming about Gramps sitting down to write that letter. I wondered how he felt, knowing his sons didn't believe him and thought he was going crazy.

Courtney wasn't moving. She didn't even whimper to acknowledge that I was awake, moving around, and talking to her. Normally, she'd have let out a little whimper that said, "I love you, but shut up, I'm sleeping." Nothing this time.

Whatever had woken me seemed dormant now that I was actually awake, staring at the partially open door. You'd have thought after reading Gramps's letter that we'd have shut, locked, and barricaded the door. But there was some debate between Courtney and me about whether what Gramps had said was true or not. She'd initially said, "Well, he was very old, Max," giving me those puppy-dog eyes of hers, trying to convince me that, perhaps, Gramps *was* a little off his rocker toward the end. Maybe he was just seeing and hearing things.

"But what about what I saw? What about what I heard?" I'd asked her. I had been trying to think back to my many times in the house. I'd been trying to think if I had ever seen or heard anything to support what Gramps said in his letter. But I couldn't recall anything out of the ordinary.

"You were tired. Maybe you imagined it," she'd said.

But I knew what I saw. I knew what I had heard that first night.

The floor was cold as my feet made contact. Before I knew it, my body had moved itself into a sitting position. Normally, I'd try to be quiet and motionless as I got out of bed, not to wake Courtney up. But if I'm being honest, I wanted her to wake up and be with me during whatever was happening.

Then, there it was—the most unmistakable sound. Someone was coming down the hallway. This time, from deeper within the house, rather than down by the staircase where I'd heard it last time. Quicker steps this time, too.

Thump. Thump. Thump. Thump.

Then they stopped.

I did my best to look through the crack in the door, trying to make out any movement or shadows.

"I heard four footsteps," I said aloud, hoping she'd wake up.

I stood up with every intention of walking over to the door, opening it, and walking out into the hallway to confront whoever or whatever was out there.

But as soon as I stood, the footsteps started coming. Faster and louder than before. More determined sounding.

"We need to see what's happening, don't we?" I asked myself.

The footsteps continued, overpowering the sound of my own bare feet on the hardwood floor in the room.

As I reached for the doorknob, a sound unlike anything I'd ever heard before came from just on the other side. Almost like a scream. A scream from the offspring of a dinosaur and a lion and a werewolf and so many different things I can't place. The scream pushed the door open against my hand, sliding me back on my heels.

Instinctively, I tried to push back against the door. It was as if, somewhere in my brain, I thought closing the door would protect us against whatever was on the other side.

The scream continued. It felt like it went on for minutes, continuously. Whatever was making it didn't stop to breathe. The sound just kept going.

I turned to look back at the bed, to Courtney. She stirred, but did not rise. She did not wake or move more than a bit.

"Courtney!" I yelled. "Wake up!" How could she sleep through the screaming?

The screaming paused for the blink of an eye before starting again. It stopped just long enough for me to push the door closed and twist the lock, which seemed like a feeble attempt to keep us safe.

As the screaming started up again, the door shook in its frame. Top to bottom, side to side, the entire door shook. As if something had a giant hand holding the entire thing and was flailing its arm around in circles. It shook so hard that I was sure the hinges were going to pop off, and the door would surely fall inward on top of me. The thing shaking it would then step inside, on top of the door, crushing me to death.

My mind raced. My heart felt like it was beating out of my chest. I couldn't catch my breath.

Courtney tossed and turned on the bed.

"Stop it," I yelled. "Stop it! Stop it! Stop it!"

The scream, somehow, got louder.

"Stop it!" I yelled louder than I'd ever screamed in my life, almost chanting the phrase. My eyes locked on Courtney in our bed, still fast asleep, as if in a trance.

The door stopped shaking, and the screaming stopped.

I looked at Courtney, still in bed, almost imploring her to wake up. To help me.

No sooner had I completed my telepathic thought to Courtney than the pounding on the door began. A knocking like someone left out in the rain, trying to be heard throughout the house—a hard, intentional pounding. An "I know you're in there, come open the door," pounding that was so hard I could feel it against the palms of my hands each time a blow landed on the solid door.

The pounding continued, its frequency growing rapidly. The knocking went from a gentle but loud knock to almost machine-gun fire. Bang bang bang bang bang, it continued.

"Stop it!" I yelled again. "Go away! Leave me alone! Courtney, wake up!" But she didn't budge. She didn't move a muscle or open her eyes even the tiniest bit.

"Go back to sleep," I heard her faintly mutter. "You're having another bad dream." She immediately rolled over, facing away from the door. I'm not even entirely sure she'd woken up to talk to me.

Then, in that moment, as if I was controlling whatever was outside the door, the knocking stopped. As if my telling it to *go away* worked.

"What now?" I said almost instinctively. My eyes were welling up with tears. I'd never cried from being scared before, but it was clear that was what was happening.

I started counting in my head. I wanted to wait at least a minute before opening the door. Don't ask me why; it just felt like a logical thing to do.

Fifty-five, fifty-six, fifty-seven. I got to sixty and stepped back from the door, simultaneously checking on Courtney to see if she'd woken up.

It seemed to take me a lifetime to psych myself up to open the door. My body quivered in fear as I stood with my hand on the doorknob, trying to talk myself into opening it. "It's nothing," I told myself. "I imagined it," I thought.

By the time I'd finally gained the courage to open the door, I could feel the tears flowing freely down my face.

The moon's glow flooded the hallway through the skylight over by the front staircase. It was bright enough in the hallway that it could have been daytime. The painting of great-Gramps seemed undisturbed and as expressionless as it had been the first time I'd seen it. The vase on the floor next to it, unmoved. I poked my head out into the empty hallway but kept my body safely in the room, clutching on to the hope that whatever had been there just a few minutes ago was now gone.

I looked left and right and then in both directions again.

"Nothing," I said under my breath. "It just seemed to vanish when I told it to go away."

I stepped out into the hallway, unintentionally letting go of the doorknob, the only thing keeping me feeling safe.

There I stood in the middle of the hallway, turning back and forth from one end to the other, looking for any clues about what had been there just a few minutes prior.

"Whatever it was," I said, "it's gone."

Part of me felt a little relieved as I went back into the room, closing the door behind me.

"Gramps wasn't crazy," I said out loud. "Court. Wake up! Gramps wasn't crazy," I yelled toward the bed, my back still against the door, which I'd closed firmly behind me. I think a little part of me had hoped Gramps *was* a little crazy, and I had imagined what I saw and heard that first night in the house. A little part of me would have felt better if it were all just make-believe.

"Hey," she said, sitting up. "What's going on? What's with all the yelling? Are you having a nightmare?"

"How did you sleep through that?" I asked, rushing over to the bed, pulling her into my chest. "That was terrifying!"

"What was?"

"You didn't hear any of that?" I asked, letting her go from my bear hug so she could make eye contact with me.

"Hear what? You yelling? I thought you were dreaming."

I didn't know how to explain it, so I just pulled her into my chest again and stroked her hair. "I was yell... Never mind," I said. "I'll tell you tomorrow. Go back to sleep."

"I don't know how I'm going to fall back asleep after you shouted at me to wake me up," she said as she lay down, her eyes already drooping.

"I'm sure you will," I said, brushing her hair back off her face. "I'm sure I won't."

She was asleep within a few minutes.

On the other hand, I stayed awake for the rest of the night. I paced quietly around the room. I looked out the window at the housekeepers' house, at Geoffrey's house, and at Otto's. Looking for a light to come on. Looking for a sign of life that would tell me they had heard the screaming there, too, and had woken up concerned about our well-being. I went in and out of the bathroom half a dozen times, looking in the mirror at myself, trying to make sure I didn't look crazy. I crept out into the hallway at one point and sat on the floor, listening. I heard nothing but the groans of old wood swaying with the breeze and settling back into where it was supposed to be. I listened to the tapping of branches on the glass of the windows in one of the other rooms down the hall. I heard the distinct sound of air flowing through the air conditioning vents as the system kicked on and then shut off when the house was as cool as it was supposed to be. I heard Courtney breathing heavily—though not quite a snore—from the bedroom.

I heard nothing out of the ordinary after the pounding on the door stopped.

CHAPTER 16
SOMETHING IN THE HALL

THERE WAS no doubt that something was happening in the house. The first time I saw and heard something, I was convinced it might be nothing. Maybe I heard something abnormal and mistook it for something else. And, likely, because I was so tired from moving that I imagined the wall pulsating across from our bedroom.

But the second time? There was no way I imagined it.

I'd been doing my best to forget about it for days. Trying not to let the anxiety of *when it will happen again* creep in. That feeling when you get a false alarm on your smoke detectors in the middle of the night and then constantly worry about when it'll happen again and scare the hell out of you? It was a similar feeling. Not a day went by that I didn't anticipate something happening. Not a day went by that I didn't peer around every corner and listen intently before closing the door to our bedroom, which we were now in the habit of locking. Though, as I mentioned earlier, the tiny lock on the bedroom door wouldn't do anything to stop whatever tried to get into our room last week. I didn't even think it'd buy us much time if that thing came back.

We were trying to get settled in the house. We were trying to make it feel like our own, using some of the cash Gramps had left behind in the mysterious box to buy some new furniture to replace his that we'd donated. Courtney even picked out a few pieces of art that she liked. Well, she called the pieces art; I think of them more like framed photographs. She picked out a killer autographed *Batman* poster to hang by the theater. Michael Keaton's *Batman*, not any of those other impostors. (Sorry, Christian Bale, if you're reading this!)

The house was slowly becoming ours. As much as it killed me, traces of Gramps were fading away. Even his smell was fading, except for his favorite spot in the breakfast nook. Every time I walked by it, I could smell him. I almost sensed he was still there, sitting, eating his breakfast, and reading the newspaper, that I was convinced he was the last person alive to have it delivered every morning. I believed in that sort of thing, so it wasn't unusual for me to get a sense of him. I liked to imagine that he was there, having breakfast with me. Courtney was never a big breakfast person and usually had to rush to get ready to run out the door for work. And that was fine. I didn't mind having breakfast alone most of the time. Even once we'd moved into Stone Way. Even more so once it felt like Gramps was there having breakfast with me.

"Sir?" Geoffrey called out to me as he came in the back door. "Good morning."

"Hi, Geoffrey," I said. "How are you?"

"I'm very well, thank you." Joy, Vanessa, and Sadie followed him in. "It must be Thursday," I thought to myself. Once I'd taken leave from work to deal with Gramps's estate, the days had all blended. And I won't lie. Once we found all that cash, I quickly decided—with Courtney's support—not to return to work. Over the years, we'd always joked that I worked for the money and she worked for the enjoyment. Meaning: I hated my job but made good money, and she loved her job but didn't get paid much. I obviously offered to let her quit her job, too, but I knew she wouldn't take me up on it. She loved being a teacher. I loathed being a salesman.

"It's floor day," Sadie said. I'd already connected those dots in my head, given that the three of them came in together. There was a unique combination of housekeepers who'd come into the house on any given day, and they'd tackle one big chore throughout the house on that day. Thursdays were the day they vacuumed the rugs and mopped the hardwood and tile. It was actually quite impressive to watch. They worked as a military unit with precision and very little wasted time.

"Ah, yes," I said, pretending to be a little surprised. "Good morning, ladies."

"Sir," Geoffrey said, approaching. "Toward the end of William's life, he didn't much require a chef anymore, so we'd let Sam go. Sam had been with your grandfather for decades as his chef. I'm sure he'd come back if you'd like." He half-gestured to the bowl of cereal I'd been eating. It hadn't crossed my mind until that moment that neither Courtney nor I had been eating very well since we moved into the house. I'd been filling the same bowl with Cheerios every morning and rinsing it out afterwards. I don't think it ever made it back into the cabinet from the dish strainer next to the sink.

"Come to think of it, a good meal might be nice," I said. "Could you arrange that?"

"Yes, sir, of course. I wouldn't have mentioned it if I couldn't get Sam back here."

"Thank you, Geoffrey."

"My pleasure, sir. As always."

"Oh, Geoffrey."

"Yes, sir?"

"I think it might be time to crack open the door to Gramps's room."

"You think so?"

"It's been almost a month since he died, and as much as I love leaving the room how he left it when he passed, it's just wasted space right now."

"I understand. Would you like some help?"

"I think I can handle it, but I'll let you know," I said. The gang of housekeepers had left the kitchen just a moment earlier, and the sound of vacuums piped up from the formal living room.

"Yes, sir, of course."

"Courtney will be home from work in a few hours, anyway. She can help if she wants to."

* * *

IT FELT WEIRD, standing there in the hallway, unable to open the door to his room. Part of me felt like there couldn't possibly be anything bad inside, but the other part of me felt like I'd open the door to find Gramps's ghost floating around in there, ready to jump out and scare me.

I must have grabbed hold of the doorknob and let go a dozen times before I was able to psych myself up and actually open it.

It creaked and squeaked as it slowly opened, kicking up dust from the hardwood floor behind it, creating a little tornado that lingered for a moment as the door finished opening all the way. "I guess they haven't been in here to clean," I thought to myself.

"Now or never," I said out loud and stepped into the room.

After fumbling for the light switch, I found it and turned on the overhead lights. Like the room we'd been staying in, Gramps's room had a massive chandelier hanging from the middle of it, now illuminating everything. The blackout drapes were still drawn, leaving the far side of the room in darkness despite the chandelier.

His room looked similar to the one we'd been staying in. Lots of oak everywhere, massive windows, though they faced the other side of the property, away from the other houses. The bed was bigger than any other bed I'd ever seen before. Much larger than a normal king bed.

I took a few steps inside, making sure not to disturb anything just yet.

On his nightstand, he had three picture frames: one of my grandmother, one of Ginger, his second wife, and one of him and me. The one of the two of us had three different photos in it: one from the first time he met me as a baby, one from my twenty-first birthday when he bought me my first official beer, and one from Courtney and my wedding.

I picked up the picture frame of us to examine it more closely, to get a better look at it, and stared at it longer than I'd intended. It made me miss him much more than I had. As I held it, I somehow felt closer to him. I felt the warmth of his presence wash over me.

Once I put it down, I moved closer into the room, needing to walk around the foot of the massive bed. Much like the other room, it had a fireplace, though it looked unused. Perhaps he'd never used it, or maybe the cleaning gang was just so good at cleaning that it looked brand new.

Unlike the other rooms, there was no dresser or armoire. I figured there must be a hidden door somewhere in the room, like the hidden bathroom in ours. I won't lie and say it felt normal to walk around, tapping on all the walls, trying to find where a secret closet or bathroom might be hidden.

On the seventh panel, just to the left of the fireplace, I found the secret bathroom. Gramps, apparently, loved secret bathrooms. This one, being tied to the primary suite, was much larger and more elegant than the one in our room. The clawfoot tub could have fit a family of five. The standalone shower would have fit the population of Rhode Island. You could have landed a plane on the vanity. And you guessed it, probably without me even having to tell you, that it had one of those fancy toilets from Japan that greets you by name and heats your butt while you sit.

"You loved living a good life, didn't you, Gramps?" My voice echoed off the tile-clad bathroom. "What other secrets do you have in store?"

I left the bathroom and continued around the room counterclockwise, tapping and tapping, looking for a closet. I knew Gramps would have a ton of clothes that could be taken out and donated. There just had to be a closet somewhere.

For a moment, I contemplated yelling down to Geoffrey, hoping he was still in the house, to ask for his help. But part of me—that little boy who grew up with *The Hardy Boys* and *Choose Your Own Adventure* books—wanted to see if I could find it on my own.

So I kept banging on the walls. Tap, tap, thud. Tap, tap, thud. Tap, tap, boink. "Huh?" I thought. "That sounds different."

My fingers ran along the outer edges of that wall panel, periodically pressing in, hoping to find the latch that would pop open what I was sure would be Gramps's closet full of his entire wardrobe.

Unlike the hidden bathrooms, this door's latch was on the left side. And it was much stronger than the bathroom latches. I had to lean into it with almost my entire body weight to get it to release.

A whooshing sound escaped from the door as it swung into the room, a hydraulic sound that made me wonder whether it was tied to an automatic-closing hinge of some sort.

What I found behind the door was not Gramp's closet. Much to my shock, it was a long, pitch-black hallway. I held the door open with my right foot, its pressure pushing back against me, wanting to close.

"Now what is this?" I asked no one.

Impatient as I suddenly felt, I waited for my eyes to adjust to the darkness. As they did, shapes appeared along the walls. Sconces as far as I could see, lining the walls.

At the far end stood a figure. A shadow. A silhouette against the faint light at the other side of the hallway. A large, hulking silhouette hid in the darkness.

I blinked my eyes a few times, hoping they'd adjust better so I could get a closer look at whatever it was. Hoping that, should it charge at me, I'd know what was coming. As if that would make a difference.

The light from Gramps's room bled into the hallway, causing my night vision not to be as crisp as it could be.

I made a split-second decision to close the door behind me to block out that blinding light, much like going out into the middle of nowhere to see the night sky better by blocking out the city lights.

Air filled my lungs as I took a deep breath and held it. I stepped inside and let the hydraulic hinge pull the door closed behind me.

My eyes fluttered as they adjusted better. It was clear as day now; the silhouette at the end of the hallway was becoming clearer and moving up and down slightly. It was breathing.

Scanning the room, I found a light switch to my left and flicked it on as soon as I discovered it. The sconces running down both walls flashed on, one at a time, stretching from where I stood inside the door to the end of the hallway.

One by one, they popped on with a hissing sound. One by one, they brought the silhouette into more and more light until the last sconce turned on.

No sooner did the last bit of light illuminate the hallway than the figure disappeared.

"That can't be right," I said to myself.

I reached to my left and turned the lights back off. As they illuminated the room, they darkened it. One by one, from the end of the hallway back to me, they went off in pairs. As soon as the last lights went out, the figure reappeared. In the same position, breathing at the same rate. Its body rising and falling in slow motion but keeping a perfect beat.

I flicked the switch again. The lights flashed on down the hallway, only to find the figure had vanished again.

I repeated the same process a few more times before realizing it must have been some odd lighting thing. Whatever was on the other end of this hallway was causing an optical illusion. And putting on my bravest Hardy Boys face, I left the lights on and ventured down the hallway to see where it led.

As I approached the other end, I felt no fear. I wasn't afraid of whatever the shadow was or wasn't. I felt relieved to be pursuing the odd parts of the house and of Gramps.

Before I knew it, I was at the end of the hallway. As I had suspected, there was nothing there. Though I felt a slight breeze coming from the left, I felt no odd presence and was not confronted by any screaming monsters, ghosts, or demons.

The end of the hallway connected to another hallway, resulting in a T shape. I looked back and forth, to the left and right, trying to decide which way I would go next. The lights in both directions seemed to be tied to the only light switch I'd seen so far, as the pairs of sconces continued in both directions, illuminating the pair of hallways.

With no knowledge of where they'd go, I followed the hallway to the left, having a sense it would lead me deeper into the house. I tried to work out the house's layout in my mind and thought it might bring me back toward the main staircases, sort of above and behind the formal living room.

The hallway was long and musty. I had to brush several cobwebs aside as I walked down it. At one point, a small field mouse ran from my right to my left, causing me to jump for a moment.

At the end of the hallway was a simple door. It looked somehow older than the rest of the house. The doorknob was one of those older glass ones you'd see in houses from the 1800s. The lock had an old-fashioned keyhole. For a quick moment, I feared it would be locked, and I would have come to a dead end.

I grabbed the doorknob and twisted. Thankfully, it opened, though the door was incredibly stubborn to pull open. I yanked and twisted. I yelled some profanity that I'll spare you from. But I finally got it open.

On the other side was a spiral staircase. The column of the staircase had been wrapped in very small, white Christmas lights, illuminating the entire way from where I stood down to the bottom. I did my best to look down and see where it led, but because of the spiral's shape, I couldn't make out what was at the bottom.

Continuing my braver-than-usual attitude, I took the first step down, planting my foot to make sure the staircase was stable and would hold my weight.

It shook a bit, but didn't feel like it would collapse, so I continued down.

The Christmas lights seemed much newer than this part of the secret hallway—or, I guess, at this point, it was more of a tunnel system.

There were thirty steps down to the bottom. Don't ask me why I counted them. I know it's not important to anything or anyone, but I did. At the bottom, there was a small landing with a light switch on the wall. I assumed it would turn off all the lights that led me to that point, all the way back to where Gramps's room had started the tunnel system.

In front of me stood a solid piece of wood. Not a door, as it had no handle and no structure like a door. It looked like just a solid piece of wood, but it was set in a door frame.

I felt around the wood, studying its edges and corners, wondering what it was, unsure of where it would lead. My body felt like it was in the formal living room. I tried to imagine leaving Gramp's room, walking down the main hallway, down the main staircase, and into the space where I was sure I now stood.

As soon as I put my weight into the faux door's wood, it moved outward. A brushing sound accompanied the door's movement, and I noticed a small piece of rubber lining the bottom. As it opened more, I could see a hardwood floor appearing under my feet. The rubber on the bottom of the piece of what I had thought was wood was preventing the structure I was pushing from scraping the floor.

By the time I realized what was happening and where I was, the wood had fully opened, pushing out into the center of the room that I immediately recognized as Gramps's old study. What I had been pushing out was the credenza with the cabinet where I had found Gramps's box and letter. It was the most secret of all the secret passageways I'd seen in the house!

"Wow," I couldn't help but say out loud. I'd sat on the floor just to the right of where I now stood, reading Gramps's letter, examining the box he'd left me, counting the stacks of hundred-dollar bills, and then explaining it all to Courtney for hours the other day. I sat just feet away from where this hidden passageway opened up and had no idea it even existed. There were no signs of disturbance on the floor. There was no draft. There was nothing you'd seen in an old movie on TNT at night that would make you even think there was a hidden passageway there. And yet, here I was. Minutes ago, I was in Gramps's room looking for a hidden closet, and now I'm downstairs in his old study, connected by a secret passage.

"If this leads here, where does the other hallway lead?" I thought.

In the fully lit study, I was able to look at the back of the credenza more closely. The "wood" I had seen from inside the hallway was, in fact, the back of the credenza. And while it was true there was no doorknob on the inside, there was a small slit in the back of the structure that could pull it closed from the inside.

I immediately ran back inside and closed the credenza, hurrying back up the stairs to head down the other hallway.

As I approached the connecting point of the T, where Gramp's room was, the lights flickered. Not one pair at a time like they had when I turned them on or off, but all at once. Flashing the entire tunnel system into complete darkness for a blip at a time. Light and then dark. Light and then dark. It kept happening as I got closer to Gramp's room.

The time the lights were off was getting longer the closer I got. The length of time the lights were on got shorter.

"Hello?" I called out, hoping it was someone playing a trick on me, though I knew it wasn't. "Is someone there?"

My sense of bravery began to fade quickly as the lights kept going out.

At one point, as I was about twenty feet from the offshoot to Gramps's room, the lights stayed out for almost a full minute. During that time, I felt someone standing in front of me. You know that feeling you get when someone's standing near you, but just out of your peripheral vision? I felt that. I felt someone's presence, but they were standing in front of me.

I did my best to get my eyes to adjust to the darkness, but it was impossible with the lights flickering off and on, over and over. Just as my eyes would adjust, the lights would come back on.

But not the last time. The lights stayed off for a minute, and when I felt the presence, I saw it there. Again. The hulking silhouette stood just before me. Mere feet from me. Breathing. Lunging up and down as if it were trying to catch its breath. I heard a small snarl, like a lion getting ready to let out a big roar. For a moment, I felt its breath on me. One long exhale that cast itself over my entire body.

I fell still, frozen. I couldn't move or speak. I couldn't even think of a coherent thought. The only thing that flashed in front of me was Courtney. If whatever this was killed me here, she'd never know. If none of the staff knew about these secret hallways, they wouldn't know to look here, and they'd never find me. I'd rot in the hallway until I was a pile of melted goo and bone fragments.

Oh God. What if it eats me, and they never find a trace of me?

"What are you? Who are you?" I managed to yell, fully recognizing that whatever it was wouldn't answer me.

It snarled again. Louder this time.

The lights flickered back on, illuminating the empty hallway in front of me.

The air felt thick and heavy. I felt a weight pressing on my back, a sense to get the hell out of there before something else—something worse—happened.

I sprinted toward the door to Gramps's room. I ran like my life depended on it, though I may have been a little dramatic. I ran straight through the door, pushing past its stubborn hydraulic hinge and right through Gramp's room to the hallway. I paused a moment before running back into our bedroom to find Courtney sitting on the bed, taking her work clothes off.

"Oh, there you are," she said, smiling.

"You will not believe what just happened," I said. "Seriously."

"Oh no. Oh, no. Tell me," she said, patting the bed next to her.

CHAPTER 17
THE BEACH

HAVE you ever felt like you were going insane? Madly, truly, deeply insane? Like everything you were seeing and hearing was not real?

I was still in a kind of shock after the incident last week with the shadow thing in the hidden hallway, even after recounting the whole thing to Courtney and asking Geoffrey what he knew about it. He claimed he knew nothing about the secret passageways. He said those hallways weren't part of the plans for the house, which he was so intimately familiar with. I didn't believe him. Something about his response felt weird, like he wasn't lying, but as if he was covering something up. I couldn't tell what, but it just led to me feeling even more insane and a little paranoid.

In typical Courtney fashion, Courtney tried to make me feel better. She held and comforted me, dragging her fingers across the back of my neck like she always did when I needed to calm down. It worked, but only marginally.

It felt like a broken record sometimes. "Are you sure about

what you saw?" Over and over, they asked me. Everyone, including Sam, who had just come back on as a cook and was worth every penny of whatever the estate was paying him. I thought the home-cooked—and very fancy—meals would have helped me feel some sense of normalcy, but it didn't help as much as I'd wanted it to.

"I think I'm going to get out of the house today," I told Courtney, as she was getting ready to head out to work. "Maybe take one of Gramps's cars up to the beach and get some fresh air."

"Oh, that's a great idea, love," she said, barely stopping to kiss me on the cheek and head toward the door.

Somehow, I knew when no one else was in the house. As soon as Courtney pulled the door closed behind her, a sense of panic washed over me. That only seemed to happen when there was no one else in the main house. Sam had been heading back out to the house he'd been sharing with Geoffrey—I'm not sure if there was no room in the house where the housekeepers lived, or if he preferred to live with another man, or if he'd headed to the daily farmer's market in town to pick up ingredients for lunch or dinner. Geoffrey usually came in during breakfast to check on us, then went back to his home. The housekeepers wouldn't usually come in until much later in the morning, except on Thursdays, because the floors took longer than other tasks.

* * *

GRAMPS HAD exquisite taste in cars, especially for an older guy. Sure, he had his classics: a '57 Corvette, a '62 Alfa Romeo, and an '81 Porsche. But he also had some modern cars in his collection, including the more-or-less brand-new Ferrari that I decided to take to the beach. I don't know what made me pick that one. It was closest to the front of the garage and would require the least rearranging to get it out.

It purred when I started it. It vroomed like nothing I'd ever driven before, and once I got out on the highway, heading north, I laid into the throttle and flew by so many other people. My favorite Spotify playlist was blaring so loudly I could barely hear the engine.

"A work of art," I thought. The car, not the playlist. Though the playlist was great.

I knew the general direction of the beach I was heading in, so I didn't bother setting up the GPS to route me there. I had nothing to do and nowhere to be. I just wanted to be out of the house for a while. To get away and clear my head. To be away from whatever was messing with me, if it was anything at all.

* * *

THE BEACH WAS EXACTLY how I remembered it. It was the same beach we'd gone to a few times as a family when I was a kid. On the few times my parents took me there, they spent most of the time in the casino while I played in the sand by myself. Though when Gramps took me, we spent the day together, building sand castles and knocking them down. He was a master at creating them. He'd bring tools. He'd make shapes. He'd get just enough water into the sand so it'd hold perfectly. And he loved doing it with me, I think.

I found the first parking spot I could and pulled the Ferrari in nose-first, worried I was going to scrape the front on the curb.

The sound of the waves immediately put me at peace before I'd even closed the door to the car.

"Nice car!" someone yelled as I stepped up on the sidewalk and began walking toward the entryway to the beach.

It was a cooler day, later in the summer, so there weren't a ton of people on the beach. The wind coming off the water made me a little uncomfortable, but I still wanted to enjoy my time.

The beach wasn't very long and not very deep. The water was just fifty or so feet from the barrier protecting the houses and businesses that lined the boardwalk. A stone wall, about six feet tall, was all that protected those buildings from surging tides. It had always felt insufficient to me, but clearly, I was wrong, as the waves never got past it and damaged any of the buildings.

Once I'd gotten to the entrance to the sand, I stopped and took my shoes and socks off. I stuffed my socks into my shoes and picked them up in one hand, letting them dangle by my side.

The cool sand felt good on my bare feet, sliding between my toes and over the tops of my feet. It felt different from the scorching hot sand I'd remembered from childhood. The tiny grains of sand felt therapeutic, almost like a little massage across my feet.

The lifeguard tower bore a red flag, though a couple of surfers ignored it and were tossing about in the waves. They dipped behind the dunes ahead of me as they cruised closer to the beach. Their heads popped up and disappeared as they rode the waves in.

Each step toward the water felt more relaxing than the last. My toes felt at home in the sand, though I only liked the beach for the beach part and not the ocean. I wasn't a swimmer, and I'd never been in the sea. Something about the salt in the water made me uneasy. The texture of it. The seaweed. The constant pushing and pulling of the tide. The water wasn't for me. The sand, though, that's where I felt the happiest and at peace.

The sun came poking out from the cloud it had been hiding behind, immediately warming my face and taking away the sting of the ocean breeze.

I felt happy—genuinely happy—for the first time since moving into Stone Way. Don't get me wrong; I was very happy with my life. I loved Courtney with all my heart. I never had to worry about money again. I had a big, beautiful home to live in and all the cars I could ever want. I was happy. Sure, I'd love a better relationship with my parents, but who wouldn't?

The sound of the waves seemed to lull me, to pull me in. Each crashing wave made its own unique sound as it thrashed upon the shore, only to retreat into the ocean and reform as something similar, yet unique.

I could feel the spray of the water as I got closer. It was colder than I expected, but still felt refreshing. It cooled my skin and counteracted the sun's rays that had been warming me up as I approached the water.

The two surfers looked to have had enough and made their way to shore, grabbing their boards and walking past me. I heard one of them say "righteous" and chuckled to myself. That wasn't a word I'd heard since childhood.

For some reason, I turned to watch them leave. Maybe curious about where they were going or how they'd get their surfboards home. Maybe just interested in general, I'm not sure.

As I turned to watch them, I noticed the two families to my left were walking toward the boardwalk as well. Their blankets, backpacks, and children's toys were all still laid out where they'd left them. The sound of their radio was still barely audible over the sound of the ocean crashing just a few feet from me. While I watched those families leave, I noticed two more families further down, doing the same thing. In fact, every family I could see seemed to leave the beach at the same time.

When I turned to my right, the handful of people and families on that side of me were leaving as well.

I jogged over to the lifeguard station—one of those tall, wooden chairs, not one of the little houses you'd see on larger beaches—and asked the lifeguard what was happening. "Where's everyone going?" I asked.

He stood on the chair high above my head, scanned the water, and then jumped down. For a moment, he stood in front of me, silent. Then he turned to his left and walked away. He didn't say a word. He just walked toward the boardwalk like everyone else.

I listened intently in case he'd said something. But he didn't. He just walked away, eventually disappearing over the dunes I'd climbed to get down to where I was.

"Odd," I thought.

The entire beach was empty except for me. I couldn't remember that ever happening before, even in the dead of winter. There were always at least a few people on the beach near me, no matter what beach I was at or what time of year it was.

A chill fell over my body as the sun dropped behind a large gray cloud that had appeared out of the blue.

I did my best to shrug it off. To not think about it. To just enjoy the feel of the sand and water on my feet. To breathe in the fresh ocean air. To let it cleanse me of whatever was weighing on me. Maybe it was a coincidence that everyone left at the same time. Maybe they got an alert on their phones about bad weather and all headed indoors while it passed. Perhaps it was something else.

The ocean water splashed up around me as I tiptoed through the waves. Their sound and feel made me more and more comfortable in my surroundings. The thoughts of shadow monsters and door-banging-screaming *things* escaped me. I thought about Gramps. I remembered the various spots on this very beach where we'd built sand castles together and played in the retreating waves, kicking water up at each other. I thought about the time I brought Courtney here and won her that stuffed monkey that she still slept with when she didn't feel well.

Suddenly, my stomach lurched. A pain in the very core of me kicked and stabbed at my stomach. I felt close to vomiting and had to bend down to put my hands on my knees. It was all I could do to keep from falling over in pain.

The world around me darkened. I think more of my eyes closing than of more clouds. The sound of the waves softened, and the sand felt coarse and painful in my toes. I took a few steps back from the water to dry sand and sat down, rubbing my temples with one hand and holding my stomach with the other.

The ocean breeze stopped as I put my head down between my knees. I couldn't feel it rushing over me anymore, which helped ease the nausea that suddenly encroached on my entire body. The sand on my feet no longer felt good, but felt painful like tiny shards of glass stabbing me all over.

"What is happening?" I yelled into the nothingness before me.

When the sense of needing to vomit passed, I lifted my head, hoping the fresh air and ocean breeze would help me feel normal again. But what I saw was something unlike anything I'd ever seen before.

The ocean was calm. Not in an "oh, it's a good day to swim" way. In a terrifying way. There were no waves. At all. The ocean had completely stopped moving. What had been just moments before a thriving, active ocean now looked like a lake. The tide wasn't moving in or out. The waves weren't rising and falling. The breeze had stopped entirely. The sun still hid behind the ominous cloud overhead.

The silence cut through my body, making me immediately forget about the pain I was feeling in my stomach. Something felt very wrong very quickly.

And then I heard it cut through the silence. A snarl. The same snarl I'd heard the week before in the secret hallway. The snarl of a lion, a bear, and an alligator all wrapped up into one. A snarl that shot fear through my entire body instantaneously.

I turned around and looked behind me. Then, next to me on both sides. Then, in front of me again, out across the motionless ocean.

There was nothing. Nothing I could see, anyway. But I sensed it. I felt its presence. Whatever it was, it seemed to have followed me. It came along for the ride. And, for some reason, it seemed to be singling me out. And on some level, it felt like it was mad at me.

CHAPTER 18
AN INTERRUPTION

SOMETHING ABOUT BEING in the attic brought me peace. When I was up there, whether I was playing with the trains, thinking about expanding the town, or just sitting quietly with my thoughts, I felt at peace. There was a calmness up there, for whatever reason. Even if I discounted how close it made me feel with Gramps, just being up there, away from life and responsibility and family drama, I felt peaceful.

There was a serene feeling washing over me that afternoon. Vivid memories of Gramps and me picking out the next passenger car at Hobby Town, rushing back to his house to unbox it, and picking where it'd go in the lineup. Would Chet get another car attached to his already impressive length? Would one of the other trains get the new car? Being a kid with Gramps was so much fun. I didn't worry about school, or my parents, or my lack of friends. There was no pressure to be anything I wasn't with him. There was no pressure at all, actually. There was just happiness.

And those memories, those feelings, carried through to the

space we'd shared for so many countless hours. To the place where I'd felt so wanted and loved. To the place where he and I spent hours building and expanding and playing and laughing. There were so many times when Gramps made me feel brilliant, but none more so than when he'd figure out some complex engineering feat we needed to work out the math for to expand the town.

I was sitting calmly in one of the old folding chairs one afternoon, thinking about what else Gramps would have liked to add to the town, when I heard the door open at the bottom of the stairs. Then, distinct footsteps climbing the stairs toward the attic.

I clenched up, worried about what might come toward me. I hated that feeling. Being scared. Especially in my own home. Especially in a place I'd spent so much time throughout childhood. The fear took over as soon as I let it—that initial wash of wonderment, excitement almost. I think on some level, we all love to be scared. We like the adrenaline rush, don't we? You hear a branch snap in the woods when you swear you're alone. You hear a floorboard creak when you're sure no one else is home. You watch a scary movie in the dark and are sure you see the little haunted doll from the movie at the end of the hallway, hiding just there in the shadows.

Something about being in the attic took that fear away, though. Sure, yes, I was still scared of any unknown sound. But I wasn't truly afraid for my life. Despite everything that'd happened to me since moving in. Despite all the weird things, all the noises and strange things I'd seen. Despite all of that, I was more curious than scared. At least initially.

The footsteps fell closer to the top of the stairs. They sounded normal, human. The tension in my jaws and temples released as Courtney's head rose above the landing into my line of sight.

"Hey," she called out as she passed through the upper doorway. I was unable to close it earlier because, once again, the humidity had caused it to swell beyond its frame.

"Hi," I called back, not rising from my chair.

"What are you doing? You've been up here all day."

"Who cares?" I snapped at her almost uncontrollably.

"I do. That's why I asked." She was approaching me now, within arm's reach. "Are you okay?"

"Of course I'm okay!" I yelled. "Am I not allowed to spend some time by myself?" I yelled even more. I found myself unable to stop screaming. I wasn't mad. I wasn't confused. But, for some reason, I was yelling.

"Of course, you're allowed some time to yourself. But you said you'd be back in a little bit."

"I know what I said, Courtney!" I was still yelling.

"That was six hours ago," she said, reaching for my hand. "I was just curious about what you were up to."

"Six hours?" I asked, looking at my watch.

"I was getting worried," she said. "Especially after what you told me about the beach."

"I'm fine," I said flatly.

"Are you coming down for dinner?"

"I don't know. Probably." I felt myself getting annoyed with the copious questioning.

"Are you sure you're okay?" she asked, now holding my hand.

I pulled away from her. "Yes, I'm fine. Can I just have some time in peace for once?" I was suddenly yelling again.

"Yes, of course." She retreated toward the door. "I know you have a lot going on in your head, but you don't have to take it out on me."

I scoffed as she tried to close the door behind herself, only to find the wood was still swollen and unable to close.

She click-clacked down the stairs, and I heard the door at the bottom shut behind her.

She'd barely asked me anything, but I felt so angry about the interruption. I had told her I'd be down when I was done, and I clearly wasn't done yet. I still had work to do. The town needed me. Gramps needed me. And all she wanted to do was bother me. To interrupt me and drag me back downstairs where we'd sit and watch some stupid show on television, or discuss what color to paint Gramps's old office for the fiftieth time. Or she'd drag me out to the furniture store again to pick out some other area rug that I couldn't care less about and had told her to pick on her own a hundred times.

Why couldn't everyone just leave me alone? In peace. Why couldn't they figure anything out without my input? *Sir, what shall I make for dinner? Sir, this bill needs to be paid. Sir, can you authorize this delivery?*

Everywhere I turned, people needed me for something. It was driving me crazy.

"Just leave me alone," I said to no one. "Just leave me."

CHAPTER 19

THE BOOK

"HELLO, SIR," Geoffrey greeted me as I entered the foyer, still reeling from the oddness at the beach the other day, unable to get the sound of the snarl out of my head. I tried to think of a movie that seemed scary, but wasn't. To lighten the heaviness of what'd happened to me, to make it less scary.

If I could correlate something that I heard, saw, or did in real life to something from a movie, I would know that the thing I experienced must be made up because it happened in a movie, and movies are pretend. That's the logic I used, anyway.

Don't judge me. My brain is weird. I know.

"Oh, hey," I said. "What are you doing?" I couldn't help but notice he was standing at the bottom of the left staircase with his hands behind his back.

"Nothing. I just came down from upstairs."

It felt odd to me that he was standing there, though I couldn't nail down why. "Do you often come into the house when no one is here?"

He thought about it for a moment before answering. "I suppose I do. Is that all right with you?"

"I suppose if it was good enough for Gramps, it's good enough for me." *But why?* The thought popped into my head without any forethought. Why did he need to be in the house when no one was there? I certainly hadn't asked him to do anything in the house that would require him to be in there without Courtney or me being home. And it wasn't like he was a housekeeper or the chef who needed to do their work.

"Have I made you uncomfortable?" he asked.

"No, not at all." I lied, albeit only a little. "You just caught me by surprise. I didn't know you were here."

"Ah, yes. I was looking for something in your grandfather's room."

"What? Like a secret passageway?" I joked, but was half serious.

"Heavens, no."

But suddenly, I felt the need to know what he was talking about. "So, what then?"

"A book."

"A book?"

"Yes, sir. An old book that I had been reading to him shortly before he passed."

"Wouldn't the book be in the library or the study?"

"It was. But once William could no longer get out of bed, I'd taken to reading it to him in his room while he was resting comfortably."

"What kind of book?" I couldn't tell what had come over me, but I suddenly felt the need to know what he was talking about.

"Just an old book. A story about another world. Your grandfather loved fiction. It's how he came up with most of the ideas for the games he made. From other people's stories."

"I didn't know that." Truth be told, I didn't know much about how Gramps had come up with the various game ideas he'd come up with. He'd told me about his inventions and patents, and that he and his friend David had made many games, but he hadn't said how they came up with the ideas. "Oh. Did you find it?"

"The book? No, sir. I was unable to locate it. I'm pretty sure I left it on the nightstand in his room the last time we'd read it. Though that was a while ago now."

"I don't recall seeing any books while I was in there cleaning out his room."

"It must be somewhere," he said, moving into the middle of the foyer.

"What's it called? I can help look for it."

"Oh, no, sir. I'll find it. Don't you worry."

"I don't mind, really. What's it called?"

"If you insist." He paused long enough that I felt like he was making something up in his head. A lie, perhaps. "Jenkinson's Tale of the Occult."

"Come again?"

"Jenkinson's Tale of the Occult. It's an old book that we'd found at an antique bookshop many years ago."

"Gramps was into the occult?"

"Not always." He paused again, as if trying to come up with something that'd appease my interest.

"I'm confused. Then why read this book to him? Especially so late in his life? He hadn't made video games in a long time, and that's why you said he wanted to read the book, right?"

He stammered as he looked for the right words. "Perhaps it would make more sense if we found the book first," he finally said.

"That doesn't really answer the question, but all right."

* * *

GEOFFREY LOOKED in Gramps's room again while I checked the room across the hall that Courtney and I had been living in.

"Nothing in here," I called out.

"Nor here," he called back.

We met in the hallway, shrugged for a moment, then moved down the long hallway to the next two rooms.

We continued down through the rest of the bedrooms, checking each room thoroughly, including the en-suite bathrooms. We checked the theater room, including under all the seats. We checked the hallway closets. We debated going up to the third floor, which I knew had nothing but the train set and storage boxes. "Oh, no, sir, I've not been up there in ages, and your grandfather wouldn't have been able to walk himself up there to bring it with him."

"You're sure?"

"There's nothing worth going up there for," he said, continuing past the door to the attic and making his way into the very last guest bedroom in the hallway.

I found myself standing in front of the door, wondering why he moved so quickly past the possibility that the book was in the attic.

"Anything?" I called out from the doorway as he kneeled to look under the bed in that last bedroom.

"I know that pesky book is here somewhere," he said. "But not in this room."

"I know you're sure it's not up there, but we should check the attic. Even to check all the boxes that are up there."

"I assure you…" He started.

"I know. It's not up there. But let's look, anyway."

He sighed. Then, he puffed his chest out a little as if he was trying to make himself feel a little braver than he had been. "As you wish, sir. It's your house, after all."

We approached the door to the attic, its door seeming more ominous than when I'd last gone up there after inheriting the house.

"I guess the housekeepers don't need to go up there?"

"Never," he said. "It's likely very dusty and very empty."

"Okay, so let's go," I said, already knowing I'd disturbed the layers of dust the couple of times I'd been up there. I assumed he knew I'd been up there, since he seemed to know everything else about the house.

He shrugged, as if to say he had no other argument about why we couldn't go up into the attic.

I was growing impatient. Even if there was truly nothing in the attic, why was he being so stubborn about it?

"I just need a moment," he said.

He walked off down the hall toward the guest rooms, where the back staircase was. Originally, Gramps had intended it to be the staff staircase, with their bedrooms being at the far end of the hall, but then he built the extra houses on the property, rendering the back staircase almost useless. It dumped you downstairs at the end of the billiard room, which was the closest part of the house to where Geoffrey's house was.

When he got to the top of the stairs, he paused and looked

back at me. I think he was wondering if I was going to change my mind about going up to the attic, but I knew I wouldn't.

I gave him a slight wave and a shrug, almost asking him what he was doing and where he was going.

He waved back, turned, and headed down the stairs. I heard his footsteps reach the bottom and then lost track of him.

* * *

I STOOD by the door while I waited for him.

"It's nothing. Just an attic," I told myself. "There's nothing up there."

I put my ear up to the door, simultaneously hoping to hear something and to hear nothing. I'm not sure what I expected. A person? The snarling thing? The hulking silhouette? But I listened intently. I held my breath. I placed alternating hands on the door, hoping to feel something on the other side. A knock, a heartbeat, anything. Something to make going up to a boring old attic I'd been in a million times a little more exciting.

"What's in there?" I asked nobody. "Probably nothing but Monica's junk." *Richard, if you're in there, can I have my credit card back?* I joked to myself. Every major life occasion called for a *Friends* reference.

Something possessed me to knock on the door. I rapped three quick times and heard them echo back from the other side of the door, far up in the attic.

Knock, knock, knock.

Knock, knock, knock came back from the other side.

I did it again.

Knock, knock, knock.

Knock, knock, knock, called back from the other side with identical cadence but slightly reduced volume.

Knock, knock, knock, knock, knock. I rapped slightly louder and slightly quicker.

The single knock in return was so loud I jumped back from the door. One loud boom, like someone had dropped an anvil on the floor right on the other side of the door.

"Sir, are you all right?" Geoffrey called out, having seen me against the wall and now rushing down the hall toward me. I leaned against the wall on the opposite side of the hallway, trying to catch my breath.

"I don't know. I was knocking and heard an echo at first. But then, that just happened. Did you hear it?"

"Hear what?" he asked.

"You didn't hear the loud knock?"

"No, sir, I didn't hear anything. I was afraid this might happen. Like your grandfather. When you got to this house, you started seeing and hearing things. Is that correct?"

"Yes. How did you know that? I didn't tell you."

"Your grandfather started seeing and hearing those things years ago."

"Is that why my father and uncles thought he was crazy?"

"I believe so, sir. It's very common when people grow old. Others think they're losing their marbles. I'm embarrassed to admit that I, too, thought your grandfather, my friend of many, many years, was going crazy. At first, he'd tell me about this shadow that he'd see out of the corner of his eye or in a dark corner. He'd tell me how he'd sense something's presence in his room, in the hallway. He'd tell me all these things that I absolutely could not and would not believe."

I chuckled.

"Is something funny?" he asked.

"I'm sorry. No. Just the way you said *'could not and would not'* reminds me of how Gramps used to say it. Go on. You were saying?"

"Ah, yes. I suppose I picked up many things from him over the years. I admired him so very much. Yes, he'd tell me these stories, and I wouldn't believe him. I'd dismiss it as an old man losing his higher functions. Perhaps he was going senile, I'd tell myself. Perhaps he was hoping for more attention. In the later years, before he struggled to walk, he'd spend countless hours in the attic with his trains. And when things got their worst, he spent a lot of time alone in his room."

"Mhmm," I nodded, still sitting on the floor across from the door, wondering what I'd heard.

"One day, maybe fifteen years or so ago, he asked me not to go up into the attic. He said that whatever he'd seen was up there and that I shouldn't take the risk."

"I see how you all thought he might be going crazy at this point."

"It was very hard," he said, turning back to me. "He was my best friend for most of my life. He took me under his wing when I was very young, and I looked up to him so much. I felt so torn between helping my friend and thinking logically. But then I thought, 'If it makes him feel better, what's the harm in not going up there?' so I honored his wishes. After that day, I never went up to the attic again. I came up only to the second floor to tend to him when he got very sick."

"Did not going up there, did it change anything?" I asked, my eyes widening.

"What do you think?" he asked, almost sarcastically. "Anything weird or unusual happening to you and your lovely wife since you moved in here?"

"I guess it didn't work." I tried to laugh, but couldn't.

"At first, it seemed to. For a short while. At least during the day. Your grandfather, just having talked to me about it, seemed to keep him from seeing or hearing anything. The days were pleasant and calm again."

"You said the days."

"Yes, the days. Night is a different story. Well, not the night per se. But the darkness."

"Darkness? Like in the hallway off Gramps's room?"

"Precisely. Your grandfather told me that sometimes, only sometimes, whatever it is, can control the lights. It seems to be stronger when it's dark."

"What are the chances the lights are on in the attic?"

"There's a switch right inside the door," he said, turning back to the door.

"I guess we're doing this?"

"You asked," he said over his shoulder as he opened the door.

We both paused for a moment to see if any sound would come from the other side.

"Wait," I said. "So, this book we're looking for…"

"Your grandfather believed it contained information about what was haunting him. I, being the good friend I am, went along with it. The hunt seemed to bring him peace."

"Okay, so this is real then? I've not been imagining weird stuff happening to me since we got here. This is real life?"

"Your grandfather certainly believed so."

"My God," I muttered.

"I'm afraid it seems like not even he can help us here, sir."

"And what about you? Do you believe any of it?"

"I've no reason to believe any of it as of now. I trusted your grandfather with my life, but I've never seen or heard anything unusual in this house or any other house."

Geoffrey pulled the door open. A rush of cold air flew down the stairs and flowed over the two of us as we stood side by side, almost taunting something to happen. He reached inside and flicked the light switch on, illuminating the plain wood stairs that led up to the attic.

"Beetlejuice," I said to myself.

"I'm sorry, sir? Did you say something?" he asked, turning to me.

"Beetlejuice. The movie. Ever seen it?"

"I believe so. The one where the funny demon lived in the miniature town in their attic?"

"That's the one," I said. "These stairs are like the ones in that movie, up to their attic." I laughed for a moment, remembering how harmless Beetlejuice turned out to be in the end.

"Shall we?" he asked.

* * *

GEOFFREY STEPPED ASIDE, gesturing for me to go up first. As scared as I was, I did.

The stairs moaned as I walked up them, kicking up more and more dust, which seemed odd, given how recently I'd been up there. My shoes seemed to land harder and harder the higher I got, causing more and more noise that I was, for some reason, trying to avoid.

Thump. Thump. Thump. I climbed the stairs to the door at the top.

"The door looks old," I called back down, having not previously noticed that fact. Geoffrey was still at the bottom of the stairs, his hands firmly placed on each side of the door frame.

"Yes. It is. Your grandfather had found it on the property when he broke ground. Literally, the first ceremonial shovel of dirt hit it. He felt like it might have been part of the home that once stood here and wanted to give it a second life."

"But knowing Gramps, it didn't fit in with his decor, so he hid it up here."

"You know your grandfather well," he said. He placed his left foot on the first step. I could tell, even from the top of the stairs, he was shaking.

"You don't have to do this," I said. "I can go in alone if you're scared."

"I'll be there shortly," he said. "As much as I wanted to think your grandfather was wrong about everything, I'm still scared of the attic."

"There's something about attics," I said. "They're all old and creepy, even if the house isn't that old."

"Basements, too," he said, now closer to right behind me.

I reached for the doorknob and noticed it was like the one at the end of the hallway behind Gramps's bedroom. The one that leads down to his study. Old and glass, coupled with an old-looking lock.

"What if something's in there when I open the door?" I thought aloud.

"Then we, pardon my French, run like hell," Geoffrey said, now on the step right below me, his hands pressed against the walls of the narrow stairwell.

"There's no time like the present," I said and turned the knob, realizing that I'd worked myself up into being scared for no reason at all. I'd been in the attic so many times over my life, and was up there as recently as just a few days ago. Something about verbalizing the fears and discussing Gramps's fears aloud made it seem more real.

The door creaked open an inch or two and then stopped. I turned and looked down at Geoffrey. His head was at my chest since he was on the step below me. I shrugged and pushed harder on the door, but it didn't move.

Geoffrey stepped up next to me and put his shoulder against the door. "Push," he commanded.

And we did. Together, we pushed as hard as we could, and the door started to move slowly open. I grunted and found myself grinding my teeth. The door felt like it weighed thousands of pounds.

"We don't have the right leverage," I said. "This doesn't make any sense. I was just up here."

"You were?" he asked. "I didn't know."

Together, we continued to push on the door. It inched open slowly, revealing the wide-planked floor covered in dust. To the left of the door, in the direction it opened, I couldn't see anything. Nothing was over there, save for a single box labeled *Elaine*—my grandmother, whom I'd never met.

The door finally lurched fully open, revealing the rest of the attic before me. I took the first step up, my hand still on the door, which now stood to my right.

The attic ran the full length and width of the house. It was a massive open space that housed the train set and its accompanying town, the box of what I presumed to be my grandmother's belongings, and boxes that were being stored.

"I see nothing that wasn't here the other day," I said, reaching down to grab Geoffrey's hand and help him get past the top step.

"I never met your grandmother," he said, pointing to the box adorned with her name. "But it's my understanding that she was a lovely person."

I nodded and took a few steps into the attic, remarking at the things I'd not spent any time looking at the last time I was up there. "I suppose when your house is this big," I said, "you have room for all of your stuff and don't really need an attic."

"I suppose that's true," he said.

"What made that noise when I knocked? Hello?" I yelled out into the emptiness. "Is anyone there?"

The emptiness seemed to swallow my voice, as there was no echo. The naked light bulbs dangling from unfinished overhead fixtures flickered for a moment but regained their illumination quickly. I flinched instinctively.

Geoffrey ducked, as if something was going to swoop down at him from the ceiling. "Please, not that. Not darkness. I'm fine with knowing something is unusual about this house. I'm fine with not coming here after dark. But I don't want to see it or hear it."

"I promise you don't," I said. "Let's go. You're clearly scared, and that's fine. And your book is clearly not up here."

Geoffrey led the way down the stairs, letting me grab the door to pull it closed. But when I yanked, the door wouldn't budge. Much like when we'd opened it, it felt heavy, immovable.

When I took a step back up into the attic and tried yanking the door again, it only moved a tiny amount. Not even an inch.

Something told me to look behind the door to see if it was stuck on something. A warped floorboard, a twisted hinge. Something. Anything.

"I found your book," I said, calling down to Geoffrey, who was now halfway down the stairs. "Well, I found pieces of your book," I corrected myself.

As I bent to examine the book jacket, I noticed the entire book had been shredded. Its contents were still trapped within the jacket, but the pages were torn to pieces. Uneven and jagged pieces fell from the spine as I picked the book up to examine it closely.

"Geoffrey, is this the same book?" I held it up in the doorway to let him get a look at it.

"Is your grandfather's name written inside the front cover?"

I flipped to the front and did my best to let more pages fall out of the destroyed book. "Yes, it says his name there."

"Then yes, that's the same one we're looking for."

Just then, I heard a snarl come from behind me. The lights flickered again, and something dark instantly covered all the windows lining the left side of the attic. The snarl got louder, seemingly getting closer to me.

"Run like hell, Geoffrey!" I yelled down the stairs, tossing the book into the air over my shoulder.

I left the door at the top of the stairs open and jumped down most of the staircase, not worried about hurting myself on the way down.

"What is it?" he yelled up in my direction.

When I landed on the bottom step, Geoffrey pulled me out of the way, grabbing for the door to close it behind me. I heard footsteps from the top of the stairs, starting to slam toward us.

The house seemed to shake around us. The floor suddenly felt uneven beneath my feet, the floorboards rising and falling in rapid succession as if something was trying to knock me off my balance.

A roar came from the top of the stairs, and that was when I first saw it in the light. A being. A creature. A thing. A thing so grotesque that I couldn't equate it to anything I'd ever seen or imagined before. The roar turned back to a snarl. Saliva dripped from what looked to be its mouth, covering the entirety of a head-like structure at the top of the thing. Rows of pointed teeth lined the opening, covering the circle entirely as it opened its mouth wide to roar again. My ears rang. Its black-and-gray skin appeared to be covered with a glaze or goo, reflecting the single light bulb at the top of the staircase. Its giant fist reached out, smashing the light bulb before roaring again.

It lifted what I believe was its foot. Its knee bent away from me, backward, bringing the foot up high, midway along its body. It bent to fit through the doorway, turning sideways.

"Sir?" Geoffrey tugged at my shirt.

The monster roared again, all of its terrifying teeth on full display, smashing its fists against the wall, leaving black streaks everywhere it touched.

I managed to regain my composure just long enough to step back from the door, grab it, and swing it closed.

"Sir? What is it?" Geoffrey asked.

"Look!" I said, pointing up the stairs, confused that he could not see the monster just a few feet from us.

"I don't see anything," he said. "But I'm scared, as you're scared."

A roar came from behind the now-closed door again, accompanied by banging—the loudest, angriest banging I'd ever experienced. Roar after roar came from the other side of the door as the creature slammed its giant black fists against it, trying to break through.

"This is it," I thought. "Courtney won't know what happened to me. This thing will eat me, and that'll be it."

"I don't understand," Geoffrey said. "But I don't need to!" He let go of my shirt that he'd been holding on to and ran off down the hallway toward the back stairs.

I watched him run and thought to do nothing but slam my fists against the door. "Not today! Today is not the day I die!" I continued pounding my fists against the door in perfect time with the monster's pounding from the other side.

The door cracked and splintered. I stopped pounding immediately. A splinter from the door flew out over my shoulder and landed across the hall. A single, solitary crack emerged in the door. Black goo oozed through it, as if the creature on the other side was pressing itself up against the door. The banging stopped, and the roar quieted back down to a snarl.

"Not today!" I yelled again.

The ooze retreated into the crack in the door. The bits that had slid down to the floor seemed to slurp themselves back up, sliding their way up the door, into the crack, and back to the creature on the other side.

Once the ringing in my ears subsided, I threw myself to the floor, exhausted from holding the door shut against the giant monster.

I sat still on the floor with my back against the door. I listened as the creature climbed its way back up to the attic. I listened as it closed the door at the top of the stairs and stomped off into the depths of the attic. I listened to it snarl and growl for what felt like a lifetime. Geoffrey hadn't heard or seen the monster, which confused me even more than I already was. But I somehow had held the door closed against the monster's pounding.

"Gramps believed in the occult," I said to myself. "Why was this thing not visible to Geoffrey?"

"What was in that book?" I asked, knowing I couldn't answer that question. I looked down at some pages that had fallen down the stairs in the kerfuffle and were resting at the foot of the door.

I managed to smile and laugh to myself, though I had no reason to be happy. "Courtney will never believe any of this."

CHAPTER 20

THE DISCUSSION

ONCE I'D HAD some time to catch my breath—and catch Courtney up on what had happened—I gathered every person who lived or worked on the property at One Stone Way around the dinner table.

Only Courtney and I knew what had happened that afternoon. Though Geoffrey had been there, he hadn't seen the monster as I had. We hadn't told the others yet. For starters, I didn't want to scare the rest of them. But, more importantly, I wanted to catch them by surprise. I wanted to see if any of them knew anything about what had happened, about that thing that was in the attic.

It wasn't even a remote surprise that Courtney didn't believe the story I'd told her. I did my best to recount what had happened and tell her every detail I could remember, but she still didn't believe I'd seen and run from the creature I'd encountered.

In typical Courtney "prove it" fashion, she made me take her up to the attic and let her explore. She found nothing but the torn-up pages of the book we'd gone up there looking for. "See? Nothing." I could still hear her words in my head as we waited for the last member of the staff to join us. It was Sam who insisted on making some appetizers because "it's inhuman to have a meeting without snacks." The more I spoke to him, the more I liked him.

Once they'd all settled into their seats, we sat in silence for a moment, looking at one another. I think they could sense something important needed to be talked about, but there's no way they could have any clue what I was about to tell them.

"Thank you all for coming," I started. "As you know, this is an unusual occurrence—us all being here together. Especially so close to nightfall."

"Some of us are anxious," Nicola spoke up.

"I know. I am, as well," I said, knowing I wasn't calming anyone's nerves by telling them I felt the same way. "Can one of you tell me why you don't like to be in the main house after dark?"

Eyes darted around the room. Brief eye contact was made among the group, but no one seemed to want to speak.

"On our very first night here, Joy and Geoffrey were insistent they be out of the house by nine. That was roughly sunset then, though now it's getting earlier and earlier as the summer wraps up. Can someone tell me why?" I asked.

"It's just…" Joy began. "It's just what we've always done. For as long as I've been here."

"And how long has that been?" I asked, genuinely unsure of the exact amount of time.

"I'd worked for your grandfather for sixteen years prior to his passing," she said.

"Fourteen for me," Margo added.

"Eleven," Nicola chimed in.

"Same," Sadie and Vanessa said, echoing one another.

"You've all worked here a long time, then. When did you start leaving before dark?"

"When I started, there was one other housekeeper," Joy said. "She told me we should never be in the house after dark."

"Did she say why?" Courtney asked.

"She said she felt uneasy being in the house after dark. But never got into the details of why."

"Did you ever press her to find out what made her feel that way?" I asked.

"She didn't say, and I didn't pry. She was an older woman. May not have been all there, if you know what I mean." She twirled her finger around her ear.

"That doesn't make sense," I blurted out. "If you're indicating you thought maybe she was crazy, why did you listen to her?"

"I didn't. Not at first," Joy said.

"When I first got here," Margo added, "Joy told me we shouldn't stay in the house after dark, and about the story Maria told her. But we paid it no mind. Ms. Maria was gone, and so were her stories."

"I'd heard those same stories," Geoffrey added. "From Maria and others who were here before her. Stories of evil around the house, lurking in corners, peering out of shadows. They were just stories. We all thought that. I tried to chalk it up to its being a big, old house."

"Do any of you have any reason to think otherwise?" I asked, motioning to Geoffrey to let the rest of the staff have their turn to speak up.

"We're sworn to secrecy," Joy whispered. "Your grandfather made us promise."

"Joy, everyone, I love my grandfather very much. But he is dead. Any promises he made to you no longer apply."

Joy looked to Geoffrey, as if he could grant her permission to speak.

Geoffrey nodded.

"A few years after Maria left, Margo and I were cleaning one of the guest rooms one evening. I don't remember why we didn't get to it during the day, but we didn't. Well, we were in there, and your grandfather came running in, screaming about how he needed help. Telling us a monster was after him." Joy said.

"He seemed terrified," Margo added. "It was so scary to see him like that."

"I'd never seen him act so erratically before," Joy said.

I turned to Sam. "Were you here then? Do you remember this?"

"Well, Mr. Max, I try to mind my own business. I like to make the food and then go about my business."

"I understand," I said. "But were you here the night Joy and Margo are talking about?"

"I was, sir. And I remember hearing your grandfather yelling through the floor. It scared the dickens out of me. The yelling sounded like he was coming through the floor. It was so loud! I dropped the frying pan into the sink and made a run for it. The girls came running down the stairs, yelling, and I grabbed them there girls by the waist as I ran by and yanked 'em outta the house. We ran clear across the field to safety."

"Where did my grandfather go when you girls ran down the stairs?"

"He followed us. Still yelling," Margo said.

"He seemed unwell," Joy added.

"Did either of you see or hear anything? The monster he'd referred to?"

"No, never," Joy said. "Not that night, and not any other night."

"But you started feeling uneasy in the house after dark? Unsettled, like Maria had warned Joy?" Courtney asked.

"We did. So we stopped coming into the house after dark," Joy said. Margo nodded in agreement.

"Did my grandfather ever follow up on this? And why did no one talk to Courtney or me about this when Gramps started talking about hearing and seeing things?"

"We tried to, sir," Geoffrey said. "I wanted to. But someone intervened. Your father."

"My father?" I gasped. "What did he do?"

"I first brought it up with him. You know, on account of William being my mentor and good friend for so long. I didn't want any surprises, since your father had been here taking care of him for many months by that time."

"What did my father do?"

"He explained it away," Geoffrey said. "He told me that your grandfather was very old and had always seen things that weren't there and heard sounds no one else heard."

"But no one else heard these sounds? No one else saw the monster?" I shook my head in disbelief. How could both Gramps and I see and hear the monster, but no one else had?

"Not me," Vanessa said. "I just trusted Joy and Margo and stayed out of the house."

"Did you ever hear anything? Ever see anything?" Courtney asked the group.

"I never stepped foot in this house after dark again," Joy said.

"Never heard or saw a single thing during the daytime when we were in here."

"Any of you?" I asked.

They shook their heads collectively .

"Okay, well, this is going to be a little hard to swallow," I started. "Geoffrey and I went into the attic today to look for a missing book."

Joy gasped. "The attic? Why? There's nothing up there but the trains and boxes. We don't even go up there."

I motioned to her to wait, trying to indicate I'd get to the explanation shortly. "I saw… something. "

"I didn't see anything," Geoffrey interrupted. "Max saw a demon. A creature. Some sort of devil. The monster William told us about."

"What did you see?" Sam asked me.

"I feel insane even saying it out loud," I said. "It was eight feet tall. Black. Covered in sludge or goo or ooze or something. It had no eyes, only a giant, tooth-filled mouth. Its hands and feet were enormous, and it used them to smash the walls in the attic as it tried to come down to get to safety in the stairwell. Its knees bent the wrong way. It was unlike anything I'd ever even thought of, let alone seen before. Nothing in any movie. Nothing from any book. And it was furious with me. It tried to come and kill me."

"Oh my," one woman—I didn't see who—cried.

"This can't be real," Joy said. "I know all about the stories from all of those years ago… but this?"

"I wish I were joking," I said. "So, all cards on the table now. If you know something about this, it's time to speak up."

"Please," Courtney added. "I think Max might be in danger."

The group looked at each other again, seemingly hoping someone had the answers.

"I know only what your grandfather told me," Geoffrey said. "He told me about this monster. He came to me over twenty years ago to tell me about it. He said he'd seen it lingering in the shadows upstairs at night. Once the night had set in and all the lights were off, he'd sense it there, looming. He'd feel it in the air. He said, "Sometimes I hear it snarl at me.""

"Geoffrey, why didn't you tell me this earlier today?" I yelled, slamming my fist on the table, scaring some women, including Courtney.

"I'm sorry, sir. I felt it would be disrespectful to your grandfather to speak ill of him. We never believed any of this. We thought he was sick."

"Okay," I said, my voice booming a little louder than I wanted it to. "No more secrets. We need to be truthful with one another. "

"Yes, sir," Geoffrey continued. "Your grandfather was fascinated by this thing. He'd told me, time and time again, that it did not mean him any harm. He was not afraid of it. He was more curious about it than anything else."

The room fell silent as we all trained our eyes on Geoffrey.

"One day, William came to me and told me he'd seen it. *The great magnificent beast* he'd called it. He said it had come to him in his room the night before—March fourteenth. I remember the date he told me. He came to me not with fear in his eyes, but with wonder. He wanted to know more about it. He insisted we know more."

"Know more?" Courtney asked. "Why?"

"William loved out-of-the-ordinary things," Geoffrey said. "In all the years I'd known him, this was the strangest thing that had ever happened. But I didn't question it. And I certainly believed what he told me. He had no reason to lie. Not to me."

"What did you do?" Sadie asked, reaching to her left to grab Margo's hand.

"Well, for starters, we kept the lights on at night. For William's safety. William knew very early on that whatever it was didn't like light of any kind. He said it didn't like light because the light made the monster weak."

"I can't believe this," I found myself repeating. "What did my father say?"

"I couldn't believe it either, at first," Geoffrey said. "Your father insisted we never mention any of this to you or anyone else. That we take it to our graves. It felt like a threat. One night last year, I heard William talking to it."

"What happened?" Sam asked.

"Against my better judgment, I came into the house after dark. To check on William. Bruce had just left, and I wanted to make sure William had everything he needed until morning. Sometimes," he looked at me, "your father wasn't the best about providing care for your grandfather when he was caring for him. Anyway, I walked up the steps and heard footsteps in William's room. Quiet at first. Then louder as I got closer. I thought someone was in there with him. It had been a few months since William had been up and walking around. I thought perhaps I was mistaken, and Bruce hadn't left yet. But when I got closer to the door, I heard William's voice. He asked, 'What are you doing here? What do you want?' I paused at the door, listening for more, but couldn't hear anything else. I retreated down to the first floor and decided that my decision to enter the house after dark hadn't been a smart one. Then, as I descended the stairs, I heard the door to

William's room fly open and heard the footfalls coming down the hallway behind me, but I wasn't brave enough to turn and look."

"You think he was talking to the monster?" Joy asked.

"I don't know," Geoffrey replied. "But I know William wasn't afraid of it. I asked him about it the next day, and all he could say was, *fascinating.* He was enthralled with the creature he'd been seeing."

"Wait," I said. "Is that why the book about the occult was in the house?"

"Yes, precisely. He must have heard about it from someone and demanded a copy. It was very hard to track down."

"And did this book yield anything that helped William?" Courtney asked.

"No," Geoffrey said. "They were old stories from ancient times. Fairy tales. Made-up stories that older brothers tell younger brothers to scare them at campfires. It was all nonsense."

The silence in the room suddenly felt very heavy.

"Gramps and I are the only ones who see this monster," I said, more thinking aloud than hoping for a response. "I don't understand why."

"I don't understand either," Courtney said. I could tell her logical mind was spinning in overdrive. "If there's some great monster in this house—not that I don't believe you, honey—why is it only tormenting you?"

"I wish I knew," I said. "I don't understand any of it. But I promise you, what I saw today was real. I felt its breath on my face. I smelled it. I can't make up a smell like that."

"I'm not sure I feel any better after talking about this," Joy said. "The sun will set soon. May we go, Mister Washington?"

I looked at my watch. Sunset was approaching. "Yes, please. Go to safety."

"Are we safe?" Courtney asked as we stood to walk the staff to the back door.

"I hope so," I said. "Geoffrey, was there anything in this book that said what the demon would do or why it might be here? Anything you recall?"

"I'm afraid not, sir. Like I said, the book was full of nonsense. Maybe your grandfather saw more in it than I did."

"Geoffrey, please go. Be safe. If you feel uneasy in the house, please don't be in here after dark."

Although Courtney had been in the attic earlier that evening and seen nothing, I still felt uneasy about the evening. I felt no closer to understanding anything that was happening in the house. What was happening to me? And why was I being singled out?

"Joy? Margo?" I called out to them as they crossed the back patio. "Did Gramps ever talk about seeing it downstairs?"

Joy thought about it for a second.

Geoffrey interrupted her thought. "Never downstairs," he said. "Only upstairs. Your grandfather only ever talked about the monster being upstairs. Sometimes in his room. Mostly in the attic. You know how he loved to spend time up there with his trains."

"Why do you think that is?" I asked rhetorically.

Before Courtney and I went back into the house, we stood on the patio for a moment. It felt calm and peaceful. The night sky above us had just one cloud that looked like Swiss cheese, which blocked out the moon periodically. Every star in the night sky was visible, and I, for the first time, felt at peace after taking ownership of the house, despite everything that had happened that day. Despite finding out that the staff knew so much, they kept it from me. Despite all that, I felt at peace. I felt safe going back into the house.

But I knew we weren't safe. Gramps had managed to keep the demon at bay and himself safe; I didn't know how he did it. I knew nothing and felt more confused than I'd ever felt in my life. I didn't know how to protect Courtney and me. But I knew I had to figure it out.

CHAPTER 21
HE'S BACK
AND HE'S MAD

"MAXWELL! MAXWELL, GET DOWN HERE!" I heard the booming voice of my father echoing through the house, bouncing off the walls and up the stairs to the hallway where I stood, just about to go up to the attic to add a new hotel to the town. Amazon had just delivered it along with a handful of other accessories I was excited to add.

I looked down at him from the top of the stairs for a moment before letting him know I was present. I waited, hoping to see some sign of why he was at the house, what he wanted. He paced around the foyer, his brown, knee-length jacket swaying behind him and swishing from side to side as he turned to pace in the opposite direction he had been. He paced so quickly, I'm surprised he didn't wear a path in the tile floor.

"You really should knock," I said as I descended the stairs, intentionally startling him. "This isn't your house, you know." I felt the words hit him and sink into his chest. I don't know why I felt the need to hurt him, but I did.

"You sniveling little shit," he said, racing over to meet me at the bottom of the stairs.

"What do you want, *Bruce*?" I knew calling him by his first name would bother him. Not so much hurt him, but the deliberate sign of disrespect would make him annoyed.

"This house should be mine," he said.

"That's not what Gramps wanted," I shot back immediately.

"At worst, it should have been a third mine. He should have left it to Matthew, Joey, and me. But he left it to you!"

I could see the spit fly out of his mouth into the air between us. Thankfully, we weren't close enough for it to hit me, but its presence felt like a foreshadowing of something worse.

"This is my house now," I said. "Mine and Courtney's. And if you want to visit, you should really call ahead. The least you could do is knock." I let the words linger in the air for a moment before taking the final step down onto the foyer floor. As we stood face-to-face—albeit eyes to forehead, since he was taller than I—I felt powerful. I felt like, for the first time in my entire life, I had power over him. I had something he wanted. And while he clearly never wanted me in his life, it felt nice to know that I had something that he wanted. The house. Gramps's estate. The fortune he'd left me. My father wanted it. He felt he'd earned it, that he'd deserved it. And it made me feel great to lord it over him and not let him have any of it.

"This shouldn't have ever happened!" he shouted, now just inches from my face.

"It did happen!" I yelled back. "Gramps left everything to me because he loved me, because he cared about my well-being. He cared about Courtney!"

"He didn't care about you!" he shouted back. I heard footsteps coming from upstairs. Courtney must have overheard us—

how could she not have—and walked out into the hallway to listen in a little closer. "He only wanted to hurt me. That's why he left you this house. To hurt me."

"You've always been an egomaniac, haven't you, *Dad*? You think the world revolves around you and everyone in it exists to serve your agenda!"

"Don't you dare speak to me that way, young man!"

It'd been a long time since he'd called me "young man". A very long time. Decades, at least. And to be honest, it used to intimidate me. I used to be afraid of him. Fearful of what he'd do if I showed any ounce of backbone toward him. If I spoke back to him or stood up for myself, he wouldn't hold back. At first, he knew where to hit so that it wouldn't draw suspicion. It started playfully when I was a little kid. He'd pick me up and throw me on the bed and "wrestle" with me. He'd charley-horse my legs, or tickle me really hard until I cried. I think I was twelve the first time he outright punched me. The first time I realized he wasn't just playing around and maybe, just maybe, he'd snapped. That for years, he'd been able to keep himself at bay and not actually hurt me. But the first time he punched me, I knew he meant to hurt me, even if it was just a punch in the shoulder.

I did my best, my whole life, to disassociate from it. I let it go because I knew if he was hitting me, he couldn't be hitting my mother. She took her fair share as well. And I knew that I'd soon be in for an extended trip to Gramps's house. That, within hours of him hitting me and really hurting me, I'd have a bag packed and be on my way to Gramps'. No one would say anything, though. The bag would just show up outside my closed door with a thump, and shortly after, my mother would knock on the door, letting me know it was time to go get in the car.

Someone must have called Gramps to tell him I was coming,

because either he or Ginger would be waiting at the door for me when we got there. The gate to the property would be open, and the outside lights would be on. Dad would pull up out front, park, and wait for me to get out. He wouldn't say anything. My mother wouldn't say anything. No one would tell Gramps or Ginger how long I'd be staying. They'd wait for me to get out, take my bag from the trunk, and walk off up to the front door. As soon as I was inside, they'd drive off.

When I was young, they'd come back for me a day or two later. But as I got older—as the hitting got worse—it'd be days or weeks until they came back. The harder he hit me, the longer I stayed away. It was like it gave him time to reset himself. He'd get angry about something, go off on me, and then dump me with Gramps until he could cool off.

"I'll speak to you however I want in my own home!" I was yelling so loudly that my throat got scratchy. "Don't you dare come in here and try to disrespect me. I'm not a child anymore." I did my best to broaden my shoulders. To tell him he couldn't just hit me and dump me anymore. I let my body language do as much talking as it could. Out of the corner of my eye, I saw Courtney on the landing at the top of the stairs.

"I'm your father," he said quietly, as if he'd just realized it for the first time in a long time.

"You've never acted like one." I couldn't believe what was coming out of my mouth, almost as if I had no control over what I was saying. "You've been a piece of shit to me for my entire life. Get out of my house!"

"You don't deserve this," he said. "This should be my house. I took care of that old fart for years. I bathed him and fed him and read to him. I did everything for him."

"We both know that's not true," I said. "That's just another lie that you think people will believe if you say it often enough and with enough vigor. But we both know you're a liar. Geoffrey took care of Gramps. You had nothing to do with it."

"I was here every week!"

"You were here every week trying to buy favor from him. Trying to get in his good graces in hopes that when he died, he'd only have those recent memories of you. The ones where you came and sat by his bedside. That he'd forget all the times you dropped your son off here for weeks and months at a time. You'd hoped you could erase the past. You're more transparent than you think you are!"

I could tell what I'd just said got to him. He reared up as if he was going to hit me, and I clenched my jaw in anticipation. I'd learned—once the punching migrated to my face—that if I clenched, it hurt less.

Courtney cleared her throat. I'd never told her about the extent of the abuse I'd suffered at my father's hands, but I'd alluded to it enough that I was sure she could connect the dots. Her making herself known to him was enough to get him to loosen his fists and back down, even if just for a moment. Much like my entire life, he didn't want anyone other than him, my mother, and me knowing about the abuse. I'm not even sure Gramps knew the extent of it.

He sulked back a bit, releasing the tension in his shoulders. "I took care of him," he repeated.

He could say it as many times as he wanted to. I knew the truth. I knew who Bruce Washington was, and I wasn't afraid to stand up for myself anymore. He couldn't hurt me. I wouldn't let him hurt me.

"It's time you left," I said. "This is my home, and you're not welcome here."

I felt the air from his mouth as he scoffed in my direction before turning around to head toward the door. "You're lucky your mother isn't here."

I wasn't sure what that meant and didn't care enough to ask him. I just let him walk off toward the door, and waited for it to slam shut behind him before letting my shoulders fall. My whole upper body hurt from being so taut for those handfuls of minutes.

"Are you okay?" Courtney called down.

I looked up at her and did my best to smile. "I'm fine."

"What'd he want?"

"To remind me that this should all be his." I gestured around the foyer to let her know I was talking about the grander *this*.

"I hope he got the picture," she said.

"What picture?"

"That he's wrong." My teeth slipped through my lips into a very quick, very subtle smile.

I knew she was right. He was wrong. The house, the estate, the staff, everything. It was ours. It was mine.

CHAPTER 22
IS THAT YOU?

"THIS CAN'T BE REAL, RIGHT?" Courtney called out from the bathroom off the formal living room.

"Court. I know you didn't see it. But it was real. I can't even put into words how real it was."

"But a demon? A monster? A *thing* that Satan rejected from hell? That's a little far-fetched, isn't it?"

"It's very far-fetched. But how else do you explain it?"

"I don't know," she said. "But I know I'm not sleeping upstairs. At least not tonight. Not after you pissed it off."

"Pissed it off? Me? No way!" But I knew she was right, at least in some way. My going up into the attic was enough to make it angry, and it wanted to come at me. Or maybe it was Geoffrey. I wasn't sure. Not yet, anyway.

"I feel safer down here," Courtney said, returning to the formal living room, where I was waiting.

"It's weird, isn't it?"

"It's a lot more than weird, Max. It's downright disturbing."

"No. Yes. I know. But I mean, it's weird that no one's seen it downstairs. No one's heard any stories of it anywhere but upstairs."

"That's what you're most concerned about?" she asked. The look she gave me was judgmental and condescending at the same time.

"No. I'm most concerned with the eight-foot-tall monster that apparently lives in our attic, that somehow hates me and wants to kill me."

"Watch out!" she mocked and pointed over my shoulder, trying to scare me.

I couldn't help but laugh. "Come on," I said, leading her through the kitchen into the still-formal-but-less-formal living room—the one without all the windows. Oddly enough, I still differentiated the two living rooms, even though the furniture Gramps and Ginger had was gone. No more couches covered in plastic that I wasn't allowed to sit on in the formal living room. No more still-new-but-less-strict furniture in the other one. We'd gotten rid of that all and replaced it with the furniture we'd had in our apartment. Each living room had a couch. Well, the formal living room had a loveseat, if we're being technically correct.

"If you think I'm sleeping on the floor, you're crazy," Courtney said as we got into the second living room. I'd turned off all the lights in the other rooms as we walked through. The rest of the people we'd been talking with just an hour ago were long since gone, back in their safe spaces away from our part of the property, safe from whatever would happen now that it was dark.

"Of course, my love. I'll sleep on the floor." I pulled one of the plethora of pillows from the couch and pretended to pick which blanket I'd want to grab from the back of the couch, knowing full well that Courtney would want the fluffy, beige one to keep her warm. Which meant I'd get the much smaller black one to cover myself with.

"I'm scared," she said quietly as I turned out the single lamp in the room. The light from the stars shone through the half-moon windows above the French doors that opened onto the backyard.

"I am too," I said. "I am too."

* * *

"WAKE UP."

The voice startled me so much that I immediately woke up and sat upright, trying to decipher where it'd come from. I looked to my left to find Courtney still sound asleep; her back to me, clad in the fluffy beige blanket she loved so much.

"It's not safe."

It came from the far end of the room, toward the billiard room.

"Hello?" I whispered as loudly as I could. "Hello?"

"Come."

Fear covered my entire body. That feeling you get when you sense something bad is about to happen—the goosebumps coupled with the instant sense of nausea. My fingers and toes tingled. I had to try to stand three times before I was able to get to my feet.

"Hello?" I called out again.

The light over the middle billiard table—the nine-ball table—flickered twice and then went dark.

For a split second, I thought I saw someone on the other side of the table.

"Come," the voice said again.

I've never walked so slowly in my entire life. Each footstep took minutes. I walked intentionally slowly, hoping the light would come on again, and I'd find Otto or Sam or Geoffrey in the other room. It was definitely a man's voice I'd heard.

It was one fifty-three in the morning, according to my watch.

"Hello?" I stopped in the doorway between the two rooms, waiting for something to happen or for someone to say something. "This isn't funny."

Courtney stirred on the couch. I looked over my shoulder, both hoping to have accidentally woken her up and also hoping she was still asleep. She was scared enough that she didn't need this additional fright. She seemed to settle back on her own, having just sat up enough to flip her pillow over to the cool side.

The same light over the same table flickered on again.

This time, I was sure I saw someone standing at the far end of the room, partially in the shadows. The moonlight had just barely illuminated his right side.

For a split second, I considered going to wake Courtney up. I thought that having another person there with me to witness what I thought had just happened would somehow make it real. But I didn't. I let her sleep, and I took two steps into the billiard room.

"Gramps? Is that you?"

The light over the far table, closest to where he was standing, came on, just for a couple of seconds.

"I don't know how this works," he said. "Come closer. I don't know how I'm doing this."

"Gramps? It is you!" I ran across the room, not caring about how much noise I'd made, and for a split second, forgetting that my grandfather had died six weeks ago.

I tried to hug him, my eyes welling up with happiness to see him. As I got close enough to him to close my arms around him, he vanished. At the same moment, the light above the pool table went dark.

"Gramps? Where did you go?" The realization that he was gone sank in again, leaving me feeling confused and empty. But man, oh man, did seeing his face for those few seconds make me feel something I can't even describe. I felt full, complete. I felt awake and aware. I felt protected.

"Maxwell, my boy." His voice came from nowhere and everywhere all at once, as if it were coming from inside me. I could feel him near me, but I couldn't see him anywhere anymore. "I'm so sorry," he said.

"What are you sorry for?" My voice got louder than I had wanted it to, echoing throughout the billiard room, bouncing off the walls and ceiling. I cringed, hoping it wouldn't wake Courtney up. I quickly looked back through the door to the living room to make sure she hadn't gotten up and turned the light on.

"I wanted to warn you," Gramps's voice said. "But they wouldn't let me. They said I was unwell. They said I was making things up."

"You weren't, Gramps. I know. I saw the monster."

"I know you did. I'm so sorry."

"I miss you so much," I said, the tears in my eyes finding their way down my cheeks.

"I miss you too, Max. I don't know how much time I have to talk to you. When it's safe and the sun comes up, go to my room. Above the headboard of my bed, press the center of the wall. You'll find everything I wanted to tell you there."

"What's there, Gramps?" But I knew he was gone. I felt a pull against my torso like someone was forcefully yanking him from me, taking him away from however he was talking to me. "Gramps?" I called out one last time.

My feet carried me back to the living room, somehow. I paused for a moment, standing over Courtney, watching her sleep. Her chest peacefully rising and falling, unaware that I'd just spoken to my grandfather. My *dead* grandfather.

Suddenly, I felt the urge to go to Gramps's room. To find whatever he was talking about. I thought I had it all figured out —he had a secret panel above his bed with something hidden inside. Something hidden for me. Something he didn't want anyone else to know about, even Geoffrey.

I shuffled my feet through the living room, into the kitchen, and found myself standing in the foyer, staring at the top of the stairs. The moonlight shone through the skylight, illuminating just a small portion of the hallway I could see. Each time the cloud moved in front of the moon, the whole hallway went dark. The painting of my great-grandfather came into view, only to disappear again a moment later.

Without thinking about it too much, I found myself climbing the left-hand staircase. I'd always used the right one because it was closer to the room Courtney and I were staying in. It never made sense for me to use the one on the left. But something felt different then. I haphazardly went up those stairs, one by one, knowing full well that I was an extra twenty feet away from the beginning of the hallway. That, should I make it to the top of the stairs, I could stand there in the moonlight—if I timed the cloud cover just right—and look down the entire length of the hallway.

"If it's safe, I'll run to Gramps's room," I told myself. "Run."

Before I knew it, I was halfway up the stairs. I climbed

slowly, one at a time. Taking very deliberate steps, like a child sneaking in after curfew. Hoping I wouldn't hit that spot on the stairs that I knew would creak or squeak. Hoping I'd make it to the top quietly so as not to disturb anything that might be up there waiting for me.

Two steps from the top, the clouds covered the moon entirely. It felt darker than it had the rest of the time I climbed the stairs. The picture of great-Gramps was gone while my eyes adjusted to the darkness. The grogginess of having been woken up in the wee hours of the morning had worn off. I was wide awake, anticipating whatever might come.

My night vision kicked in, rendering the darkness less of an enemy. From my vantage point, I could see down the hallway to the other end. All the way down to the staircase that brought you down on the complete other side of the house.

The hall was still. The air was thick and silent, and my chest felt heavy as I stepped up the final step.

I paused a moment, listening intently. The sound of a field mouse scurrying through a wall. The wind blowing that massive maple tree back and forth just outside. My chest rising and falling.

Then I heard the faintest, tiniest, almost inaudible scratching. Just two little scratches at first. One, two. Very quick. Had I not been standing still, I wouldn't have heard it.

Then two more. Longer. Louder.

Then, a loud bang.

I did my best to try to figure out where it was coming from. But I knew. As soon as the second loud bang happened, I knew it was coming from the door to the attic.

The moonlight hit the hall again, just in time for me to see Gramps standing there, right across the landing from me.

"Daylight," he said. "It's safe in the daylight."

And then he vanished again. The banging grew louder, and I heard the attic door splinter. I couldn't figure out how the door was holding it in, especially if it was more powerful at night, like everyone had said. I also couldn't figure out how it had come out the other night, and I pounded on the door to our room. "If it's trapped, how does it get out?" I asked myself, knowing I had no answer.

"Tomorrow." I heard Gramps's voice call out again and felt a hand on my shoulder, turning me back toward the stairs, almost ushering me to go down.

"Tomorrow," I said. "In the daylight." The faint smell of cinnamon filled the surrounding air.

I didn't care how much noise I made going back down the stairs. If the banging hadn't woken Courtney up, I doubted my footsteps would.

When I got back to the living room, she was sitting up on the couch, wrapped in her blanket, looking confused.

"Where were you?" she asked.

"I saw Gramps. I followed him upstairs. We have a task tomorrow. I saw him," I said, fluffing my blanket on the floor. "He was here. He was real. Don't worry, everything will be okay. Let's go back to sleep."

I had no idea if I'd just told her a lie. But I knew after seeing Gramps and talking to him, I felt more at ease. I had no idea what this monster wanted to do, but I knew, at least while we were downstairs, that we were relatively safe. And that was enough for me to fall back asleep, even over the sound of the monster stomping around above us.

CHAPTER 23

QUIET TIME

THE NEXT MORNING, the calm and peacefulness of seeing Gramps stayed with me. I slept so well the rest of that night that I felt rested and ready when the sun found its way through the tiny crack in the curtains. In hindsight, I should have lain the other way so that the sun couldn't hit me. But I suppose there were worse problems I could have.

I stood and stretched, keeping quiet. I didn't want to wake Courtney.

As great as seeing Gramps was, I needed to feel that connection again. And soon.

Passing through the kitchen, I grabbed a Danish from the tray on the island that Sam had made well before the sun had come up.

"Breakfast?" he asked as I scurried through, holding the danish up as if to say, "No, I'm good. I've got this."

I'd rounded the corner and started mounting the stairs to the second floor before I heard Courtney call out to me. "Max?"

"In the foyer," I yelled back. "Going up to the attic to spend some time with the trains."

She must have responded too quietly for me to hear, but I waited a minute to see if she said anything else. "Love you," I called out as I got halfway up the staircase.

Before I even approached the door to the attic, something caught my attention. The door was ajar. Just a tiny bit. Just enough for the sweet smell of cinnamon to waft through and find me standing there at the top of the landing. There are so few smells that can transport me back in time to a specific point in my life. But the cinnamon smell from Chet was one of them. So much so that the morning Sam had made cinnamon rolls as part of breakfast, I reminisced about sitting around the train set in the very early days of the town Gramps and I would eventually build together. I got lost in the memories.

The scent filled my lungs, increasing my desire to get up to the attic and spend some more time with the memory of Gramps. And though I found it odd that for the last few decades I hadn't cared much about the trains, I found them bringing me peace since Gramps's passing.

I pulled the door open as I scarfed down the last of the Danish I'd grabbed, licking the last of the strawberry jam from my fingers. The door's hinges creaked as I pulled it closed behind me. The stairs beneath my feet groaned and whined as I climbed the steps to the top and used my shoulder to push through the door that had been stuck shut due to the summer's humidity.

The sun illuminated the entire space from floor to ceiling, despite there being only a few windows. The massive attic immediately felt warm and welcoming. The town of Williamsburg drew me in and sprang to life as soon as I flipped the master switch. Its shops came to life, its residents began their predetermined paths throughout, and the cars, buses, and trucks began heading to their destinations. Chet stood waiting idly by for me to throw his switch and set him free to take his cargo of passengers to their next stop. Chet's friends—who'd never gotten their own names, for some reason—stood waiting for their cue to get going on their routes, as well.

As usual, I flicked Chet to life first. He sprang to, making the silence of the attic a thing of the past. He chugged and chooed as he made his way to the first stop, the commuter rail station where he'd "pick up" some passengers. The technology didn't—and still doesn't, I don't think—exist actually to board the tiny people onto or off the train, but I often suspended my disbelief when playing with the train. Chet let out a big puff of smoke as he rounded the corner where I stood, making his way toward his next stop.

Once Chet cleared the second stop on his route, I let loose the other trains. They flew off in opposite directions, their routes carefully planned so they wouldn't collide. Though I had to be aware of a few possible collisions happening, the town would mostly run itself for my enjoyment while I sat back and watched it.

"Thank you for this, Gramps," I said aloud, hoping he could hear me, but not having seen any sign of him. Being there with his trains and town and thinking about him brought a smile to my face.

Chet zipped by a moment later on his second revolution around the town. Once again, as if on cue, he let out a puff of smoke right in front of me. Chet was an old locomotive—I think Gramps had said his grandfather had given it to him as a child —but he still purred along. His engine was powerful, and his cargo was a set weight. I knew he could continue pulling that load much longer than I'd be around for.

The trains zipped around, slowing down just enough for the railroad crossings to drop their gates and pause traffic. The people walked to and fro. The cars obeyed the rules of the road. The town was alive, just as I knew Gramps would want.

At that moment, I decided to do my first improvement to Williamsburg since Gramps's passing. Something he and I had talked about when we first moved the town to the attic, but something he'd never done. Perhaps he didn't want to do it once I'd lost interest in the town. Perhaps he forgot. Maybe he couldn't physically do it. But he'd prepared for it, that I knew.

I dug around under the town, pulling various boxes and containers out of the way, kicking up years and years of dust. I slid Chet's original box past me, out into the sunlight. I tossed aside dozens of tiny boxes that once housed miniature people and cars and trucks. I pushed and pulled through enough boxes that I'd just about come out the other side of the town when I found the bag from HobbyTown. It'd been Gramp's favorite place to buy train stuff since they opened right around the time I turned ten. Its old logo had faded from age, but I still recognized enough of it to know it was the bag I was after.

Once I'd slid it out and kicked most of the boxes I'd displaced back under the town, I re-hung the curtains we'd put around the entire edge of Williamsburg. A soft brown color that had faded more on the Eastern and Western facing sides of town, where the sun hit them through the windows. When we first bought the curtains, I joked that they looked like poop. Gramps quickly scolded me and corrected me, telling me they were, in fact, the sides of the mountain that the town rested upon, high above the rest of the world.

The handful of boxes of string lights flopped out of the bag onto the floor at my feet. I cringed a bit, hoping my shaking them out of the bag hadn't damaged any of them.

"Williamsburg will finally have the stars we talked about," I said to Gramps as I pulled the step ladder from against the wall and propped it open in the middle of the room, as close to the Northern edge of Williamsburg as I could get without climbing on top of the town. The unfinished ceiling in the attic made it easy to string the lights along. In addition to the dozen packages of string lights, Gramps had also bought a number of boxes of thumbtacks from HobbyTown.

Each thumbtack sunk into the wood of the rafters with ease, and the string of lights clung to it like they were a match made in heaven.

I finished stringing as many of the lights as I could reach before I had to move the ladder. I repeated the process a number of times before realizing that I needed to get myself over the town itself, rather than continuing to string the lights around the outer edges.

"Here's hoping we built this sturdy enough," I said aloud before putting all of my weight onto the foot I'd positioned about two feet in from the Western edge of the town. I jostled myself back and forth a bit before placing my other foot on the plywood. I made sure not to step on any of the fake trees, the people, or the other accessories. I ensured the plywood would hold all of my weight before I let go of the top of the stepladder.

Quickly, I moved my arms above my head, nervous that the structure would collapse at any given moment. Thumbtack. Lights. Thumbtack. Lights. Connect the string of lights to the next one.

I stepped around the town, reaching further and further

above it, still nervous—but less so—of its potential collapse. Before I knew it, the whole sky above Williamsburg was lit. As I climbed back down the stepladder and admired my handiwork, I immediately groaned at myself. Had I planned it better, I could at least have tried to mimic some of the constellations.

"Oh well," I said. "At least it's done." From then on, the sky above Williamsburg would forever be clear and filled with hundreds of tiny, twinkling lights. "Hope you like it, Gramps," I said.

The people, cars, and trains all continued chugging along on their routes as I admired the entirety of Williamsburg. The sense of accomplishment washed over me. It was the first time I'd personally contributed to the town in at least three decades. It felt good. It felt like a connection to Gramps. To the thing he spent countless hours building and working on. To the thing that brought him such joy. A thing that was now bringing me the same amount of joy.

As I slid the last of the boxes back in under the curtain, a piece of paper flew out into the open. It seemed to have been tucked away on a small ledge under the table.

It flew across my feet out into the open space at the back of the attic, landing face down. As I took a step toward it, the door at the opposite end of the attic slowly swung open.

My mind started racing, wondering if it was Gramps coming to visit me again, or the monster coming out of hiding to scare me, or worse.

"Ignore it," I told myself, taking the last steps toward the piece of paper. As I got closer, I saw the words "Bill and Max, 1986" scribbled on the back. I didn't recognize the handwriting and guessed that it was my grandmother's or Ginger's. Remembering exact timelines of my childhood wasn't my strong suit.

When I picked it up and flipped it over, I found it wasn't a piece of paper at all. It was a photo of Gramps and me from my birthday. Judging by the year written on the back, it was my seventh birthday. I stood next to Gramps, his left arm draped around my shoulder, holding me close to him. I came up to his sternum. Had I been a little taller, my head would have tucked into his armpit. At that moment, I couldn't remember if I was an abnormally tall seven-year-old or if Gramps, perhaps, wasn't the tallest of men. I hated that I couldn't remember how tall he was. It felt as if he was slipping away.

For a moment, I felt glad that he had kept a photo of us so close to the town we'd built together. It made me happy to know that even when I wasn't right there with him, he still had something to make him think of me. It was kind of how I felt in that exact moment. Gramps was gone, but he was still there with me. Both in his spirit, and now in the same photograph he'd kept to remember me.

I brought the photo up to my face to get a closer look at it, finally seeing that we were standing in front of Williamsburg, though downstairs, before we'd outgrown the extra bedroom it'd originally resided in.

As I scanned the rest of the photo, looking for any signs of what the town had been in 1986, I noticed two trains next to each other on the track. Their headlights, for some reason, were red. The camera captured a double image, reflecting the trains' headlights above town and creating two eerie red lights floating in the air.

"Ha," I laughed to myself. "It looks like eyes." I pulled the picture away from my face for a moment and scanned the entirety of Williamsburg. At present, no train has a red headlight, let alone two. And to the best of my knowledge, there had never been a train with a red light of any kind on it. It's not like trains have brakes, after all.

"It looks like eyes," I said again, to no one. And although I can't prove it, I heard a faint chuckle. A tiny, incredibly brief laugh. And just as I jolted my head up from my investigation of the town's trains and their lights and lamps, the door to the attic slammed shut, causing an unnerving echo throughout the almost empty room.

"Gramps? Is that you?" I called out.

I got no answer. Only the silence of the room, somewhat shattered by the choo-chooing and chugga-chugging of Chet and his friends.

As I made my way around the town to where the master power switch was, I looked up at the lights I'd just finished hanging. Their twinkles were slightly obscured by a cloud of smoke from Chet, giving the sky above Williamsburg a hint of a foggy night.

I smiled as I made my way cautiously toward the door. The room around me was completely silent now that I'd shut down the town and its trains. The creaks and cracks of the floorboards echoed throughout as I took step after step toward the door. It whined as I opened it.

Before I could scare myself any more, I ran down the stairs and closed the lower door behind me. I stood for a moment in the now-dark hallway with my back against the attic door, thankful that nothing else had happened. But also sad that while I was in the attic the entire day, I didn't get to see Gramps again.

CHAPTER 24
GRAMPS' TREASURE

THE NEXT MORNING, the sun found the absolutely perfect sliver of space between the blinds in the living room—where we'd still been sleeping—and hit me right in the eye just after sunrise. I flipped over, then tossed and turned on the floor for a bit before giving up and deciding to get up.

"Court?" I called out after discovering she wasn't still asleep on the couch above me.

6:31, my watch informed me.

"Court?" I called out again. Silence.

The floor was colder than I expected once I stepped off the pile of blankets I'd made into a bed, so I played an impromptu game of The Floor is Lava—cold lava, as it were—and hopped from the bed over to the area rug where I'd taken my socks off. I slid them on while still scanning the room for signs of Courtney.

Though I wasn't certain, I thought I could hear faint sounds of life coming from above me.

As I went from room to room, I called out her name, trying to find her, growing slightly more panicked as I approached the foyer and eyed the grand staircases.

Despite it being morning, I still felt afraid to go up. I lingered at the bottom of the stairs for a moment, trying to work up the courage to go upstairs. The voices of everyone from last night played through my head, both comforting and terrifying me. *Never heard or saw a single thing during the daytime*, I heard Joy's voice say, and I mustered up the courage to climb the stairs.

One by one, I paused, listening. Both hoping I would and would not hear the monster.

"Courtney?" I called out from the top step, letting my voice echo through the hall in both directions.

A moment later, she appeared in the doorway of Gramps's room. "Oh, hi! You're up. Get in here!"

"What are you doing?" I asked, but she had already gone back into the room.

"Come on," she shouted.

For some reason, I felt cautious as I walked down and across the hall toward his room. I combined tiptoeing with long slides in my socks like I'd done as a kid in that same hallway.

"What are you doing?" I asked again as I entered the room to find Courtney sitting on Gramps's bed.

"You were talking in your sleep."

"Okay. I ask a third time. What are you doing?"

"You kept talking about the treasure above Gramps's bed. I couldn't sleep anymore, so I came in here to find out what you were talking about."

"What's that song?" I asked, realizing there was music coming from somewhere.

She pointed to the record player on top of the dresser. "Moon River," she said. "Sit, I'll explain."

I climbed onto the bed and sat down next to her. My legs dangled right along hers, though mine touched the floor, and she just grazed it.

"I'm ready," I said.

"As I said, you kept talking about the treasure above Gramps's bed. Can you tell me what that was all about?"

"I saw him last night," I told her. "After you'd fallen asleep, he seemed to have summoned me. He told me there was treasure above his bed, and I needed to find it." I looked around the bed. Between us, next to us, and behind us was an assortment of so many things. Papers. Records. A few boxes. "What is all this? And what's that music?"

"Gramps left quite an assortment of stuff in the hidden cabinet there." She pointed above the bed, where I'd failed to notice a door had been propped open, held up against the wall with what looked like an empty paper towel roll. That little paper tube held the wood panel up and out of the way, exposing an approximately six-foot-long cabinet that appeared empty.

"Did you take everything out?" I asked.

"Yes, it's all here," she said, motioning around the bed.

"What is all this stuff?"

"Well, here, read this first." She handed me a letter and the envelope it had been sealed in.

I took them both, flipping the envelope over to reveal my initials written on the front. The back had the same safety mechanism as the other letter he'd left me—a single piece of Scotch tape with his initials written on it in marker, now smudged, presumably from Courtney opening it.

"Was it opened before?" I asked.

"I don't think so. It was sealed before I opened it."

"What's it say?" I asked momentarily forgetting I knew how to read.

"Read it," she said, pulling my hands up near my face, almost shoving the paper into my nose.

> My dearest Maxwell,
>
> By now, you know I'm gone. Especially if you're reading this. Though I have no control over what happens to you in your new home, I've put some things in motion that should hopefully help you.
>
> Things that should help reveal the truth, and in the proper order. If you haven't yet found the package I left in my old study, please get it. It's in the cabinet on the left-hand side of the credenza along the southern wall. If you've already gotten it, please continue reading.
>
> No cheating! Go. I'll wait.
>
> Welcome back, maybe. If you've found this hidden cabinet, you've found a number of my things. Things I consider valuable. Maybe not monetarily, but personally.
>
> "Moon River" was your grandmother's favorite song. I know you didn't know her, but please play that record from time to time. I used to think

she could hear it, and it would bring her peace.
I could feel her near me when I played it.

Please take great care of these items as
they are important to me. Much like you are.

All my love,

Gramps

"I'm assuming that's 'Moon River' playing?"

Courtney nodded. "Gramps said to play it, so I did. Sorry if the music woke you up."

I shook my head. "What is in those boxes?"

"Well, Gramps was quite the joker," she said. "He said his treasure wasn't monetarily valuable, but these three boxes are full of cash."

"More cash?" I slightly gasped.

"And there are a bunch more records, too. I put the ones I recognized over there behind you, and the others are over here."

"Anything else?"

"That's it, I think. But I didn't look very closely at all the boxes."

I grabbed the one closest to me and dumped it out on my lap. It was chock-full of cash, like Courtney had said. Stacks of hundred-dollar bills, banded together into ten-thousand-dollar stacks. There were sixty-five of them in that one box.

I couldn't believe my eyes. "This is a ton of money," I said. "Why would Gramps keep so much cash hidden away?"

"I was trying to figure that out myself," she said. "I have no idea."

"Maybe he didn't trust banks."

"Or maybe he didn't want anyone else to know how much money he had."

"Are the other boxes like this?" I asked.

"They are."

I flipped the other two boxes over where they were, spilling out their contents onto the bed. Another seventy-eight bands of bills.

The last box also had a key at the bottom.

I picked it up and gave it a once-over. On one side was the number 929. On the other was a tiny inscription that I couldn't make out at first until I brought it closer to my eyes.

"Bank of America, Pittsburgh," it read.

"Hmm," I said. "Why would Gramps have a key to a bank?"

Courtney laughed. "You dummy. It's not a bank key. It's the key to a safe deposit box." She took the key from me. "Box nine-hundred and twenty-nine at a Bank of America in Pittsburgh."

"I guess we're going for a drive," I said.

* * *

ON THE DRIVE TO PITTSBURGH, Courtney and I reminisced about Gramps and laughed at our newfound knowledge of his oddness. I'd never really gotten to know him as an adult. It hadn't really crossed my mind until Courtney brought it up, just as we'd crossed over the line into Pennsylvania.

"About another three hours," she said, looking at the map on her phone.

"It's weird, isn't it?" I asked.

"What is?"

"I never knew him as anything other than my grandfather. I didn't really know him other than that."

"That's not weird," she said. "That's how relationships with grandparents are. To you, they're *only* your grandparent. They're not a person. They have no personality other than how they interact with you. It's completely normal."

"But why? I spent plenty of time with him after I became an adult. Why didn't I ever get to know him?"

"You just don't," she said. "It's just the nature of how we are with them."

"Did you know your grandparents well?" Both sides of her grandparents had passed before we'd met, so I never got to know them. I loved how much she loved Gramps, but I was always a little sad for her that she'd lost both sets of her grandparents when she was so young.

"Not really, now that I'm thinking about it. I just knew how they were with me."

"Right? Isn't that weird? To me, as a kid, Gramps was just this fun-loving guy who played with trains and bought me tons of Christmas presents."

"My dad's mother made the best lasagna," Courtney added.

"I wish I had known who he was," I said. "It might make a lot of this weirdness easier for me. Maybe we wouldn't have to drive three states away to open a secret safe deposit box. Maybe I'd just know what was in it because he'd have told me."

"We'll be there before you know it," she said.

* * *

"I'M SO sorry to hear that, and for your loss." The bank manager had greeted us promptly once we'd told the teller who I was and why I was there. "He was a wonderful man. In the few times I'd had the pleasure of helping him, he was always so kind. I was sad to learn about Ginger's passing all those years ago, as well."

"Thank you," I said, doing my best not to seem impatient.

"If you'll follow me," he said, motioning to the security guard to open the locked door separating the lobby from the teller area.

We followed him through, waiting for them to coordinate closing the door behind us. The security guard then pressed a button under the counter, which emitted a buzzing sound, and the door to the back room swung inward, allowing us to continue following him.

"I'm Jillian," he said. "And yes, I know it's not usually a man's name. My mother had an unusual sense of humor." I could tell he'd said the same thing a thousand times in his lifetime, having to explain why he had a girl's name. Elementary school must have been hell for him.

We both shook his hand as he held open the outer door to the vault area, ushering us past him. We stopped at a stainless-steel table in the middle of the room, surrounded by hundreds of safe-deposit boxes of varying sizes.

"It's just like in the movies," Courtney said. I couldn't help but chuckle. *Where's Robert De Niro and Tom Sizemore*, I thought. Surely they'd be in to rob the bank at any moment, like in *Heat*.

"If you will," Jillian said, motioning toward the wall farthest from where we stood. I could barely make out the numbers in the nine hundreds. Courtney took the key from me and followed Jillian across the room.

Courtney slid her key into the left lock, and Jillian pulled his matching key from his keyring and inserted it into the right lock. As if coordinated, the two of them turned the locks to a satisfying clank, and the door slid open, revealing a long, silver case inside.

"It is just like the movies," I said.

Jillian pulled the case from the safe deposit box and carried it over to the table, placing it down in front of me. Courtney marveled at its perfect reflective surface, gazing with wide eyes.

"When you're through, just press that button there," Jillian said, pointing to the left of the door we'd just come through. "I'll return posthaste. This bag should suffice, should you want to depart with any of the box's contents." He reached under the table and pulled out a medium-sized duffel bag, and slid it across the table to me.

I waited for him to leave the room and for the door to latch shut before I flipped open the massive lid. The surface caught the light just right, and a beam of light shot across the ceiling and down the wall to my left.

Inside was a collection of things I'd never have thought Gramps would have, let alone keep in such a secure place.

More cash. I slid the stacks of hundreds out of the way.

"I didn't know Gramps liked comic books," Courtney said, pulling a stack of old-looking ones from the case and spreading them out on the table.

"They're all from the thirties and forties," I said. Admittedly, my knowledge of comic books was limited to the Marvel and DC films I'd seen in my lifetime, which weren't many. As much as I loved Batman, I couldn't tell you whether the stack of comics in front of me was of any value or not. I only assumed they were, because why else would they be locked away?

"These are patents," I said, pulling papers from the next layer. They seemed old and fragile, so I did my best to take care of them as I placed them down next to the comic books.

"From his inventions," Courtney said. "Look, his name is on most of them in the bottom right corner." She flipped through them to show a few to me before I lost interest and returned to scavenging through the rest of the box.

"His social security card." I smiled as I looked it over. He'd clearly signed it as a small child, something I didn't think they had you do anymore. I pictured him as a little boy, not knowing what he was doing, but following his father's orders to sign the blue paper with his name and some random numbers.

"A marriage license," Courtney said, pulling out a rectangular piece of paper and examining it. "To your grand-mother." I pushed some of the remaining pieces of paper around, trying to see if the license for his second marriage, to Ginger, was there, but it wasn't.

"She was the love of his life," I said. "I get why that's here."

The rest of the papers comprised his birth certificate, some bonds, and stock certificates to companies I'd never heard of. A handful of old photos from when he was a boy. I put one aside to take with me that I was sure was of him and his parents. The back was dated July 1929. He looked to be about six or seven, which lined up with how old I knew he was.

"You recognize this?" Courtney asked, holding out a single, slim, gold band in her palm.

"No. It looks like a wedding ring. But Gramps never wore one. Not that I knew of, anyway."

"Maybe it was from when he was married to your grandmother."

"Maybe?" I put it in the pile of things to take with us. I slid the pile of comics into the takeaway pile, figuring there was no sense in leaving them locked up forever. "Someone who would love them should have them," I said when Courtney gave me a puzzled look.

At the very bottom of the box was a single flash drive. Though it looked so old, it was likely called a thumb drive back then for some technical reason I surely didn't understand.

I picked it up and examined it. There were no markings on it other than 1GB on the front and a faded logo that said something *disk*.

"I wonder what's on it," I said aloud, mostly talking to myself. I plopped it in the pile of things to take with us and gave the box a once-over to make sure it was empty.

The items we decided not to take were gently placed back inside before we closed the lid and buzzed for Jillian to come back.

While we waited, I packed up the duffel bag with the items we would take, careful not to damage any of the comic books. Despite being encased in hard plastic, I was still worried I might damage them. I knew enough to know any damage would destroy their value, and while I didn't have to worry about money, whoever would be lucky enough to get the stack of comics likely would care about their value.

"All through?" Jillian's voice startled me through the door to the vault.

"Yes, thank you," I said, picking up the bag and motioning for Courtney to lead the way out of the room.

"Thank you," she said as she scooted past Jillian.

I shook his hand and thanked him again as he entered the vault to return the box to its locked drawer and retrieve his key, which still hung in the lock.

"I wish I'd brought my laptop," I said, gently dropping the duffle bag onto the floor behind the driver's seat.

Courtney plopped herself into the passenger seat and pulled up the map to get us back home. "This is an adventure!" she said gleefully.

"Hey, you guys!" I did my best Sloth impression as I backed out of the parking spot, eager to get back to the house to find out what was on the drive.

* * *

NO SOONER HAD we entered the house than I rushed into the living room to grab my laptop.

I effortlessly slid the drive into the USB port, only to get a pop-up saying it was incompatible with my Apple laptop.

"Are you kidding me?" I scoffed. "What does that even mean?"

"Let me try my laptop," Courtney said, rushing out of the room to fetch hers from wherever it was.

"Okay," I yelled, hoping she could hear me, as I didn't know how far she'd have to go to get her laptop.

Her computer dinged as soon as we plugged the drive in, and a window popped up showing a single file. PlayMe.wmv

"It's a Windows file," Courtney said, clearly more technical than I. "That's why your laptop couldn't open the drive. Gramps didn't have a Mac."

I nodded as if I knew what she was talking about. "Click it! Click it!"

An application opened on her screen, and within a second, Gramps's face was there before us, frozen still.

"You do it," she said. "Press play."

My hand trembled as I reached out to the computer to click

the play button. In that moment, I felt hopeful and frightened at the same time. I hadn't seen Gramps move or heard his voice since before he'd passed, and something about the anticipation of hearing his voice again gave me pause.

"Go on," Courtney urged.

I closed my eyes for a second and then clicked play. The frozen image of Gramps immediately came to life in crystal-clear, vivid color.

"No one would have thought to look at the thumb drive," he said. "That's why I didn't password-protect it. I knew only you'd look at this, Maxwell. I knew you'd find the key and would be curious to come and see what I'd left in the safe deposit box. I'm sure Courtney is there with you as well. Hello, dear. "

I blinked away the feeling of confusion for a moment. Never in my life had I seen a video of Gramps, and it felt strange to see him on recorded media.

"I'd love to tell you that there's a hidden message here. I'd love to let you know that there's a secret of some kind. But there isn't. This video is solely to tell you, to remind you, of how much I love you. How much I love both of you.

"It's no secret that part of me died when your grandmother passed, Max. But as you and I got older together, I found a love in my heart that I'd thought was gone. You brought me such joy and light, and I wanted to leave this to you as a constant reminder of how much I love you."

I found myself tearing up and reached for a tissue on the end table.

"By now, you've found a lot of my secrets throughout the house. You've heard the stories, likely from your father or his brothers, about how I'd lost my marbles toward the end. You've probably had your doubts about me as well. Both of you. But know that I am of sound mind as I record this, and nothing has ever been clearer than my love for you. It's why I left everything to you. It's why I wanted you to have it all."

His eyes darted off-camera for a brief second as a shadow moved across the screen, briefly covering his face.

"I love you, Maxwell. I love you, Courtney. I always will, even though I'm gone."

He smiled directly at the camera. That dimple on his left side popped through, just as I'd remembered it. He raised his hand to wave to us, just for a moment, before he mumbled one last thing.

"What'd he say at the end there?" I asked, hoping Courtney had heard it.

She shrugged and grabbed the laptop to rewind the video. Before pressing play, she turned the volume up as loud as it could go.

"There, now he knows." His voice came through quiet and humbled, but at an incredibly loud volume.

"Who was he talking to?" I asked rhetorically.

"Someone off camera. Who would have been in the room with him?" Courtney asked.

"Probably Geoffrey, or one of my uncles. Someone who would have helped him record the video?"

"You're probably right," she said. "We'll ask Geoffrey when we see him."

It felt odd. The way it ended. It was so heartwarming to hear his voice again, to see his face in something other than a photograph. But the way the video ended didn't sit well with me. Who was he talking to, and why did he say it the way he said it?

It felt like he was under duress. Like someone was forcing him to say what he said. It didn't make any sense, given how positive and loving the video was. Thinking about it made my head hurt.

CHAPTER 25

MOM AND DAD

"CALLING A PRIEST IS STUPID," I said. For the first time in as long as I could remember, both of my parents were in the same place. That place was the living room at One Stone Way. And for the first time in even longer, neither of my parents was yelling at each other or at me. Historically speaking, someone was usually yelling when we were together. Now, though, they were both calm. It seemed like—at least to me—they were both playing the role of good cop.

It was the first time my father had been back at the house since we'd had our little war or words a couple of weeks prior. As usual, he'd either forgotten it had happened or he was putting on his best mask in front of my mother and Courtney. Even though everyone knew—or had their suspicions—of what kind of man he was, he wasn't that man when others were around.

"Have you literally never seen a horror movie?" Courtney added.

It'd taken some considerable time—and testimony from the

house staff—to convince my parents that Gramps wasn't crazy. That the sounds he'd heard and the things he'd seen were real and that there was something in the house.

"Maxwell," my mother began. "These things are usually unholy."

"A priest could help," my father said, standing and beginning to pace laps around the sofa. Flashes of so many horror movies about possessions and hauntings popped into my head. *The Exorcist,* the most notable.

"That's almost as ridiculous as saying, 'There's a monster in my attic,' out loud to people who haven't seen it or heard it. But here we are."

"Max, don't get sarcastic," my mother said.

"I'm sorry, Mom, but I don't think a man coming in here with some special water and saying some things in Latin is going to help any. No one believes me that the monster is real, anyway."

"If movies have taught us anything, that just makes it worse," Courtney said. I knew she didn't believe me, and it didn't matter anymore.

"Why are we talking about movies?" My father stopped at the back of the couch, leaned over, and put his hand on my mother's shoulder. "This is real life, isn't it? We can't compare real life to a movie because movies aren't real. Max thinks he's seeing monsters. My father thought he was seeing monsters, so let's call in a professional."

I ignored that comment and fought back the urge to point out that *some* movies are real.

"Dad," I started, but he interrupted me.

"I want to see it."

"You want to what?" my mother asked, turning to face him

and, coincidentally, shrugging his hand off her shoulder. "It's not real."

"I want to go to the attic and see this thing with my own eyes. Prove to me it's real, Maxwell."

"Dad, that's crazy," I said.

"He's right," Courtney added. "You need to trust him. Max has seen it."

"I want to see it with my own eyes," he said. "Have you seen it, Courtney?"

"I haven't seen it," Courtney said, taking my hand.

"Bruce, no," Mom said.

"Ellie, hush. You stay down here. Let's go, Maxwell."

"It's not safe after dark," I said.

"All the better," he said. "Then there's no chance I won't see this *thing*."

* * *

HE LEFT ME NO CHOICE. He stormed out of the room, pausing only for a second in the doorway to wait for me to catch up with him. I gave Courtney and my mom a shrug, telling them I had no choice.

My father had always been the type to do what he wanted and sometimes ask for forgiveness later. Asking for forgiveness wasn't common. Often, he'd gaslight you into thinking you were the one who did something unusual and that he was being the rational one.

"When did you see it?" he asked as we ascended the back staircase.

"A few days ago. Geoffrey and I were looking for the book Gramps had been reading before he died."

It was the first time I had said *died* out loud. It felt so harsh. Passed. Moved on. Shuffled off this mortal coil. There are so many less harsh ways to say someone had died. The word *died* felt so impersonal, so cold. But I'd said it, and it didn't even make my father flinch.

"Describe it to me," he said, walking faster up the stairs.

"Tall. Very tall. It didn't fit through the doorway at the top of the attic stairs, either height-wise or width-wise. Its shoulders were too big. Its whole body was covered in a black goo, or ooze, or something. It dripped onto the floor and the walls. It didn't have eyes. The whole face was one giant mouthful of more teeth than I've ever seen outside of a shark's mouth. Its knees bent backward, and the things I think were its hands were enormous."

"How did it move?"

"What do you mean?"

"Did it move fast? Slow? Did it jump around? Did it run?"

"It was fast. But deliberate. Like it could have moved faster if it wanted to, but it moved slowly at first to intimidate us."

"What did it sound like?"

"It growls a lot. Like a lion, tiger, or other big cat. And sometimes it yells, screams almost. I don't know how to describe the screams."

"Try."

"The Tyrannosaurus Rex from *Jurassic Park*." It was the closest thing I could think of. "But meaner. Deeper." I knew he'd remember the reference. He'd taken me to see it when I was about fourteen. I remember the theater asking him if he was really sure he wanted me to see it, because "although it's PG-13, it's very scary."

"Oh my," he said. "And it didn't hurt you, right?"

"No. I feel like it wanted to, though," I said as we reached the top of the stairs and began walking toward the attic door, which felt like it was a mile away.

"This is bonkers," he said, stopping in the middle of the hallway. "There has to be some other explanation."

"I felt the same way at first. When I just heard weird noises, it was easy to shrug off. It's a new place I'm living in, so it could have been the house settling, an odd tree branch, or something. It could have been many things. But once I saw it with my own eyes, I knew Gramps wasn't crazy. Or if he was, I had become crazy living here, too."

We stopped at the door to the attic.

"What do we do?" Dad asked.

"What do you mean?"

"If it's up there."

"It's up there," I said matter-of-factly, as if I were some world-renowned expert on haunted attics.

"So, what do we do?" he repeated.

"We tread lightly. We don't go too far into the attic."

"What's up there?"

"Nothing but the train set. The town Gramps and I built."

"Of course that's all that's up there," he said. "He loved that stupid train set more than any of us."

Any of you, I thought to myself.

"Okay, let's go," he said and swung the door open.

For some reason, I expected the hallway up to the top of the stairs to be pristine. For the door at the top to be perfect and unmarked. You know, what always happens in horror movies. The main character sees the *thing*, and the thing throws a TV at the wall or something, but then the next day, when the main character brings his friends to see the thing, the TV is fine, and the wall is undamaged. I expected that.

But it wasn't.

As soon as the light flickered on, the damage to the door was clear. It sat crooked in its frame. Splinters and big chunks of wood lay across the stairs below it. The walls on either side of it were covered in the black goo that covered the monster's body. A smell washed over me that almost made me vomit instantly. The spots where the goo had been slathered across the wall from its hands had begun to rot, to corrode through the plaster and blue board down to the studs. Insulation poked through the goo in spots where the wall had been completely eroded.

"Do you smell that? What is it? I don't know. I think it's from the goo," I said, answering my own questions and pointing to the wall to draw his attention to it in case he hadn't seen it on his own.

"Listen, Max, if this is some joke you're playing, like when you were a kid, it's not funny anymore."

"I wish it were a joke, Dad. But it's not."

"I'm scared," he confessed as he took the first step up toward the attic.

Just as I stepped up next to him, I felt it—a low grumble at first. Almost like the growl I'd heard too many times already, but silent. I could feel its presence growing closer, but couldn't yet hear anything.

"Do you feel that?" I asked. "That's it."

"That's what? That's the monster?"

"That's the monster."

We took another step up, in unison, toward the top, and the feeling grew stronger, vibrating through my core. It felt like I was on a roller coaster that I didn't want to be on. My body quivered unintentionally.

As we took the third step up, I felt the hallway around and under us shake. One loud stomp from the attic seemed to have caused it. The monster knew we were coming and was coming to meet us.

Each step we took toward the top was met with another thud from behind the barely there door at the top of the stairs. The walls around us shook. Plaster fell from the ceiling above us, creating a dusty haze that made it hard to see. The smell of the rotting goo grew stronger as we got closer. I tried to hold my breath but couldn't. Fear kept pushing the air from my lungs.

I felt Dad grab my arm the first time the monster snarled. He turned to look at me before freezing in his tracks. "Is it up there?" he asked.

"Where else do you think it would be?" I said more sarcastically than I had intended.

No sooner had I finished talking than the banging on the door in front of us started. Dad jumped back at the first thump, yanking me down two steps with him.

"It's there!" he shouted. "It's on the other side of the door!"

My stomach dropped, though I don't know why. It's not like this was new to me. It's not like I hadn't seen the monster before or experienced its growling and snarling and oozing. But I was still afraid, especially since I'd never been so close to it before, with just the remnants of a flimsy wood door between us. A door that was already on its last legs, ready to disintegrate at a moment's notice.

"Believe me now?" I asked. "Believe Gramps now?"

I could hear him gulp over the sound of the growling. He

was frozen solid, still grasping onto my arm, still holding on for dear life.

The light under the door darkened, and the shadow of the monster blocked out what little light the attic windows let in. Its presence hulked before us, seemingly ready to burst through the door and destroy us both.

"Can we go now?" I asked. But Dad didn't respond. He just turned his head back toward the door and took a step closer.

The monster screamed as if it could sense Dad getting closer. It didn't seem to faze him at all.

Its shadow under the door disappeared and reappeared with louder and louder banging. It was jumping up and down. It was excited by Dad's presence. It seemed to enjoy Dad being there and being so close to it through the door.

"Dad?" I yelled over the monster's excited screaming. "Dad! Let's go!" I finally reached out in front of me and grabbed him, tugging him in a trance-like state away from the door and almost throwing him down the hallway.

"No!" he yelled. "I have to see it! I need to see it!"

Before I knew it, he was running back up the stairs toward the door. I slipped trying to catch up to him and fell hard, smashing my shin on the lip of one of the stairs.

"It's glorious!" Dad yelled as I looked up. The door had opened, and my father stood eye to chest with the monster. A foot separated them. The beast stood over my father. It seemed to lean down and smell the top of his head. It screamed with pleasure and jumped up and down, shaking the entire hallway around me and causing the remaining pieces of the door to crumble to shrapnel around its feet.

"Dad!" I yelled. "Get back!"

But I was too late. The monster grabbed my father with its

huge, gooey hands. The black ooze slid down its arms, across its hands, and started climbing up Dad's torso and arms.

Like when Venom takes over Eddie for the first time, I thought.

"Dad!" I yelled again, racing up the stairs in a futile attempt to help him.

The ooze flowed faster over Dad. He screamed in pain. The ooze melted away his skin much quicker than it had eaten the drywall in the attic hallway. The sound of his skin burning sizzled in the air. The stench filled my nostrils as I grabbed at his legs, trying anything I could to get him away from the monster. I yanked and tugged and pulled at his legs, but it was too late.

As his upper body melted away to nothing, the monster flew up into the air, yanking Dad away from me. The ooze slid down its arms faster and melted the rest of my father before I could even comprehend what was happening.

The silence imploded where my father's screaming had been. The monster snarled and bent down toward me, letting the last remnants of Dad's legs fall to the ground.

I froze, barely able to even quiver.

It reached out one of its arms and paused its hand in front of my chest for a moment. Then, just as I was able to move again, to flee for my life, the monster flicked me backward. A tiny bit of ooze burned through my shirt as I flew down the stairs into the hallway below, rapidly trying to remove the ooze from my chest before it burned through me as it had just done to Dad.

When I landed at the bottom of the stairs, my entire body was numb, but I was still in incredible pain. I looked to the top of the stairs as the beast stood back up to its full height. Dad's legs—what was left of them, from the knee down—were in each of its hands. Its giant mouth opened wide, letting its tongue come out and spread like a massive lightning bolt around Dad's remaining limbs. It flicked its head to the right, tossing the last remains of my father against the wall. They landed with a thunderous smushing sound.

I stopped for a moment, listening. Wondering if everyone else was rushing up to see what the commotion and yelling were about. I waited. But no one came. Were they too afraid? Were they running for their lives? Did they even hear what had happened?

The monster looked pleased with itself, and I swear—even if I'm mistaken or crazy—it laughed; a small chuckle combined with a growl, but a very distinct laugh.

It killed my father and was taunting me about it.

CHAPTER 26

DAD'S GONE

DESPITE TRYING to compose myself before going back downstairs, I couldn't. I spent what felt like ages trying to dry my eyes, to stop hyperventilating, to stop screaming. I did my absolute best, but I couldn't. I had barely managed to get back down to the upstairs hallway, shut the attic door behind me, before I collapsed. The monster was still up there, growling and howling and cackling like it was happy about what it'd done to my father. I could almost sense its excitement. I could feel its satisfaction at having killed my father.

And let's be clear, as I've alluded to many times, my father was not the best man. He was greedy and self-centered and probably a bit of a narcissist, but he was my father. Even though he wasn't there for me for much of my life, even though he didn't make the best decisions and do the best things, he was still my dad. He taught me to throw a football. He pushed me to go to a good college. He ensured I had everything I needed in life, even if those things were bought or provided for by someone else, namely Gramps.

Despite all his shortcomings and downfalls, I felt an immediate and overpowering sense of emptiness. I tried reasoning with myself. I tried telling myself that it'd been years since he and I spent any quality time together, one-on-one. That it'd been years since he and I had seen eye to eye on things. That it'd felt like a lifetime since he told me he loved me. But my heart hurt. Let's not even factor in how bizarrely insane what just happened was. Let's try to ignore the fact that a demon from some other world literally just melted and ate my father. Let's forget that. No, idiot, how can I? How can I ignore the fact that someone so important to me was here a minute ago and is now gone? *It's like when Barb disappeared on Stranger Things.* Here one minute, gone the next.

The feeling I get when I'm about to throw up slid its way up my body, finding a resting place right in my upper chest, lower throat. Locked in place, nauseating me. My head dizzied. My palms were sweating. My feet and lower legs started shaking. I knew I had to get up, race down the hall, get to the bathroom, and throw up. I told myself what to do. I yelled at myself. But I couldn't move. The anxiety, fear, and nausea froze me in place. And for a moment—a quick, fleeting moment—I thought I was going to choke on my own vomit. *Like Jane in Breaking Bad.* Except I had no Walt standing over me, watching me die.

"I can't," I whispered to myself. Barely audibly. The words escaped past my lips, wet with tears but stinging from panic. The monster just two doors away and up a flight of stairs wailed. It heard me. Or sensed me. Although it knew that I was there, it did not acknowledge me.

My feet stopped trembling long enough to force myself to stand. The vomit feeling crept past my chest, settling into my throat. A feeling that I truly only felt at the worst times in my life. A feeling I hated. A feeling that meant I wasn't in control. And I hated not being in control of my body.

Step after step, I slowly trudged down the hall toward my bedroom. Thump after thump, the monster wailed. My stomach lurched. My spine tingled, and my fingers twitched. My whole body felt a compulsion to throw up.

No sooner had I arrived in front of the toilet than it started. A long stream of black vomit. Pouring out of my nose and mouth, burning. It had a foul stench, like rotten eggs. The smell made me throw up more. It turned from black to grey, then back to black.

"Oh my God," I thought to myself. "What is happening?" The vomit poured from my mouth, quickly filling the toilet bowl and overflowing onto the floor.

I did my best to avoid it with my feet, but it ran up over my socks. It poured out everywhere.

When it stopped—which I was not in control of—the entire bathroom floor was covered in a slick, black coating. The base of the toilet was buried in my vomit. The smell of the room was overwhelming.

I rushed out, sliding on the hardwood floor and almost falling to the ground before regaining my balance. I quickly yanked the vomit-covered socks off and pulled my pants down once I realized the ends were also covered in puke. I slid new pants on and slowly put a sock on each foot, sitting on the edge of the bed, trying to regain my composure again. And trying to shake off the rest of the nausea that I was feeling.

* * *

WHEN I MANAGED to get back downstairs, Courtney, my mom, and Geoffrey were waiting for me in the kitchen, sipping their tea or coffee or whatever they had.

"Where's Dad?" my mother asked.

"Max?" Courtney said, somehow recognizing that I was not all right.

"Sir?" Geoffrey added.

I collapsed into one of the empty chairs, still silent, unsure of what the right words were to say. My face fell to my hands. The smell of vomit flew up my nose, and that feeling hit my chest again, only to quickly back down once I pulled my hands away from my face.

The words escaped me.

"No one goes into the attic," I said. "Ever."

"Where's Dad?" my mother asked again.

"The monster," I started. "It took him."

"Took him?" Courtney asked.

"It grabbed him and squeezed him. He got covered in the black ooze and started melting."

My mother shot up from her seat. "What?!"

"The monster killed him, Mom. Melted him and then ate him."

"This can't be real," she said. "Where is he? Is he playing a joke?" She walked out of the kitchen toward the foyer.

"Mom. Stop. He's gone."

"I don't believe you," she said.

"It's true," I said with more insistence.

"What happened, sir?" Geoffrey asked.

"We went up to the attic so I could show him the monster."

"What happened, Max?" Courtney took my hand and squeezed it.

"It melted him." I didn't know what else to say. I couldn't put into words what had happened before my eyes just a few minutes ago. I couldn't articulate the monster's actions, what it'd done to Dad, how it had eaten what was left of him after it melted most of him. I didn't know how to tell them the full truth. I didn't even know if there were words for what I'd just seen happen.

"Oh God," Geoffrey said, standing and pacing around the kitchen island. "Your grandfather warned us about this."

"You knew about this?" my mother yelled.

"No, ma'am. Not entirely," he said. "William had been talking about the monster that lived in the attic for quite some time before his death."

"And what?" Mom asked.

"And we just thought he had lost his marbles," Geoffrey said. "We thought he was going senile, as so many do in the later stages of life."

"No one believed him," I said. "He wrote me a letter, and he said no one believed him. But I've seen it. I've seen and heard and experienced the monster."

"Oh, Max," Courtney said. "I'm so sorry." She squeezed my hand tighter, oblivious to the fact that I reeked of vomit.

"What do we do now?" Geoffrey asked.

"I don't know if there's anything we can do," I said. "But no one should go up to the attic. It's not safe."

"I need to go," Mom said, snatching her purse from the island and bee-lining it for the front door. "I can't be in this house any longer."

"Mom, wait." I chased after her, not really knowing why, but feeling compelled to.

She stopped in the foyer, staring up the stairs toward the landing.

"It's up there," I said. "With what's left of Dad." I hugged her, squeezing her tight. I knew deep down that Mom loved me unconditionally. I had always felt like she'd have been around more if Dad hadn't been in our lives. That she'd have been the mother I wanted if she hadn't prioritized being his wife instead. If it were just the two of us, things would have been very different.

"I love you, Maxwell," she said, shrugging her shoulders to break free from my hug. "But I need to go."

"I'm so sorry, Mom," I said, letting her go before opening the door for her.

She stopped at the bottom of the front steps, turned back, and looked for a minute. From behind the sunglasses she'd slipped on, I couldn't tell if she was looking at me or something else. But I felt her sadness. I felt it mix with mine. I felt the two of us connected for the first time in a long time.

CHAPTER 27

IT'S SAFE DURING THE DAY

"ARE YOU SERIOUS?" Courtney had practically yelled at me loud enough for anyone and everyone in the house to hear her.

"What's the problem?" I asked, genuinely not understanding her immediate frustration with the news that I was going to the attic to work on Williamsburg.

"Max. Listen. I trust you. I love you. I believe you when you say a demonic monster lives up there and killed your father last week. I believe all of that."

It was the first time anyone had said it out loud, other than when I told them all my father was gone, that the monster that lived upstairs had killed him and turned his body to a goo-like substance. It'd been almost a week, exactly, since it'd happened. For the first couple of days, the house was silent. The housekeepers stayed away. Geoffrey was scarce. Sam only showed up to make meals for Courtney and me. Otto was as elusive as Otto always was. Courtney and I barely spoke to one another. If I'm being honest, on the first day after it happened, I lay in bed all day, weeping. Visions flashed before my eyes of the monster tossing Dad from side to side, slamming him against the door-frame, its goo flowing down Dad's body like the world's most disgusting river. I couldn't shake the images. I couldn't forget the sound. The slurping. I'll never forget the slurping.

But by the seventh day, things had mostly returned to normal. I even think I laughed at one of Geoffrey's terrible jokes over breakfast earlier that morning. I don't recall exactly what it was, but something to the effect of "the police wouldn't believe us, anyway," when someone else had mentioned calling the police about Dad's grisly demise.

"There's nothing left of him," I told them over and over again. "He's gone," I repeated when any of them asked to go up to the attic to see.

I knew there was a bit left of him up there, but I didn't want anyone to suffer the horrors that I suffered in having to see it for themselves. No one else needed to live that horror. It was some-thing I was confident I could carry on my own. Especially once the initial shock wore off. Once I made it through that first day, the memories of the demon's mouth opening and eating parts of Dad weren't so vivid anymore. The sound in my memory faded into obscurity. Not gone, but not roaring loud in my ears all the time.

"I have to go up there at some point," I told Courtney. "It might as well be now."

"Why now?" she asked, almost pleading.

"It's been long enough," I said. "And besides, Gramps said it's safe during the day. I have plenty of hours until nightfall."

"Please be careful," she said. "I don't know why you love that silly train set so much, anyway."

"I told you. It's what Gramps and I built together. It's our town. I named it after him. It makes me feel better to continue it for him. In his memory."

She came closer to me and put her hands on my hips. This was a common Courtney tactic to distract me from whatever I wanted to do that she didn't want me to do.

"I love you," I said, kissing her on the forehead as I had a million other times. "I'll be down in time for dinner."

I knew that by telling her I'd be down before dinner, she'd feel better about my going up. In mid-summer, the sun wouldn't set until close to nine, so I'd have plenty of light up there until well after I returned to the first floor. Plenty of light to keep the demon away.

* * *

THE DOOR to the attic remained closed, just as I'd left it a week ago. With the smell of the goo and the remaining bits of my father safely tucked behind the door, away from where it could sully the rest of our beautiful home.

For just a moment, I paused at the door. My hand tentatively held onto the handle, ready to unleash whatever was behind it. I listened intently, hoping to hear something. But more truly, hoping to hear nothing and hoping that all was quiet on the other side of the door. That the monster or demon or whatever it was, wasn't there at this moment. That Gramps was right, and whatever it was couldn't harm us during the day.

There were so many questions. So many things I wondered about. So many things I didn't understand. There was so much about the whole situation that made no sense.

"You won't get answers if you don't ask any questions," I told myself as I swung the door open.

A foul stench hit my nostrils as soon as the door brushed past my body. It seemed like the door had created some backdraft, and the fresh oxygen mixed with the stench of the monster's leftovers and the remains of my dad.

I retched. I felt the vomit come up and sit in my throat and mouth, but could barely choke it back. I felt nauseous immediately. The hallway around me and the stairs before me spun violently. The walls seemed to warp in and out like some cheesy effect from *The Twilight Zone*. I put my hands on the frame of the door, trying to steady myself, hoping the feeling would pass as I adjusted to the smell. Hoping that my body would eventually accept the stench as normal and let me get past it.

The longer I stood, the worse the smell seemed to get, though steadying myself against the door helped the room stop spinning around me.

"One foot in front of the other," I said. "For Gramps."

As I climbed the stairs, the black goo that had slid down the monster's arms onto my father lined the walls. My sneakers got stuck in it, like thick mud or tar, making it increasingly difficult to reach the top. The sound of rubber snapping away from the gelatinous goo reminded me of the sound of my father's limbs as they separated from his body. I wretched again, this time unable to stop the vomit from escaping my mouth and nose. I turned my head a split second too late, creating a sprinkler effect of vomit across the door at the top of the stairs, and all along the wall to my left, and eventually down a few of the stairs behind me.

The smell of my own vomit mixed with the stench in the hallway somehow made it better, less foreign.

I pushed my shoulder against the door at the top of the stairs, doing my best to move it from its stubborn frame. It was stuck more than usual. The humidity in the attic must have been higher than usual. "Old wood," I told myself.

When I finally managed to push my way through the door, the familiar smell of cinnamon hit my nose, immediately canceling out the vomit, goo, and melted flesh smell that had been so overpowering just moments ago.

My eyes stung. The attic was full of smoke. But the smoke alarm made no sound.

For a moment, I stood in the doorway, letting my eyes adjust and waiting for the little flashing light on the smoke detector to go off, to let me know it was still operational. And after what felt like forever, it did. The light flashed and then flashed again.

"It's not real smoke," I said out loud. "It's from Chet. It'll be fine."

When I looked across the gap between the door and where Williamsburg started, I could see Chet moving around the track. The rest of the town was dark; turned off. But Chet was still alive, following his predetermined path to his pickup and drop-off spots.

"That's not possible," I said to myself, trying to remember the last time I'd gone up to the attic. I'd never, for as long as I could remember, turned off the majority of the town, but left one of the trains running. I couldn't make sense of why I would have done that.

The first step I took toward the town was interrupted. I tripped and fell to the floor. The haze of smoke had created a blind spot by my feet, causing me to trip over my dad's shoe.

As I quickly scrambled away from the shoe and whatever part of his leg was still attached to it, I bumped my head against the underside of the town. The smoke seemed to lighten for a moment, but just enough that I could see the torn end of Dad's pants and the bare skin of his ankle and shin. I threw up for the third time. This time, down my chest and onto my stomach.

Chet's choo-choo rang out and made me jump, hitting my head on the underside of the town again.

I quickly turned my back to dad's foot and lower extremity. Somewhere in the back of my mind, I made a note to figure out what to do with what was left of him. What's the protocol for when a monster eats most of your dad? Burial in the backyard? Actually, call the police and hope they believe you? Burn it in the massive fireplace in the formal living room?

Once I couldn't see it anymore, I felt better. Though I knew it was still there, I was able to convince myself that it wasn't something I needed to worry about at that moment. That I could, in fact, deal with it later, and there'd be no difference.

Chet continued his route, but without me at the controls, he didn't stop at his commuter rail stations. He just plowed on and on around the track in a continuous loop. All the railroad crossings were up. All the pedestrians were positioned out of the way. All the cars and trucks were in places where Chet wouldn't hit them.

It seemed impossible that I'd have done that without remembering. It would have taken time and planning to ensure that everything was out of Chet's way. Had I just turned off everything else and left Chet running, he'd have eventually run into a car on the tracks or a railroad crossing that was down. It was just the nature of the way Gramps and I built the town. Turning the power off and having all of those obstructions out of the way was statistically impossible.

"There's no way," I said aloud, waving my hand in front of my face to push the cloud of smoke aside.

When I got to the other side of the town, where the controls were, I toggled Chet off. He immediately shut down; his headlight dimmed instantly, and the sound of his whirring stopped.

The lights I'd hung a couple of weeks prior were still lit, but the smoke from Chet's smokestack had all but made them invisible. I could see only one or two lights at a time as the smoke moved around the ceiling.

I coughed a few times. Though the smell of the faux smoke was sweet, it hit hard in the throat and lungs. The burning felt like I was smoking the worst cigarette I'd ever smoked. Which, admittedly, wasn't very many, and not since my friends and I tried them when we were teenagers.

"What'd you do, Chet?" I asked the train, as if it had a mouth it didn't have, to answer me.

"Oh, hi, Maxwell. I just thought it'd be fun to drive around by myself and fill the room with smoke," I said in a mock ridiculous voice that I, for some reason, added a Cockney accent to. Apparently, Chet, the train, was partially British.

"Stupid," I said. "Stop being stupid."

Again, I waved my hands in front of my face, forcing the smoke to clear long enough to make out the town before me. Chet had stopped just a few feet away and now lay silent and dark. The rest of the trains were back at the train yard, carefully parked in their appropriate places, like I'd always left them.

Despite trying to tell myself not to, I glanced over toward the door, catching a glimpse of my father's leg and the stairwell light's reflection shining off a pile of goo to the leg's right.

I forced myself to look away, but felt myself fall to the

ground. My elbows found my knees, my hands found my face, and I wept.

Gobs of snot fell from my nose as my weeping turned into hysterical crying. "How could I let this happen?" I yelled out to no one. "Dad wasn't perfect, but he was my dad."

"You hated him." A voice I didn't recognize came from nowhere, echoing throughout my core.

I pulled my hands from my face, swatting the smoke from the air in front of me, hoping something would make sense. "Who's there?" I called out.

"Your whole life, your father was a terrible man," the voice called out again.

"Who is that?" I yelled louder than the first time.

"You'll thank me later," it said before erupting into a loud but quick laugh.

"What is this?" I asked, hoping for some answers.

Silence fell over the room again. "Hello?" I called out. "Are you there?"

But I saw no one. I heard nothing. I continued swatting at the smoke, pushing it past my face and wondering why it hadn't cleared up on its own yet. The smell of cinnamon had faded shortly after I'd turned Chet off, but the smoke was still thick in the air. Though it was still daytime, the smoke clouded the room, making it feel like dusk. The light from the windows had only just started to shine through again as the smoke thinned. The lights on the ceiling eventually became visible to my stinging eyes.

As the room became brighter and less smoky, I looked around, hoping to find someone playing a joke on me. One of the housekeepers doing a grisly voice, perhaps. Or maybe I'd see

Otto popping out of one of the far corners of the room I previously couldn't see.

There was no one. There was nothing. Once the smoke cleared, all I could see were the remains of my father, the puddles of black goo strewn about beside him, and the piles of my vomit that I'd dropped along the way as I crossed the room.

* * *

"I KNOW WHAT I HEARD," I told Courtney.

"I'm starting to worry about you," she replied, taking both of my hands in hers.

"Worry? About me? Why?"

"You've been a little off lately, that's all."

"What do you mean?" I asked, genuinely not knowing what she was talking about.

"I didn't want to bring it up. But now you're hearing voices upstairs? In the attic?"

"I know what…"

"I know. You said that," she interrupted me.

"There's something up there," I said. "But it's safe during the day."

"Why haven't I seen it?"

"What do you mean?"

"You've seen this *thing*, you've heard it, you've experienced it making noise just outside our bedroom door. But I haven't seen or heard any of it."

"I don't know," I said. "I don't have an explanation for that."

"Doesn't it seem odd to you?" she asked.

"I guess I hadn't thought about it."

"Will you let me come up there with you? During the day?"

"I don't know, Court. What if it tries to hurt you? What if it tries to kill you?"

"Has it tried to hurt you?" I could see the look of concern in her eyes deepening. Though we had chosen not to have kids, the motherly look in her eyes made me feel judged.

"Well, no," I said. "I guess it hasn't. But what it did to my father was unbearable to watch."

"We need to do something about that," she said. "The hallway near the attic door smells like death."

"I know, but I'm not sure what I should do. The police won't believe me, will they? The whole thing sounds like insanity."

"You're right," she said. "I think we all know that. Have you spoken to your mother?"

"Not since she left that day," I said.

"I talked to her yesterday when you were in the attic. She's worried about you, about us."

"Why is everyone worried?" I asked a little louder than I'd intended. My frustration was seeping through my usually calm demeanor. The fact that it seemed like people were doubting the monster's presence was starting to bother me, but I couldn't put my finger on why.

"Why wouldn't we be? You say there's a monster living in our house and it killed your father."

"Gramps saw it, too," I immediately said, trying to dissuade Courtney from starting down a path that might lead me to believe she thought I was crazy.

"I know." She squeezed my hands tighter and brought her face closer to mine. The cushion on the couch sagged under the weight of both of us.

"I just need to figure out what it wants," I said, suddenly having an epiphany of how I could deal with the monster. If I knew what it wanted, maybe I could give that thing to it and it'd leave us alone. Maybe, just maybe, there was something it needed or wanted, and I could befriend it by getting that thing. The wheels in my brain started turning, and I jumped to my feet.

"Max, please," she said, trying to tug my arm back down to the couch. But it was too late. I was already heading out of the room toward the kitchen. "Where are you going?"

"I have to take care of my father," I called back.

CHAPTER 28
THE COVER UP

THE SMELL of death didn't bother me as I bounded up the attic stairs and through the not-so-stuck door. I burst right past the remaining limbs of my father and slid under the drapes surrounding Williamsburg. The last time I'd rummaged through the boxes and other stuff under the table, I'd come across a handful of curtains that Gramps must have bought to drape the edges of the town. You know, to hide all the junk that was underneath it.

He must have been planning to make it bigger, and thus needed more curtains.

I tossed empty box after empty box out from underneath the town. Plastic bins full of old spare parts slid across the attic floor in all directions as I made my way closer to the center of the structure. Though all the trains were quiet and had been still since I was last in the attic, the sweet smell of cinnamon still hung in the air. A constant reminder that Chet was only a flick of a power switch away from springing back to life.

Gramps had been quite the packrat. The storage space under

Williamsburg was full of virtually every single thing he'd ever bought for the town. All of their boxes, all the packaging. He even kept the receipts, dating back to the seventies, when he started the original train set downstairs.

Eventually, I found the package of curtains I'd remembered seeing previously and slid out from under the town with them in hand. Kicking past the boxes and containers and debris I'd scattered around the space, I made my way over to Dad's limbs. My immediate reaction was to vomit. Between the smell coming off of what was left of him and the sight of the maggots and flies on and around his body, I felt queasy. I did my best to shoo the flies, but they just circled and continued their touch-and-go landings on Dad's remains. There was nothing I could do about the maggots.

Despite knowing I needed a more permanent solution, for the time being, I draped the two curtains from the package over Dad's remains. I did my best to tuck them underneath him without touching too much of the rotting flesh. Piles of maggots fell to the floor as I shifted one of his shoes up off the ground to get the final corner of the curtain underneath it. I cringed. Not just at the bugs and smell, but at the act of what I was doing. I knew I couldn't explain what had happened to the police. They wouldn't understand what was happening. I knew that for a fact.

Something about covering for Dad made me feel uneasy. The sheer act of sliding those curtains on, around, and under him made me shiver. I felt like someone was watching me, but I knew I was alone. Since the last incident with the monster, I hadn't let anyone else up into the attic, even Courtney.

Once I was satisfied that Dad was fully covered, I took a step back from the spot where he lay. Had I not known what was there, it would have just looked like a pile of dirty laundry. The blood from each of the remaining body parts had dried up already, so nothing bled through the curtain to expose what was under it. And, yes, I realize I just used the word *bled* in a silly way. Don't worry, I smirked to myself at my amazing cleverness.

As I made my way back over to Williamsburg, an eerie feeling fell over me. For a moment, the strings of lights I'd recently hung all flickered, as if something had interrupted the power to the attic. A moment later, the sun was blotted out by passing clouds, leaving the entire attic in complete darkness. The sound of my heartbeat, rapidly increasing, reverberated up through my body, into my temples, and eventually into my ear canals. "The Telltale Heart" popped into my head for a fleeting moment.

The clouds outside moved quickly, causing the darkness in the room to come and go. And while I did my best to forget about the remains of my father just a short throw away from where I stood at the edge of the town, I kept turning back as if I expected his legs to come back to life and charge me. The fear suddenly consumed me, leaving me feeling as though something were about to happen.

I did my best to shake it off, to ignore it. I walked around the far side of the town and flicked the light switch on the side of the table, illuminating the town's streetlights, stoplights, buildings, and movie theater marquee. It was very little light in the grand scheme of things with the rolling clouds outside, but it helped illuminate the room enough to lift some of the heavy feeling that had been consuming me.

For a moment, I stood at the edge of the town, admiring it. And though it was illuminated, it sat motionless before me. None of the other switches or levers had been thrown, leaving the town still. Its inhabitants, both people and machines, sat silent. Frozen in time, for lack of a better explanation. Moments like that made me reflective about life and about myself.

Just as I was thinking of a fond memory of Gramps, the pit of my stomach turned. A pain so instant and so sharp that I doubled over. With my hands placed firmly on my knees, I cried out in pain. The pit felt like it was twisting and turning, as if something inside of me was trying to get out, to free itself from the confines of my stomach. The pain was almost unbearable. I cried out in pain again, hoping my yelling would somehow help alleviate the pain. But it didn't. The pain got worse, and I fell to the ground.

At first, I lay on my side. The left side of my body pressed firmly against the hard and cold wooden floor of the attic. My legs flailed from side to side, uncontrollably from the rest of my body. My hands pressed into my stomach like I was a little boy who couldn't poop, and pushing on my stomach might help force my body to evacuate my bowels. I pressed hard. I slid my hands across my abdomen, up onto my chest, and then back down and around. The pain grew worse.

I writhed on the floor, tears streaming from my eyes. "This is punishment," I told myself. For what I had let happen to my father. For covering the remains of his body with cheap Dollar General curtains with the most hideous octagonal pattern on them. "Dad deserves better than those green things," I yelled.

My body convulsed, and my eyes closed. The tears continued to flow down my face, but I could no longer open my eyes. I felt frozen, like the town sitting just a few feet above my head.

The pain in my stomach grew even stronger. So much so that I felt like I was going to die. I felt like I was on my final breaths, that life would soon end, and all I could think of was Courtney, how she'd eventually come up to the attic and find me. How she'd subsequently find Dad's remains under the curtains. How she'd have clung to my dead body and cried. How she'd have thought *I told you there was a reason to worry.*

And just like that, in the blink of an eye, the pain stopped. Control of my limbs was given back to my brain, and I was able to open my eyes again. I felt perfectly fine in an instant.

As I regained control and could stand back up, I leaned on the edge of the town for balance. Though my body felt fine, my head was dizzy. The room spun for a moment as if I'd just gotten off a serious rollercoaster and needed a moment to regain my composure. As if I were still being tossed around on sharp corners and losing the sense of gravity on a steep drop.

When I could finally shake the dizziness, I stood fully upright and surveyed the room. First, I looked out the window and saw that the clouds had cleared. Then I began scanning the room. Starting at the back, I found that all the boxes and containers and debris I had scattered previously still seemed undisturbed. The town lay still before me. The door to the attic was still open, the light from the stairwell illuminating the landing at the top, just inside the door.

I blinked rapidly, making sure what I was seeing was what I was seeing. The spot where I'd covered Dad's remains with curtains was empty. Vacant of the pile of dirty laundry I'd left there just a few short minutes ago.

"What?" I called out. "Where?"

I was flabbergasted, but not surprised, to see things suddenly go from eerie to terrifying.

I scanned the rest of the room, though in my mind I knew there was no way Dad's limbs could have moved themselves, let alone the curtains I'd placed over them. I looked under Williamsburg, nothing. I looked down the stairs toward the hallway on the second floor. Nothing. I looked behind the door. Nothing. I looked in all the dark corners that the sunlight couldn't illuminate. Nothing. The pile of Dad was gone.

And just as I turned back to turn off the lights of the town and hightail it out of the attic, I ran smack dab into the curtains. They stood before me, the size of a man. A man taller than me by a good foot. The unmistakable shape of a ghost from an old movie or television show. All that was missing were the cutouts for the eyes of the actor under the sheet.

But there were no eyes. This was no sheet and certainly no movie. The hulking figure stood before me, looming over me, yet silent.

I froze, and I'm not too proud to admit that I peed a little. I'd never felt a terror so strong before, even when watching a literal monster melt and digest my father before my very eyes.

The figure moved closer to me, almost leaning down on top of me. I'm sure I imagined it, but I felt a cool breath wash over my face, as if it had exhaled onto me.

Paralyzed by fear, I could do nothing but stand there and wait, hoping that what I was seeing would disappear. That whatever this was would stop, and I'd realize it was all a dream. That I imagined this.

"You hated him," the same voice from before had come out of the curtain before me. The shape of the man grew taller, now almost reaching the ceiling. As I looked up at the figure, the lights I'd hung from the ceiling temporarily blinded me. I squinted and held up a hand to block the light so I could keep track of the figure. I waited for it to speak again, for it to tell me something. For it all to make sense.

But nothing happened. I blinked a few times to get my eyes to adjust to the bright lights from the ceiling, and on the last blink, the figure was gone.

Immediately, I raced over to where my father's remains were. I flung back the curtains, accidentally tossing maggots and whatever other bugs were crawling on him into the air, scattering against the windows and walls.

And there he lay. Still, and yes, I realize the double meaning of the word *still*. What was left of Dad was exactly where I'd left it before, covered by the world's most hideous curtains. Still motionless. Still rotting and still smelling disgusting. But still there. It hadn't gotten up and moved around the room, and it certainly hadn't spoken to me.

"I'm going crazy," I thought, as I made my way down the attic stairs, closing the door firmly behind me. "I should tuck a towel under the door," I thought to myself. As if it would make the stench in the hallway less obtrusive, somehow.

For a moment, I sat on the third step down. I plopped my head in my hands, and I cried. The feeling of being overwhelmed washed over me, causing a slight panic attack, which resulted in the only thing I was capable of doing in that moment: crying.

CHAPTER 29

I DON'T FEEL GREAT

"DO YOU EVEN HEAR YOURSELF?" Courtney had been grilling me since I came down from the attic, attacking me as if I were some crazy person.

"Of course I hear myself!" I yelled.

"And you still think what you're doing is fine?"

"It's as fine as it can be. My father is dead. Can you not show an ounce of sympathy?" Again, I yelled at her. Something I don't think I'd ever done before over our entire relationship. But yet, I couldn't stop myself. I was overwhelmed with emotion and fear. Full of anxiety and terror.

"Max, I know that. You've told me. You've told us all," she said, trying to calm me down.

"But it's not your father who's dead!" My voice grew louder as my patience vanished.

"Please calm down, Maxwell. You're scaring me," she said, taking a few steps back from the bed where I sat, toward the door.

"Good! Then maybe you'll feel an ounce of what I'm feeling.

Maybe you'll understand how terrified I am about what's happening in this house!" What had just been fear had turned to rage. That feeling, they say, you get just before you see red, was hitting me, consuming me. The rage flowed up from my feet into the pit of my stomach, sitting there like a rotten watermelon I'd mistakenly eaten. It burned and cramped. It twisted and flopped around. It crunched my insides until the pain was unbearable.

"I don't feel great," I said, trying to express my physical and metaphorical discomfort about what was happening. The pain almost caused me to writhe around on the bed. The discomfort of my yelling at Courtney felt palpable in my mouth. A taste I found both disgusting and invigorating. A feeling I'd never felt before, but one I was sure I wanted more of. The anger and hatred I felt for her in that moment were certainly unfounded, but it felt incredible. It felt like it was something I'd been holding onto.

"Maxwell, please calm down." She took a few steps backward, almost standing in the doorway. "You're really scaring me."

Suddenly and without control, I leapt to my feet and began pacing the room. "You have no idea what this has done to me." My words were so loud that they echoed past Courtney out into the hallway, bouncing off the portrait of Great Gramps and hitting me back in the face. My own voice washed over me in a warm and embracing hug. My anger grew to a point where I felt like I wanted to break something or hit someone. It felt uncontrollable. It felt unlike me. "But I feel so good," I said, clenching my hands into fists. My nails dug into my palms, causing little half-moon-shaped blood blisters to appear. The pain didn't faze me.

I went to the bathroom and instinctively ran cold water over my hands. Normally, I'd have done that to calm the pain of a cut, but this time, I did it because I felt like I was supposed to do it. There was no pain. In the pain's place I should have been feeling, all I felt was more rage.

The water pooled in the sink, turning a very light shade of pink. I let it run clear and then dunked my hands back under the running tap. Again, the water turned pink and pooled at the bottom of the sink.

"Are you okay?" she called out to me from the bedroom.

"Do you even care?" I snapped back. "Like at all? Do you care?"

"Maxwell, of course I care." She was calling me by my full name. Again, which she only did when she was mad at me. It didn't happen often, but it wasn't completely abnormal. It always reminded me of the episode of *The Office* where Toby tries to calm Andy down and keeps repeating his name. *We're your friends, Andy.*

"It doesn't feel like that. It doesn't feel like anyone cares." I looked up at myself in the mirror hanging above the sink. My eyes were red with rage. The white parts were filled with blood vessels that had burst. My vision was poor at best.

And then, over my shoulder, in the reflection, I saw the monster. At first, it hid in the shadowy corner near my nightstand. Between where the curtains that normally covered the window bunched up when they were open and the space next to my nightstand. It lurked there, waiting.

My first instinct was to tell Courtney to run. To make her flee for her life. To save her from the same fate that my father had suffered. To protect her.

But I froze. The cold water still flowed over my hands. They were almost numb. In my peripheral vision, I could see half of Courtney reflected in the mirror, hovering in the doorway, unaware. She leaned from left to right, shifting her weight from one foot to the other, clearly uncomfortable and uneasy. I wasn't sure if she'd yet seen the monster.

I did my best not to let it know I saw it. I gently turned the faucet off, allowing the excess water to drip off my hands and swirl down the drain in a pink flourish. My gut said to turn and run, grabbing Court on the way out the door, hoping I could beat the monster, should it spring from its hiding spot and lurch toward either her or me.

For the slightest moment, I froze. Its reflection became clearer in the mirror the more I glanced at it. The outline of the monster became more pronounced, as if the slight light from the window found the creature and wanted to show it to me.

"Are you okay in there?" Courtney called out. I ignored her, focusing on the monster. Focusing on my plan to escape with Courtney into the hallway.

"How is it here?" I mumbled to myself. "It's daytime." What was happening was against everything I knew about the monster. Gramps had assured me it didn't come out during the day. That it wasn't strong enough to get out of the attic during the daytime.

And then it hit me. While I was up in the attic with Chet and the rest of Williamsburg, the monster had escaped. It didn't need to be strong to fight its way down the attic stairs and through the door on the second floor. It didn't need any strength, because I'd left both of those doors unguarded while I mucked with the stupid town and its stupid trains. Those dumb trains were going to be the death of Courtney and me.

"You can't be here!" I yelled out. "You have to go." I wasn't sure if I was talking to the monster or to Courtney. But either of them needed to leave. Her to safety. It back to the attic.

I squinted, trying to make out its features more, though it still stood in the shadow. It knew I saw it, though. It must have. It smirked a tiny bit, showing the top row of its teeth, which caught the light from the window just enough to cause a little lens flare. *J.J. Abrams loves his lens* flares, I thought to myself.

"What's happening?" Courtney yelled.

"You have to go!" I yelled just as the monster stepped out from the shadows. Its hulking figure stood tall in the room, almost touching the ceiling with the top of its head. The wooden floors beneath its feet groaned with pain, nearly crying from the weight of it. "You have to go!" I yelled again.

"Fine! I'll go, but this isn't over!" Courtney yelled as she slammed the door.

I felt thankful that she'd gone, but worried that she was still in danger. Having no other choice, I turned and faced the monster. A dozen or so feet separated us, and I knew, from having seen it demolish my father in the blink of an eye, that it could be on me in a heartbeat. That, should it want to, it could leap from its spot and land on me, flattening me like a pancake. Crushing every bone in my body into nonexistence. It could do that without even losing its breath. Bam, it's over. I'm gone. I'm dead.

It could destroy me without even caring.

"You cannot be here!" It was the only thing I could think of saying. I repeated it over and over in my head. Trying to wish it away. Hoping that by saying it enough, it would leave. That it'd retreat to the attic to recharge or something. Perhaps the sunlight weakened it. Maybe I was lucky, and it was powerless to kill me because it was daytime. I'd never hoped for something so much in my life.

The pain in my palms suddenly showed itself. The eight tiny slivers where my fingernails had pierced my skin started throbbing. Most of the blood blisters had ruptured and were forming little blood droplets that I repeatedly wiped on my jeans.

It let out its first sound since emerging from the shadows. A low, faint growl. The tiniest growl followed by a hissing sound. Like a cat that isn't super angry, but is getting close. Just a quick warning sound to let me know it was about to be really pissed off.

I clenched my fists into balls, but I couldn't tell you why. Was I going to fight it? Was I going to punch it? Did I even have a chance at fighting this ten-foot-tall monster from hell? But what other choice did I have?

The only other thing I could think to do was to close my eyes and prepare for it to attack me.

The floor groaned again as it took a step toward me, nearing the edge of the bed, and coming closer to the door to the bathroom. With my back pressed firmly against the sink, I waited. I held my ground, only hoping that if it killed me, it'd buy enough time for Courtney to flee the house. To get downstairs and out the door to safety. That she, and all the other humans who lived on the grounds, would be safe. That my life, my sacrifice, would be enough to save them all.

My breath stopped. My heartbeat slowed down to the point where I could feel each pulse of blood rush up through my body and flood through the veins and blood vessels in my ears. That faint whoosh sound you hear when you lie awake at night, head on the pillow, in silence. The sound of your own blood flowing through your body.

Whoosh.

Whoosh. Whoosh.

Whoosh.

I waited.

I held my breath longer. Waiting for the monster to take another step. For it to reach out with its massive arms and rip me in half.

I knew it was coming. It was toying with me. It was playing a game that I didn't understand.

Whoosh.

Whoosh.

The blood slowed down.

At that point, I was sure I was already dead.

Despite my best judgment, I opened my eyes, expecting the monster to be right in front of me, waiting. I expected it to be there, bending down with its giant mouth open, ready to consume me. That it would be face-to-face with me, prepared to end my life.

But it was gone.

I looked left and right, turning around to check the mirror behind me.

But it was truly gone. The monster had vanished.

It hadn't run out of the room, for I heard no creaking floors. It didn't jump out the window, as it wasn't broken.

It had simply vanished from sight.

Whoosh.

Whoosh.

The blood started flowing back into my body, and my limbs got that tingling feeling like I'd been sitting on the toilet scrolling Instagram too long. The pins and needles stabbed and poked all of my limbs and extremities simultaneously.

I let out a small gasp, trying to catch my breath.

Whoosh. Whoo. Wh.

The sound of my blood flowing slowed and disappeared. My heart returned to normal rhythm as the pins and needles disappeared.

The pain in my palms raged. The tiny cuts felt like someone had dumped hydrogen peroxide all over them, screaming out in agony.

Tiny cuts in the palms of my hands had never hurt so badly before in my life. They throbbed and pulsed. I turned my palms toward me to look at them and found them full of blood, as if I'd been trying to collect it, to make it pool up in my hands.

* * *

"MAX, ARE YOU OKAY? MAX?"

Courtney stood over me as I opened my eyes. The cold of the bathroom floor felt like an icebox as I lay there. My limbs felt stiff; my back throbbed. The spot right above my kidneys that always hurts when I stay in bed too long was on fire.

"What happened?" I asked, still unsure of where I was or how I'd gotten there. "The last thing I remember was being in the attic."

"You were," Geoffrey said from the doorway. I was on the couch in the living room. The room was dark and quiet. I could see Joy and Vanessa flanking Geoffrey. Looks of concern covered all three of their faces.

As I focused in on Courtney's face, I saw a look of concern there as well.

"Is someone going to tell me what happened?" I asked, trying to sit up.

"You were in the attic," Geoffrey said, taking a few steps toward the couch. My head throbbed, and I felt weaker than I'd ever felt before. "When no one saw you for a while, I came looking."

"We were worried about you," Courtney added. "You were gone all day."

"Was I?" I couldn't remember. The only things I could concentrate on were the pain in my body and the throbbing in my head.

"Thankfully, though this house is massive, there are few places you like to go, sir," Geoffrey said.

Joy and Vanessa backed out of the room, seemingly feeling better now that I had woken up and made a feeble attempt at sitting up.

"Geoffrey came and found me once he'd found you," Courtney said. "You were unconscious on the floor by the train set."

The news of where and how I was triggered a brief memory. I looked down at my hands and found them bandaged in more gauze than was probably necessary. Though somewhat numb, I could sense the cuts on my palms. I could remember digging my fingers into them, almost against my will. I could feel the pain I'd caused myself. And suddenly, I sensed the panic I must have caused in everyone when they couldn't find me.

"We carried you down to your bedroom," Geoffrey said. "But after it got dark that night, you mumbled you couldn't be upstairs."

"You were mumbling about the monster," Courtney said.

"The monster. Right. I remember." I didn't remember. I remembered the monster, of course, but not the events of the day. I didn't remember what had happened while I was in the bathroom or how I got to the attic, not even in the slightest.

"So we brought you down here," Geoffrey said.

"Three days ago," Courtney said.

"What? Three days ago?"

"Yes, honey," she said. "You've been out for three days."

"We had a doctor come and check on you. Doctor Louveen. The same doctor who we knew would make a house call, as he'd been here a number of times for your grandfather toward the end."

"What did he say?" I asked in the general direction of both of them. Though Geoffrey was still a few feet away from me, Courtney sat right next to me on the couch, holding my hand and steadying me as I continued to try to sit up.

"He said to keep an eye on you," Courtney said. "He gave you an IV and has been back a few times to check on you, change out the bag, and give you medicine."

"He'll be glad to know you've woken up, sir. I'll go call him and let him know." Geoffrey was gone from the room before I could even process what they were telling me.

"Three days?" I asked again, squeezing her hand as best I could. "I'm so sorry," I said.

"You had me very worried," she said. "Very worried. You kept talking about the monster."

"It's starting to come back to me now," I said. "I think it was up there with me. When I was in the attic."

"The monster isn't real, Max."

"Of course it's real," I said, almost shouting. "I've seen it so many times."

"But no one else has," she said, stroking the back of my hand through the gauze.

"Gramps did."

"Gramps was sick," she said. "You know he was sick near the end."

"I've seen it, Court."

"It's not real," she said, kissing me on the forehead. "But regardless, I'm glad you're okay now. How do you feel?"

"How do I feel? I feel like nobody believes me. I feel like my body's been run over by a truck. I'm seeing a monster that lives in our house, which tormented my grandfather and now torments me, but no one else has seen it and thinks I'm crazy. How do you think I feel?" I hadn't realized it, but I was yelling.

"Max, please calm down."

"You calm down!" I yelled at her. "You all need to calm down!"

"Max, the monster isn't real."

"You're wrong. You'll see," I said, doing my best to turn my back to her, as it was all I could do. "You'll all see."

"Talk to me, please," she implored. "I'm worried about you."

But I couldn't talk anymore. I had no words left to use to convince her of what I knew to be true. Is this *The Sixth Sense*? Am I dead or something? This can't be real, can it? I tried to pinch myself, but the combination of being face-first into the back cushions of the couch and my hands being wrapped in gauze prevented me from doing so. I closed my eyes and tightened them as much as I could. They watered until tears streamed down my face. I clenched them so tight, hoping to close out the world, that it caused my headache to worsen.

"Max, please," Courtney said. Her weight lifted from the couch, and I rolled back toward the floor slightly. In that way you move on your side of the bed when your partner gets up before you in the morning. "Fine, I'll leave you be," she said, storming off.

"Why does she get to be mad at me?" I asked myself. Why does she get to basically tell me I'm crazy and then get mad when I don't want to talk to her about it? That's garbage. That's not fair. I'm the one who should be angry. I'm the one who should be seething. I'm the one being haunted or whatever by this monster that literally ate my father.

They must have seen the body. They were in the attic. They must have. Despite my best efforts to keep them from seeing it, they must have peeked, right? They came up there, found me, saw the sheet with Dad's remains under it, and tore it back, revealing his gruesome remains. Who wouldn't? Who would be in that situation and not want to look at it? Who wouldn't want to confirm all the weird things I'd been telling them were true? That was the solution, wasn't it? I didn't want anyone else to have to suffer through that the way that I did. It wasn't fair to them.

I dry-heaved just thinking about Dad's legs dangling there up under the sheet. And then dry heaved again from the sound of my first dry heaving. The human body is weird.

I shut my eyes tight again, hoping to fall asleep. Hoping that I'd doze off and wake up in the morning to find this was all a nightmare. To find that I was in my bed, Courtney next to me, sweetly holding my hand. I hoped to fade out the day and start fresh again.

CHAPTER 30

AN INVESTIGATION

"MAX?" a voice called out, waking me. I found myself still on the couch with no sense of what time it was or how many days had passed since I'd fallen asleep again. The feeling in my back had returned to normal, but my hands were still in dire pain. The IV drip that had been previously tucked into my left inner elbow was gone, replaced by a small, round band-aid.

"Hello?" I tried to open my eyes, but they were tight. I had been asleep for longer than a single night, I could tell.

"Max. Hello. My name is Detective Thomas. Are you able to sit up and talk to me?"

"No one's name is *Detective*," I snapped. I could sense him laughing a little, knowing I was right.

"That's fair. Greg Thomas. I'm a detective."

"What are you doing here?" I fought a little harder and finally managed to open my eyes. The morning sun hit me as soon as I did, causing a searing pain in both eyes. I pulled up my gauze-laden hand and blocked as much of it as I could until I adjusted to the light. It was definitely morning, based on the sun's position. A cup of coffee sat on the table in front of me, with what looked to be a day-old Danish. Cherry. My favorite.

"Your wife called us," he said. "And your doctor."

"Why?"

"I told you I was worried," Courtney called out from behind the couch.

"Ma'am, please. I said you could stay in the room. I didn't say you could interrupt."

"Why?" I asked again, ignoring Courtney's interruption.

"You were unconscious in the attic. Is that correct?" He ignored my question and responded with one of his own.

"Don't ask questions you already have answers to," I snarked again.

"Let me rephrase. Why were you unconscious in the attic?"

"I don't know," I said truthfully. "I don't remember what happened."

"You've been telling your wife stories about some monster. You have your staff more scared than worried at this point."

"Not a question."

"This is real life, Mister Washington. This isn't a movie."

"Make a point."

"Monsters aren't real," he said. His frame loomed over me, though I couldn't tell if he was much larger than me, or if it was just the perspective of him standing and me partially sitting up on the couch. But he felt intimidating in either case. Something that he probably felt gave him an advantage over me.

"Okay. You're right." I intentionally laced my words with as much sarcasm as I could, like Iago from *Aladdin*. "Are we done now?"

"No, sir. What can you tell me about your father?"

It caught me by surprise. He knew. They must have told him.

Someone must have. Or, worse, he'd seen the remains himself. How would I explain this? "What do you mean?" The sarcastic tone continued unintentionally.

"Your doctor called first," he said. "He was worried about you. We didn't know anything about the specifics until your wife called later that same day."

"The man who helped create me was hateful. He was anything but a father." It was all I could think of to say. If he wanted me to paint a picture of him, that was the best I would do.

"What do you mean?"

I felt Courtney stirring around behind the couch. Some of the thoughts that flowed through my head are things I was never even able to tell her. The things I had repressed memories of that had started coming back up the longer we were in One Stone Way. The feelings that had resurfaced about my parents, specifically my father, were feeling all too real lately. Part of me wanted to open up to the detective. Part of me wanted to see if I could get up and run out of the room. All of me felt trapped.

"He hated me," I said, not able to stop the words from coming out of my mouth. "He hated me from the moment I was born."

"Max," Courtney spoke, but the detective held up his hand as if to shush her.

"Continue," he said.

"My earliest memories are of his leaving. Of his taking my mother away on a trip. A trip that my grandfather, his father, no doubt paid for. Trips that happened all the time."

"What kind of trips?" he asked.

"Trips that would take him anywhere I wasn't."

I could see Courtney starting to cry out of the corner of my eye.

"Go on," he said.

"From a very young age, I knew he didn't want me. Just him. My mother loved me. She thought the world of me. I knew she loved me. She told me all the time. But she loved him, too. So she let him take her away from me. To send me here, to stay with Gramps. For days. Weeks. Months. He sent me here so he wouldn't have to see me. He left me because he hated me."

"Why do you think he hated you?" he asked.

"I ruined his perfect life. I was unwanted. Before I came along, he and my mother had it perfect. He loved their life. He loved that they could do whatever they wanted. He loved that they had no responsibilities. He loved that he was free."

"And then you came along, and he had to be responsible?"

"Ha! Responsible? Him? The great Bruce Washington? Get real. The closest thing he ever did to being responsible was coming back from the trips. They'd go off for a while, and then he'd come back. And you'd think he'd try to make up for being gone. You'd think, right? 'Come on, Max, let's play catch' or 'Do you want to go to a movie together, son?' Nothing like that. He'd come back and go straight to his office or the yacht club with his friends. He might as well have stayed gone."

"What about your mother?"

"She was under his control. His spell. Like he had something over her. He controlled her. I'm pretty sure he hit her sometimes, too."

"Did he hit you?"

"Is that a serious question?" I scoffed. "It was the eighties. All fathers hit their kids."

"Did he hit you more than your friends' dads hit them?"

"What friends? Gramps was my only friend."

"Would you say he was abusive?"

"What was abusive then is not the same as it is now. Back then, they called it discipline."

"I get it," he said. "I grew up at the same time. We're roughly the same age. My dad walloped me with a belt from time to time when I misbehaved."

"That's just it," I said, not able to stop my mouth from spilling the rest of the story that I'd kept to myself for all those years. "I wasn't misbehaving. I never did. I knew deep down that if I were a bad kid, it'd be even worse. No, not me. My dad just hit me because he wanted to. He hit me because he hated me. He hit me because it made him feel powerful and made me feel weak and small. He hit me because he could. Because I ruined his perfect life by existing. He hit me all the time, and he seemed to enjoy doing it. He was a terrible man, and no one knew it. Not even Gramps. My mother never told a soul. She'd just go to the kitchen and bake. She'd turn on the radio and turn up the volume so she couldn't hear it. She'd pretend it didn't happen while it was happening. She'd escape from it. And then, when it was over, she'd get me, bandage me up, tell me some story about how he didn't mean it and that it wouldn't happen again. She'd tell me all those lies, even though she didn't believe them herself. She'd put ice on my eye or bacitracin on a cut. I'm pretty sure we kept the Band-Aid company in business back then. And then she'd help him. She'd check on him to make sure he hadn't hurt his hand beating on me. She'd actually leave me in the kitchen, listening to the radio, to check on him. Can you believe that? I never once understood it. I didn't get why she never took me away. I never got why she didn't save me from him.

"She'd come back to the kitchen after a while with some story about how I'd gotten into a fight at school or the park. She'd tell me repeatedly so I could remember it, so I could tell Gramps when I'd see him, or tell the teacher at school. Teachers weren't as smart back then; no one knew what signs to look for. They didn't know what the signs of abuse were so that they could report it. She just helped cover it up. She helped him because he controlled her. And I hated him so much for it. I hated him for what he did to me. I hated him for hating me."

"Is that why you killed him?" The room froze. My heartbeat rose into my ears, flooding my brain with fresh blood. What did he just say? Did he ask me if I killed my father?

Courtney continued to pace behind the couch, her shadow from the morning sun floating over me and then disappearing as she paced. The sound of her hyperventilation was the only thing I could hear above the sound of the blood flowing through my brain.

He thinks I killed my father. Why wouldn't he? Why wouldn't anyone? The monster did it, and I knew that. I knew the monster did it because I saw it happen. I witnessed it. It happened right in front of me. I can still hear it happening. I can still smell the black ooze that flowed down Dad's body and disintegrated him. But no one else had seen it, so why would they believe me?

"Is it?" he asked, snapping me back out of my own thoughts.

"Excuse me? I didn't kill anyone," I said. "The monster killed my father. I told my wife that. I told everyone that."

"Did you report this to the police?" he asked, already knowing full well that I hadn't.

"The monster killed him," I repeated. "The monster."

"There is no monster," Courtney managed to get out through

her tears. Her voice sounded frail and weak. She sounded defeated and scared at the same time.

"There is a monster!" I yelled, lunging from the couch to my feet. "I can prove it!"

"Mister Washington, please sit back down," he commanded, his right hand positioned over his service pistol, ready to defend himself should I lunge toward him.

"I can prove it! Let me prove it!" I yelled. "Come with me."

"Sir, please!" he said. "Please sit back down." But I had no intention of doing so. I left the room, not waiting for them to follow me, but hoping they would.

"Max, stop," I heard Courtney's faint voice as I rounded the stairwell and started up the stairs.

Their footsteps clanked on the tile floor as they made their way through the foyer and onto the stairs. Just as I exited the top of the stairs and was about to open the door to the attic, I saw them out of the corner of my eye.

"You're not well!" Courtney shouted. "Please stop!"

But I couldn't. I had to prove to them that the monster had killed my father, and it wasn't me. I had to show them the body. I had to explain what had happened. If they could just see. If they could have understood what had happened, they'd have had no choice but to believe in the monster. They'd have no choice but to see what I saw.

"Come on," I shouted, bounding up the stairs toward the door that I'd hoped wouldn't be stubbornly swollen shut.

They followed me, though Detective Thomas kept Courtney behind him. He'd drawn his weapon at some point between when I left the living room and then. His trigger finger was a blip away from taking my life.

The door before me burst open, swinging fast toward the

wall of the attic. The lights in the sky over Williamsburg were still lit, casting a faint glow throughout the attic. The faint smell of cinnamon floated in the air from the last time Chet had made his rounds around the town. The sheet where Dad's remains lay was there, undisturbed.

"See?" I yelled. "There!"

"Max. Please. Don't," Courtney begged as I got closer to the sheet. Hundreds of flies buzzed around the room. I noticed the sheet moving slightly. Was he alive under there? What was happening?

When I got within arm's reach of the sheet, I kneeled, scared —terrified, even. The smell hit both nostrils at the same time, and I threw up to my left. The rotten smell of human flesh is the vilest thing you can imagine ever smelling.

As I yanked back the sheet, I found Dad's remains covered in maggots. Millions of tiny, slimy, white maggots crawled around on his body. They were what was moving the sheet. There were so many of them it seemed like my father was moving under the sheet.

Courtney screamed like a teenage girl in any horror movie made in the nineties.

I heard Detective Thomas throw up a few times.

"Step back," he said once he'd regained his composure. "Step away from the body."

I turned to look at him, making eye contact. "See?" I said, imploring him to see what I'd seen. Begging him to see the black ooze that I'd seen. I wanted him to see the missing parts of my father that the monster had eaten.

"Step away from the body," he said again, more demanding the second time.

But I couldn't. I needed him to see. I needed them both to see the wrath of what the monster had done.

I turned back to Dad's remains, hoping I could pick up a leg and wave it at them. That my directly showing it to them would make them understand. What else could I do?

And that's when I saw him.

Dad. My father.

All of him.

Every piece of his body was covered with insects, so badly decomposed that I wouldn't even have known it was my father if I hadn't watched him fall in that very spot and die. There were no missing limbs that the monster had eaten. The parts of him I'd seen melted and swallowed were present, but decomposed.

"I don't understand," I said. Years of pain and emotion suddenly poured down my face as I fell to the ground, pushing myself as far away from the body as I could. The sound of the flies filled the room, drowning out my own thoughts. The smell hit me again, over and over.

"Max, please," Courtney said. "Please step away and tell us what really happened."

But I couldn't. I didn't know what had happened. Nothing made sense. I watched the monster kill him. I saw it happen. I saw its ooze flow over him. I saw it eat him. I saw the look on his face when he knew he was about to die. He saw me as I did nothing.

"What happened here?" I said just before I blacked out.

CHAPTER 31

THE REVELATION

"WHERE AM I?" I said as I woke up feeling groggy and confused. The light in the room blinded me immediately. I felt cold. The blanket covering me did little to stave off the frigid temperature in the room. There were three people in the room. The only one I recognized was my mother. She stood in the doorway, shrouded by the other two unrecognizable people, with her back to me. But I'd recognize her tint of auburn hair anywhere. The same color of L'Oréal she'd been using my entire life, thanks to bad genetics, turned her hair gray when she was in her twenties.

I couldn't hear their voices, and I don't think they heard mine, so I took the opportunity to look around the room. It seemed I was in some medical facility. The walls were stark white, marked only with scuffs and dents from where untrained orderlies accidentally bumped the walls as they wheeled beds in and out of the room. The faint beeping of a machine to my left, which I couldn't quite make out, kept time with my heart. Voices from the hall sounded like panicked nurses running to and from various other rooms. The fluorescent lights overhead hummed just loud enough for me to hear them when the machine wasn't beeping.

"Hello?" I called out a little louder. My mother's body froze, its language telling me she suddenly felt unsafe.

I raised my left hand to wave to the two other people facing me, but was unable to raise it more than a few inches. The sound of metal on metal clanging caught my attention. When I looked down, I found that my left wrist was hand-cuffed to the metal rail that ran along the whole side of the bed. I jangled it, like in an old episode of Magnum P.I. I'd seen with Gramps as a kid. I jangled it some more to draw more attention to myself.

"What's happening? Where am I?" I yelled out loud enough that none of the three people in the room would be able to ignore me.

Finally, my mother turned to face me. The look of terror on her face made me pause. I waited. Hoping she'd come closer to me and explain what was happening. Again, I jangled the hand-cuff as if to say, "What *the hell is this*?"

"Max," she started. "My boy."

She approached the bed but kept her distance. She got just close enough that she could lower her voice, so I'd be the only one who could hear her.

"Mom, where am I?"

"You're in the hospital," one of the unknown men said. He flipped the folder he was holding shut and approached the side of the bed opposite my mother and my handcuff. "Can you tell me the date?"

"The date? Who cares about the date?!" I was loud, but not quite yelling. "Where am I? Someone tell me what's going on!"

My mother put her hand on the back of my hand, which I'd found unknowingly gripping the metal bar I was cuffed to.

"Max, you're in the hospital. You blacked out. Do you remember?"

I ignored the question. "Where's my wife?"

"She's here. In this building," the other man said, still keeping his distance. "You'll see her soon."

"I want to see her now!"

"Max, it's important we talk about what happened," the man further away said.

"Do you remember what happened?" the man with the clipboard asked.

"No." I was honest. I didn't remember anything that had happened. After finding my right hand free from handcuffs, I raised it to my head and wiped the bead of sweat that had formed on my brow. The touch of my own skin felt cold and caused my head to throb with pain. The lights were killing me.

"Do you remember your father?" My mother asked, pulling her hand away from mine.

"Of course I remember my father!" I shouted. "How could I not remember him?"

"That's not what I meant," she said, a single tear falling from her eye.

"What are you talking about?"

"Max, my name is Doctor Horton. I'm the head of Psychiatry here. We want you to know that we're here to help you."

"Help me with what?" I asked.

"Everything," the other man said. "I'm Doctor Ryder, head of Neurology. I'm working with Doctor Horton on your case."

"My case? What case?" My head throbbed more as the lack of understanding set in.

"Can you tell me what happened to your father?" Doctor Horton asked, scribbling something down in the folder he'd reopened. The sound of the pen scratching against the paper was much louder than it should have been, almost with an echo.

"When?"

"The last time you saw him?" Doctor Ryder added.

"The last time I saw him?" My mind flashed back to the memory of him standing at the top of the stairs.

"Take a deep breath," Doctor Horton said. "Try to remember."

"Try not to think about what you told people," one of them said, though their voices blended once I'd closed my eyes, and I'm not sure which of them said it.

"I don't remember," I said, still trying to be truthful. I didn't remember the last time I'd seen him. I remembered him at Gramps's funeral. I remembered him coming to One Stone Way a few weeks later and storming off. I couldn't remember having seen him after that.

"I'm going to step out and find Courtney," my mom said. "I'll tell her you're awake and with the doctors."

Her heels clacked their way across the tile and out of the room. The soft hydraulic hinge made a puffing sound as she closed the door behind her.

"Max, remember that we're here to help you," one of the all-too-similar-sounding voices said. "We want to understand."

"The police will be here soon, and we need to help them understand, too," the other voice said. I think it was Doctor Horton, based on the direction of the sound.

"I don't know," I said again.

"Did you love your father?" a voice asked.

"What kind of question is that?" I snapped back.

"Again, we're trying to understand," one of them said. Doctor Ryder, this time, I think.

"Understand what?"

"Why you hurt him."

"I hurt him?" And then, in the blink of an eye, it all came rushing back to me. The conversation with the detective. What was his name? Williams? Raspse? Something. I can't remember. He asked me why I'd killed my father. He'd accused me of doing it. But it wasn't me. Was it? No, it was the monster. Right. I remembered. There's a monster living upstairs at my house. In the attic. The house my grandfather left me when he died. Wait. A monster? Did I just think that? A monster? In my house? A monster? Was I blaming something on a monster? And expecting people to believe me? What the hell was happening?

Just as I was having a revelation, the door to the room opened. My eyes instinctively opened, and though I'd hoped to see Courtney come to save me from whatever was happening, it was the detective whose name I couldn't recall.

"Maxwell, I'm glad you're awake," he said as he entered the room and closed the door behind him.

"Detective something," I said.

"Thomas. Yes. How are you feeling?"

"Confused. Very confused."

"That's understandable," he said. "Doctors, may I have a moment?" He gestured toward the end of the bed, though it was clear they all knew I'd be able to hear what they were talking about.

He lowered his voice, but I could still hear everything he said to them.

"Once the coroner removed the body, I met with the forensics team, and we combed over the entire attic and the rest of the house. We went through every inch with help from his wife and staff. It took some time, but we eventually found this in the attic."

From his pocket, he pulled a large plastic bag. The outside was covered with a white label bearing my name. The top was sealed with red tape, with white letters spelling out 'evidence' in capital letters across the whole thing.

I couldn't tell what was inside. I tried to move my body to the side some, to get a better view around Doctor Ryder's massive shoulders, but I couldn't. Thankfully, I didn't have to wait long.

"Lionel liquid smoke," one of the doctors said, but with their backs to me, I couldn't tell which.

"It's from the fifties," Detective Thomas said. "It's eighty-five percent Ethylene Glycol," he paused as if that was some giant revelation that would cause both doctors to applaud or panic.

"I don't understand," Doctor Horton said.

"Ethylene Glycol is harmless," Doctor Ryder said. "Unless inhaled in large quantities."

"Max, can you tell us what this is?" Detective Thomas asked, holding the bag up so I could see the white bottle through the clear part of the plastic.

I squinted, but I knew what it was immediately. "It's the smoke we use in Chet."

"I'm sorry, who's Chet?" Doctor Ryder asked.

"Chet is the train. The main train in the train set."

"What's happening?" Doctor Horton asked.

"There's a massive train set in the attic of the house," Detective Thomas said. "He and his grandfather built it over many years."

"Decades," I interjected.

"Decades. They built it together. When his grandfather died, he left the whole property and his fortune to Max and his wife."

"Oh my God," I blurted. It hit me like a sledgehammer.

"We think he had been spending a lot of time up there with the trains to feel connected to his recently deceased grandfather," Thomas said a little under his breath.

"I was!" I shouted. "The trains and town we built made me feel like Gramps was there with me! It made me feel him!"

"Max, did you use this smoke in Chet a lot?" the detective asked.

"Every time I was up there," I said.

"And how often was that?" Doctor Ryder asked.

"I don't know," I said, wracking my brain, trying to remember. "A lot."

The memories all flooded back. The countless days and nights in the attic, building up the town that Gramps and I had started, all while Chet zipped around, making his stops, puffing out his sweet-smelling cinnamon smoke. Drop by drop, I poured into the smokestack whenever it ran dry. The hazy fog that had covered Williamston had done something to me. My head throbbed, and my eyes watered.

"What have I done?" I cried out.

"Forensics thinks he spent so much time up there that the hazardous smoke—which they stopped producing this way in the seventies, by the way—poisoned him. I spent some time talking to folks at Lionel and researching it online. It was known to cause hallucinations, which is why they changed the formula. His grandfather must have bought it in bulk way back when, and they'd just never run out of it."

"What?" I called, simply unsure I'd heard him correctly.

"We think the smoke from Chet poisoned you," Detective

Thomas said loudly and clearly. "We think it made you crazy." He twirled his finger around his ear.

I couldn't believe what I was hearing. Though no one had said it out loud, I pieced everything together quickly. Everyone in that house—Courtney included—had been telling me that there was no monster, and I refused to believe them. I'd seen it. I watched it torment me, and I watched it kill my father. I watched it destroy what was left of him and then laugh at me.

"There was no monster," I said aloud suddenly.

"That's right," Detective Thomas said. "There was no monster. You were hallucinating."

The door to the room flew open, and Courtney came running in, immediately clutching my free side when she got close enough. "I knew I should have been worried about you!" she shouted.

"Courtney, I'm so sorry," I said, not knowing what else to say. "I'm so, so sorry!"

"I know, honey, I know." She clung to my side, squeezing me as if she could erase everything that had happened.

The doctors and the detective took a few steps back, clearly trying to give us privacy.

"There was no monster," I told her quietly, almost in a whisper.

"No, Max. There was. You were the monster."

What she said connected the rest of the dots. All the rage and anger I'd been bottling up against my father for decades of abuse and neglect came out of me. It filled me up until I reached a boiling point and exploded. The hallucinations from the chemical poisoning had simply allowed me to find a way to blame someone else. Some*thing* else. A monster I'd made up. Gramps had seen something as well and had planted the idea of this monster in my head. Maybe he was using too much of Chet's smoke, too. Or perhaps he'd just gotten old and confused, as everyone said. But he planted the idea of the monster, and the chemical poisoning built the rest of it in my head. It was all in my head.

"It felt so real," I said, sobbing into Courtney's shoulder.

"I'm sure it did," she said, trying to stifle her own crying.

"So I..." I started, not sure I could even say the words. "I killed him?"

"That's what they think," she said. "Your father's neck was broken. They're pretty sure you did it."

"I'm pretty sure I did, too," I said, though I wasn't completely convinced I had it in me.

"Whatever he said to you in the attic must have been the last straw," she said. "You flew into a rage and couldn't control yourself."

"But I'm not a killer," I said. "I could never."

"You would never," she said. "Not when you're yourself. You weren't thinking straight. You were poisoned from all the hours you spent up there inhaling the toxic smoke."

"The more time I spent up there, the worse it got," I said, more of a confirmation of what Courtney had just said, and as a revelation to myself.

"With every breath of the toxic smoke, you became less of you and more of the monster you'd made up," she said, now sitting back and looking me in the eye.

"The stronger the monster became, the less I could control it. Oh God. Does my mother know?"

"She does. She feels terrible. We talked earlier, after Detective Thomas told us their theory. She blames herself."

"Why?" I asked, genuinely confused.

"Despite sending you away to Gramps's all the time, it wasn't enough to save you from your father. She said that Bruce was a terrible man, but she couldn't stop loving him. She blames herself for all the abuse that spilled over from her to you, but wouldn't elaborate on any of it."

"So she tried to save me by sending me away? By sending me to Gramps's house?"

"Right," she said. "It wasn't your father who sent you to Gramps's house all those times. It was her."

"She tried to protect me," I mumbled to myself repeatedly.

"She did. She did her best," Courtney said, squeezing me to find some sort of comfort, some sort of relief.

"Courtney," Doctor Horton said. "Why don't we let him rest?"

"Okay," she said, holding up one finger to ask the doctor for another moment. "I'll come see you again as soon as I can," she told me. She kissed me on the cheek and stood up in one motion, making her way toward the door.

Before leaving, she turned back and smiled at me. A look that told me she loved me, she believed in me, and she knew better than to think I'd have done any of it on purpose. It brought tears to my eyes.

And then, just like that, I was alone in the room. Left with my thoughts. Left trying to piece together the events that happened at the top of those attic stairs. The events that happened upstairs. How I went from simply hating my father to ending his life.

CHAPTER 32
IN CONCLUSION

SHE WAS ALREADY WAITING for me when I got to the visitation area. She was dressed in her Sunday best, as they say, seated on the opposite side of the glass that would separate us. As I sat, she reached for the phone we'd use to talk to one another.

"I'm so sorry, Maxwell. For all of this." It was the first time my mother had apologized. She'd hardly spoken to me throughout the trial. She'd only visited me once while I was going through that whole thing. She'd hardly ever call or text when I had access to my phone. It felt nice to hear her say that she was sorry. However, I was honestly hoping for a little more than just a blanket apology.

Her voice came through the handset, tinny and faint. The sound of other prisoners easily overpowered my mother's frail voice. The man to my right was talking to his "baby mama, "as he put it. They were having some sort of dispute over his paternity. The woman to my left was talking with her lawyer, trying to get a retrial.

By this time, I knew the visitor area all too well. Courtney saw me almost every day for the three years I'd been in prison. Despite the best efforts of my legal team—I know how pretentious that sounds, but Gramps's money was put to good use—to plead insanity, I still had to go to jail for murder. Murder in the second degree, technically. The judge sentenced me to 10 years but said I'd likely get out in 5 with good behavior. I was being the best I could be. After all, there were no trains in jail to make my brain turn against me.

Mom stared through the thick glass at me, as if she were waiting for me to say something. To forgive her. To let her get peace from the situation. But the truth is, I had already forgiven her. Maybe she just wanted to hear me say it out loud.

"It's okay," I said. "You don't have to apologize."

"I could have protected you," she said.

"You did. You tried."

"I should have tried harder." Tears were flowing gently down her cheeks.

"This isn't your fault," I told her. "This is just a perfect storm of craziness."

"I hate that I knew your father wasn't a good man."

"Me too."

"I hate that I didn't protect you."

"Mom, really. Water under the bridge."

"It's not. You wouldn't be here if I'd just protected you. Like a mother should."

"You tried your best. You sent me to Gramps's house. I know that now. I know how you tried to keep me away from him so I'd be safe."

"I could have done more."

"Be that as it may," I said. "It's all in the past now. I forgive you."

The tension released on her face. The crow's feet and frown lines loosened. I could tell she'd been waiting for me to say those exact words. That I'd forgiven her.

"Are you okay in here?" she asked, clearly trying to change the subject.

"I'm doing the best I can. It's about as bad as you'd think it was." My mind flashed to *My Cousin Vinny*, when they first go to jail after getting arrested and there's yelling and hollering at the "new fish". And then I thought about *The Shawshank Redemption*. I felt a lot like Andy Dufresne over the last three years. Like I didn't belong. Like I had to get out. That on some level, I was innocent.

"That's all you can do, really," she said. "Be on your best behavior and get out of this place and back to your life."

"How's Court doing?"

"I've been checking up on her, as has Geoffrey. She seems okay."

"She puts on a good front. Don't let her fool you." I knew that on some level, Courtney was struggling. We'd been so reliant on one another over the years that I knew she had to be struggling as much as I was without her.

"I'll make sure to spend more time with her, Max."

"Thanks, Mom. And thanks for coming to see me. It means a lot that you feel the way you do."

"Of course," she said. "You're my baby and always will be."

* * *

SO MANY DAYS I sat in my cell, reading, writing, thinking. I spent countless nights awake in the dark, listening. Hoping that the monster wouldn't show itself again. Fearful that perhaps, just perhaps, it wasn't the liquid smoke that made me crazy. Worried that I was, in fact, actually crazy. I waited night after night, week after week, year after year, to hear the growls. Waiting to hear it come back, to call to me. To make me hurt someone else. Someone I didn't loathe with every fiber of my being.

During the trial, so many doctors had testified for the state about how the liquid smoke poisoned my mind. We even called one as part of my defense, hoping it'd sway the jury to know that we believed the same thing the state did, but that I wasn't of sound mind when I did what I did.

Jeez, even after all these years, I struggle to write down what I did.

I know what happened. They recreated the scene with a court-appointed animation for me to watch back during the trial. I know what I did.

But I still see it differently. The memory of what I thought had happened was burned so deeply into my brain that I can't shake it.

I still see the monster I created. I still see its ooze. I still see it grabbing my father and melting him, eating him. I know that none of that happened. I've worked through it with my prison-assigned psychiatrist. I've talked it out ad nauseam. I know the truth about what happened. Sometimes when I'm actually able to fall asleep, I can see it how I thought it happened. Like a vivid memory of something that never happened. It was almost like I was dreaming of it happening.

Most nights, as I lay awake well after dark, I listened. I

waited and sometimes hoped that I'd hear the monster again. That it would find me in prison, and it would tell me that what I thought happened really happened. That I wasn't crazy. I hoped for that bit of peace. That tiny shred of assurance that it wasn't me who did something wrong. That whatever lived upstairs actually existed, and it wasn't just my imagination running wild and making me do unintentionally drug-induced violent things.

Though wish as I might, hoped as I may, no monster ever visited me again. No growls at a distance were heard. No visions of creeping shadows. No hidden things that only I could see. Just me in my cell, waiting for my sentence to be over. For my life to go back to as close to normal as it could. To get home to Courtney and resume our lives.

I worried that my life would never be the same. That thought crossed my mind almost every waking minute of every day. That I'd be labeled a murderer by people who didn't understand what had happened. Sure, I'd made the news. I'd been in the papers and even made the cover of the National Enquirer at one point. **Toy Train Drives Man Insane**. They thought they were so clever. And while they told most of the story correctly, no one took it seriously because of the publication it was in.

Courtney had been wonderful and supportive throughout the whole trial. She was there for me every step of the way. She held my hand during the sentencing. She'd coordinated with other friends of ours to be there on a rotating schedule, so I was never alone in the courtroom. She shone in her role as my support system. I'd known for decades that I'd picked the right partner, but this whole situation had really reinforced that knowledge.

I know that when I get out of here, things will be tough. Life won't be the same. I'll have a lot of changes I'll need to make. Of course, I'll need to find some new, less insanity-inducing liquid smoke for Chet. I'll have to try harder to be the best person I can be.

Hopefully, I can get out of here sooner than I should. I'm not a bad person. I know that. Therapy has taught me that. I am a good person who made a terrible decision. Did I, though? Did I decide? I don't even know anymore. These are the things I think about as I stay up most of the night, unable to sleep in this hell-hole, while I write, to the best of my recollection, everything that had happened, exactly as I remember it.

I hate knowing that Gramps had the same problem I did, though not to the same extreme. He'd seen the monster himself. Or thought he did, I'm sure. He was convinced it was real, much like I was. He wrote me letters about it. He warned me that people wouldn't believe me. And he was right, with good reason. I hated knowing that he must have felt so alone in his last years. I should have visited him more. I should have spent more time with him. All he had were the trains. And they, as they did to me, made him a little crazy. The only bit of reprieve I have is that he must not have spent as much time up there as I had. He wasn't trying to reconnect with someone like I was. He wasn't trying to feel his Gramps up there. And as such, he didn't get as poisoned as I had. I'm thankful for that. Thankful for that bit of relief, knowing he wasn't as crazed by the whole thing as I was.